The Blood of the Shroud

A NOVEL

D.B. SANDERS

Sanders, D.B.
The Blood of the Shroud: a novel / D.B. Sanders.
ISBN-13: 978-0-9885506-1-2

For my wife Kaye who always knew I could do it—even when I didn't.

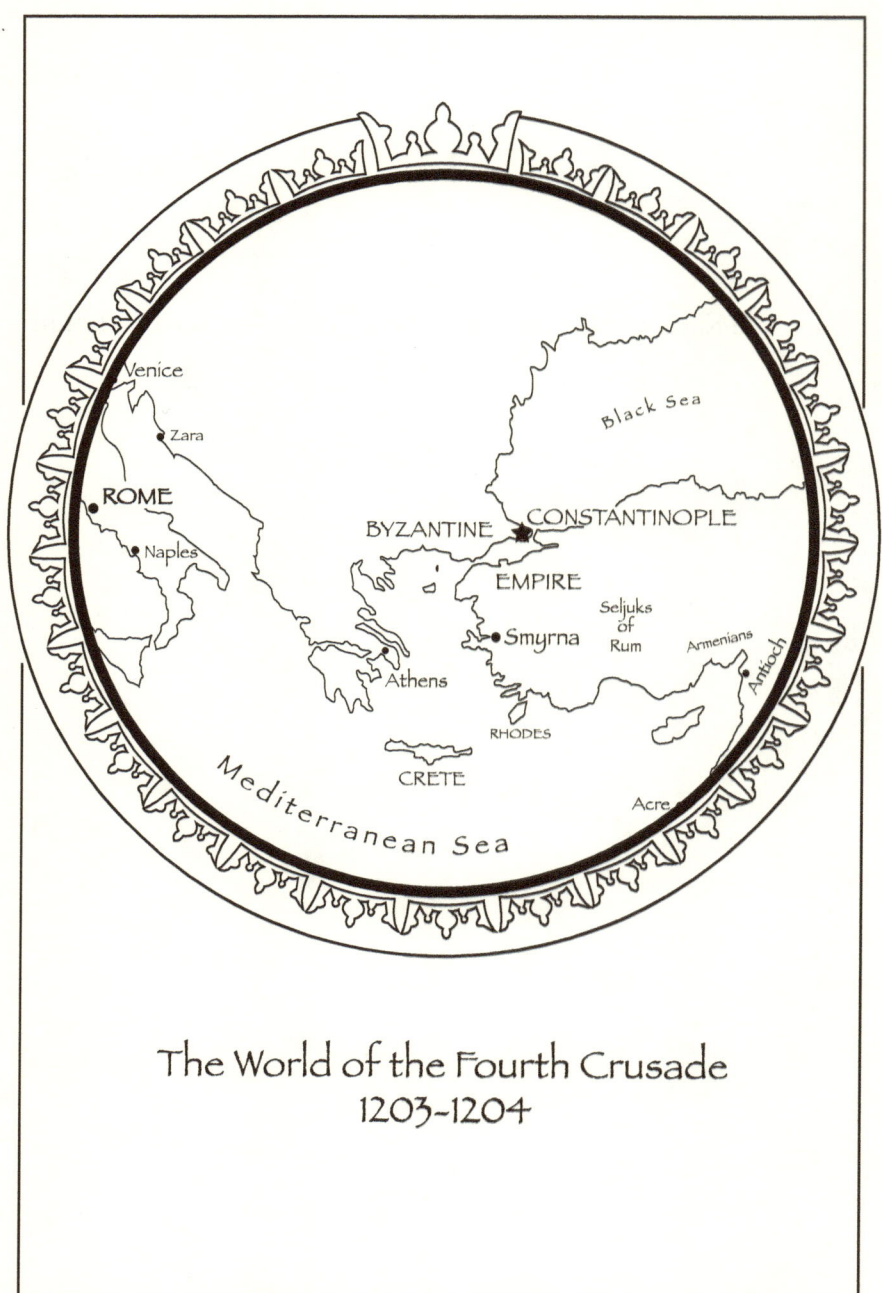

Venice
Zara
ROME
Naples
Black Sea
BYZANTINE
CONSTANTINOPLE
EMPIRE
Seljuks of Rum
Smyrna
Armenians
Athens
Antioch
RHODES
CRETE
Acre
Mediterranean Sea

The World of the Fourth Crusade
1203–1204

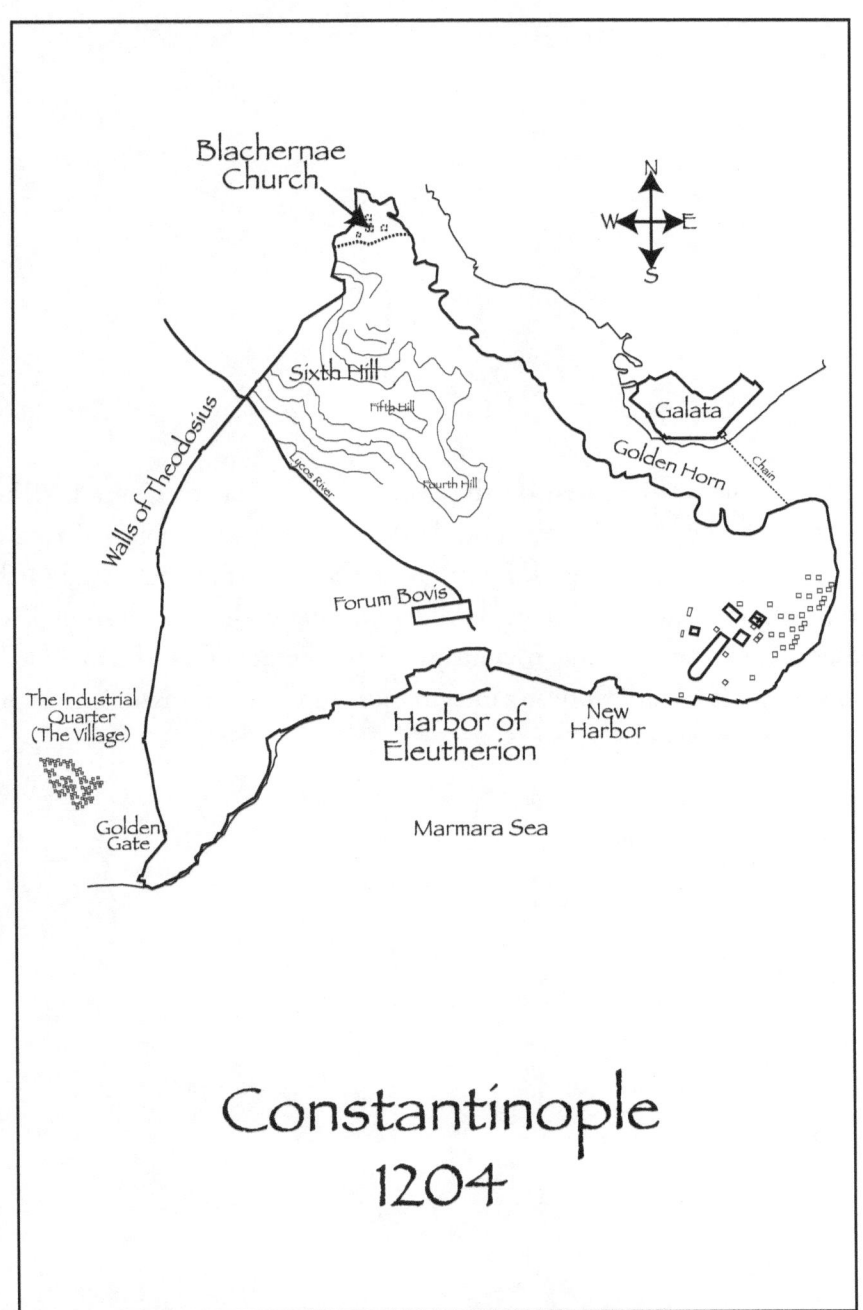

Blachernae Church

Sixth Hill

Fifth Hill

Lycos River

Fourth Hill

Walls of Theodosius

Galata

Golden Horn

Chain

Forum Bovis

The Industrial Quarter (The Village)

Golden Gate

Harbor of Eleutherion

New Harbor

Marmara Sea

N
W   E
S

Constantinople
1204

Author's Note

The book was inspired by the events of the Fourth Crusade. The dates when confirmable were used fairly accurately. The epigraphs were inspired by an ancient lexis. I summoned some of the characters forth from history's multihued past to do my bidding without hesitation. The others came from my unconscious mind and demanded to be included. However, it is a work from my imagination and as such it is all invention masquerading as reality.

The Blood of the Shroud

The Kingdom of Acre, part of the Crusaders States – 1203
ONE - WORTHY OF LIVING.

"I am tired of this life of death," William Arc whispered to himself.

His entire life had been dedicated to the religion of peace and yet he had never known any, forced into a constant campaign of hate against heretics and Muslims by every Pope to lead in his lifetime. Now the petition for action had been provoked again. His gaze strained over the Mediterranean in an effort to see his current desire fulfilled. "There he is," Gerald of Wales said, pointing to the small galley riding into view on the phalo blue Mediterranean Sea. If William was the Wolf of Acre surely Gerald was its hawk, possessing eyes that could perceive the slightest movement at distances far from the thoughts of others. Here had come William's passage to yet another of the Pope's glory and honor campaigns. His intention this time was not to join, but rather to fight against it.

William was to meet Philippe de Plessiez, the newest Templar Master, in Naples in an effort to strategize the Templar's position before the start of Innocent III's crusade to dismantle the Muslim stronghold in Egypt. William wanted no part of this crusade of blood, a fight he was sure would stain the hands of his Templar brothers forever; he was intent on persuading Philippe to ignore this folly from the fool in Rome. William had once believed in the papacy that preached that Christ had not come to bring peace upon this earth, but to bring the sword to the wayward, but William's doubts had grown since the battle of Arsuf, those many long years ago, *did not Christ command, love one another, as I have loved you?* He wondered where his love had gone.

"Stephen, arouse yourself from your daydreams and gather our camp, we leave for the shore within the hour," said William. Stephen looked up sheepishly and moved at a pace far too slow for William's liking. "Stephen it is in the trying that we grow, now move boy or you will make me regret taking in my brother's son!" William said, much to the amusement of his Templar brothers. Stephen could only muster a weak, "Yes, William," and a trifle more speed before tripping over his own feet in an effort to please. This intensified the humor of the men, but William put a stop to it instantly and cautioned Stephen, "Stop when your passions rise, it will only lead to your confusion and dishonor. Templars pull actions from their skill, not their zeal." Stephen pulled himself up and began carefully wrapping the weapons and provisions of the knights for travel. With the camp broken and the horses loaded the five warriors for Christ made their way to the shore.

As they drew closer, William's friend Gerald said, "The old Greek has found us a sea shield." William studied the outline of the approaching vessel and agreed, "Yes, hopefully that will cloak us from the Bedouin pirates, but if they are hungry nothing will dissuade them." All distances were deceptively close in the clear air of the Mediterranean, while the shore appeared to be at arm's reach, in reality it was a good twelve miles away and it would be an hour before they reached their rendezvous with the old Greek Gaius. "Gerald, set pace for us and keep a watchful eye for our friends with the arrows," William said. Saracen archers continually tried to take down a few careless Templars outside the city walls as sport. There was a truce between them but at best it was only a truce of deception prone to endless skirmishes. While William was the best warrior in battle, Gerald with his keen eyes was always best in the forward position.

The Blood of the Shroud

The air was calm and the sun was now fully crested above the horizon bringing with it the heat that could caress or kill. The pace was brisk but it did allow for chatter among the knights.

"I hate the sea."

"That is because you swim like a rock…"

However, William paid no attention to any of it. His dreams had been bothering him again. Dreams of war were a constant with him, but these had been different and while less violent, far more disturbing. He had repeatedly dreamt of Christ for the past month—it was always the same—Christ would speak from a distance, but he could not hear him; as he attempted to reach his side he would awaken suddenly. It made him uneasy, he felt he was being summoned, but for what he did not know.

Stephen interrupted William's thoughts with a question, "Uncle, will we return to Acre?" "We must learn to shut off our tomorrows, as well as our past if we are to shoulder our load today Stephen. I cannot say what the Lord will bring for us, but I feel it will take all of our concentration to make this journey successful," William said, as he kicked into his horse to catch Gerald.

The pace and motion of his own horse had a hypnotic effect upon Stephen and soon he became lost in his own thoughts. Stephen knew William to be a serious, but patient teacher in the year he had been with him, but lately he seemed preoccupied with something terribly troubling. He had seen him awake from sleep at all hours in the night. He was tense in the day and was sometimes angry without reason during his training. He feared he was not meeting William's expectations: after all, he had not chosen this path of the Knight. He had wanted to follow his father's path. He longed for the confines of the workroom to be near his father and mentor, Gregory Arc, the greatest of the Byzantine weapon makers. His father's death weighed heavily upon him and the burden of his failure had not lessened in the year he had been with his uncle William.

The memories of his beginning were so intertwined with his father's stories of his life that Stephen could no longer distinguish between the two. And, in this oblique view of his past, his mind's eye returned him there, to live it again, as he rode towards the shore.

~

Gregory's workroom was the epitome of mystery and science. The walls were covered with years of handcrafted tools of every size and shape. Stores of chemicals, metal, leather, wood, and stone were carefully sorted by size, color, and type. It was a cornucopia of strategic materials for the production of the finest armaments available in the Byzantine Empire. Gregory Arc's reputation for quality was known from England to the edges of the Mongol Empire; he had designed and built the best: swords, crossbows, lances, spears, axes and daggers and more, for more knights and kings than any man alive. He employed a minimum of fifteen craftsmen at all times, but none but himself were ever allowed in his private sanctuary where he would often work seventeen hours a day, taking meals only when his wife violently insisted. He had not strived for fame but rather excellence and so his fame in the empire grew with his every step. It was inside this crucible that Stephen learned the craft and use of weapons while hearing the often-repeated story of his father's beginning.

Gregory Arc was born into the Order of the Temple in 1131. As a 17-year-old Templar Knight he had served in the Battle of Damascus in 1148 under King Baldwin III, in which the defeated Christians suffered fatalities in the thousands that day. It was here that he lost his left eye. Gregory's poorly tempered sword broke on him in the pitched battle against the overwhelming Muslim forces, allowing his opponent's sword tip to slice his eye, forcing him to fight half blind, in order to defeat him and survive the day. For weeks after, as the great defeated Christian army retreated, he studied the sword taken from the Muslim who blinded him. He marveled at the blade's surface that resembled grains of wood. It was lighter and stronger than anything he had ever seen or used. It was a Damascus sword and it had broken his. It was here that he vowed to build weapons for the Christians that would not fail, that would match the man for whom they were built and survive the centuries after they were buried.

When Gregory reached Antioch he asked the Templar Master to grant him leave so that he could return home, which was given with little hesitation as Gregory was highly respected in the order. But Gregory did not return home. In disguise, dressed in the manner of the poorest Saracen, he left Antioch under a full moon with intentions to travel throughout the Muslim empire and learn the language and manner of his enemy. Taking the name Nain al-Din he traveled everywhere trading his youth to gain knowledge, until he could no longer be seen as anything but Muslim. He was then ready to travel to Damascus to steal the secrets of their swords.

Once in Damascus, Gregory had no trouble finding the factory, as the billows from the crucible fires that produced the steel were evident from any part of the city. He secured work easily there, tending the fires, as few workers survived longer than a few months working under the blazing Syrian sun, stoking the furnaces that could melt iron in a matter of moments. Here, Gregory would remain for four years before he was allowed into the secret chambers where the iron masters worked forging the legendary blades. The insides of the workshop were hotter than the outside. It required men who could survive the work outside to have a chance of functioning in an environment that to Gregory's mind was hell envisioned.

Gregory's accession to the ranks of the secret chambers was not a promotion based on his devotion or skill, but merely the happenstance-of-location. The dung-man dropping dead from exhaustion a few feet from him was all that was necessary for him to earn the eye of his whip-handed master; who now facing a manpower shortage, turned to him, pointed his whip and declared him the new dung-man. He was given the assignment of collecting bird droppings from the hundreds of birdcages outside the workshop and then deliver them to the workers who melted the iron. The feed of these birds were mixed with ground iron, and it was thought that their droppings infused the metal with special properties. To the molten iron, a mixture of these special bird droppings, carbon, sand and sulfur were added. Another year would pass before he was trained to tend the mixture and it was then that he learned that two mixtures were prepared—one with less carbon and one with more. One gave the iron suppleness, and the other hardness. From these mixtures flat billets were made. Three special ironsmiths would hammer under heat the two billets of metal together, folding them when they had elongated to the proper length. Repeating the process no more than fifteen times. He bribed one of the ironsmiths to be allowed an opportunity to learn this technique and was permitted a chance to slave at the anvil. It took Gregory working seventeen hours a day, in a pit of hell-fire, five years to perfect the hammering technique.

If all had gone perfectly to this point, the sword could still be ruined in the final step when the blade was quenched cool by plunging it into goat urine. It took the Damascenes five decades to find the perfect fluid to quench their blades—water, wine, oil and blood were all tried until they had discovered urine. If quenched too slowly the blade became weak, too fast, brittle. Only urine gave them perfect blades. The quenching process required a series of heating and cooling cycles; and required the ironsmith to judge by approximations the correct amount of heat and the proper speed to plunge the sword into the urine so that it would cool properly. This took Gregory another year to learn.

Once the blades were properly formed and quenched, the swords were then turned over to the engravers and polishers to add the artistic elements that would embolden the new owners to greatness. Adding an hour to his day Gregory mastered the art in a mere year, greatly impressing his employers. Now, Gregory felt ready to depart with his knowledge.

Joining the league of ironsmiths was simple in comparison to leaving the order. It had only required surviving and pretending to be a Muslim for more than thirteen years, under conditions that would kill ordinary men from heat exhaustion in hours. Learn perfectly eighty-two different manipulations that turn a lump of iron into a finely polished weapon of unsurpassed quality and when it was all done have the fortitude to plunge it into the body of a muscular and active slave—so that the metal would be infused with their strength. It was this final rite of passage that unmasked Gregory. This final secret of the Damascus sword that was not revealed to any who had not reached the pinnacle of the craft. It was the final act and secret rite that would bestow upon the ironsmith his status as supreme craftsman.

The ceremony took place, on a barren hilltop north of the city, under a sickle-shaped-moon once a month. Gregory had been aware that some action requiring the attention of the senior ironsmiths had taken place each month, but he had never been invited before. The three ironsmiths and Gregory rode on camels to the appointed destination carrying thirty new swords with them. When they arrived, Saracen warriors guarding a wagon carrying chained men greeted them. A large fire roared to the side. Gregory's warrior-instinct came flooding back to him with a horrible sense of foreboding. Gregory eyed carefully the chained men and could instantly make out the crusaders amongst the slaves. The ironsmiths quickly explained to him what was to transpire and the chained men were dragged from the wagon and lined up before the smiths. By now Gregory was so entrenched in his role that he was no longer recognizable as a Christian to the prisoners. The first man was unchained and the head ironsmith praised Allah and plunged the sword through the man's belly under loud praises from his companions and the other warriors.

The ironsmiths took Gregory's horror as fear and told him that the passage would be easy if he would only remember that these men were his enemies as he plunged the sword in.

Gregory quickly surmised the situation as a Templar warrior. Five Saracen warriors and three strong ironsmiths, the odds did not favor his survival. He would need the assistance of at least one of the crusaders. The dislike and fear of Templars amongst the Muslims was well known. The chances of at least one skilled Templar in the group were likely. Other knight orders were usually ransomed, but Muslims feared Templars and death upon capture was a certainty. Gregory feigned interest to his fellow smiths that he would like to kill a Templar. The warriors and the ironsmiths took delight in his desire and proceeded to unlock three more men for Gregory's inspection. The ironsmiths stood behind him and the sacred weapons lay to his right. His victims were before him with three Saracen warriors behind them. The final two Saracens guarded the balance of the prisoners to his right, at the end of the wagon. The fire raged to his left. He walked calmly and picked up a weapon as to inspect it and then another as if to choose between them. He ordered his victims closer to him and the Saracens pushed them forward on his command. It was then that Gregory acted, moving between the Templars and slicing off the outstretched arm of one Saracen and then the hand of another. In Latin he screamed to his Templar brothers, "Take arms and fight for your freedom!" The Templars moved quickly to the weapons on the ground as Gregory continued slashing at the last of the three confused Saracens severely wounding them with the help of the chained prisoners attacking them from behind.

However, the ironsmiths were not distracted moving at the freed Templars and tossing them off the swords easily, as if they were children, then arming themselves to engage them. The chained men had now fully realized the opportunity and attempted to find the keys to unlock themselves among the dead Saracens.

Gregory turned to find himself under attack by two ironsmiths. While they were strong they were not trained as warriors giving the one-eyed Gregory advantage. The one on his blind side slashed at him, but had misjudged the distance, forcing from him a longer reach than would be desired against an opponent of Gregory's skill. Gregory twisted to his left in order to present a smaller profile and then took off the forearm of the outstretched arm; he continued around until he faced the more clumsy of the two, who was now holding his sword high above him when Gregory lunged his sword through his belly with his right hand. Leaving the sword in place he then sliced at the ironsmith with the sword in his left hand targeting just above the man's knee, severing the tendon, and causing him to drop instantly. The third ironsmith in a blind rage was consumed in hacking a Templar repeatedly before one of his Templar brothers could arm himself and kill him.

The scene was horrific. Fifteen men lay suffering or dead. Gregory was covered head to toe in blood. Some of the prisoners had run off while others were picking at the corpses for anything of value. Gregory called his brothers to order and they chased off the thieves. After a brief explanation, Gregory and his two Templar brothers fled Syria on horseback that night, heading back to the Byzantine Empire.

Armed with the secret knowledge of the Damascus sword and the assistance of his two rescued Templar brothers, Gregory set-up shop in Milan and married a widow, Heloise, half his age, whose former husband had broken his neck in a game of street ball, which the resemblance to war was missing only because they did not pass out weapons beforehand. Gregory's reputation as a sword smith grew swiftly, as did his fortune and he soon expanded his business into all areas of weapon manufacture attracting the most skilled craftsmen of the empire to his side. In ten years he was one of the most renowned manufacturer of swords in the empire, rivaled only by the sword makers of Damascus and Toledo.

Heloise gave him four sons in rapid succession. Only the youngest, Stephen, survived. When Stephen arrived Gregory was nearly sixty. Because of this, Stephen was treated all the more sacred by his father and from the beginning Gregory demanded that Stephen be present in his workroom as much as his mother would allow. And, in this odd nursery Gregory nurtured his son in the ways of men and war. From the earliest moments it seemed to Gregory that Stephen did not just watch his every movement but showed an understanding of what was being done there. Stephen's presence became so natural in that nursery-of-war that Gregory took on the habit of talking to him, as one might an old companion, discussing his plans and ideas for this or that, so it came as no surprise to Gregory when Stephen uttered his first word, "Dagga," before his second birthday, as Gregory rounded the edge on a small wooden blade for his son, replying back, "Yes Stephen, a dagger, for you." Gregory in his concentration would only realize the significance of the event hours later.

By the time Stephen was four he had already learned to sort the various objects around the workroom into their proper containers. By five he mastered the art of placing an edge on a small weapon and by six he had the intellectual ability to explain the forging process even though he was not yet sufficiently strong to wield the tools to do so. Stephen's first lesson of manufacture came at eight.

"Your first duty will be to build yourself a weapon of my design: a special crossbow. Lighter than any ever made, it will carry five quarrels, four internally and one in its breach. By means of a special lock it will be unable to fire holding a loaded quarrel in place and yet let its possessor, at will, quickly change that and allow its deadly cargo to fly. Its bow will be pulled into position by means of an integrated lever and it will fire across a large meadow with great accuracy. It will carry easily upon your back with the aid of a strap and padded blocks. I have also devised one special quarrel for it that will ignite upon passage by means of a special flipping plate at its front. It will be both a thing of beauty and perfect annihilation. By this means you will learn every method I know. However, we must still continue to earn for ourselves so I expect this to be done after your daily work. It should take two years to complete," Gregory had explained to him.

Stephen completed the crossbow in a year and spent the second perfecting its use. When he was finished his father said upon its inspection, "The malice in men are many, but this will surely hold them at bay."

While the manufacture of small arms consumed the time of Gregory's craftsmen, his greatest success came from the design of siege weapons, siege towers and trebuchets capable of throwing the largest stones hundreds of yards. He also had created a particular potent variation of Greek fire for sieges.

"Stephen we are one of the keepers of a great secret," his father said, while taking from his hiding place a manuscript written on sheepskin vellum.

"This is the Epitome de Rei Militari—the Digest on Military Matters by Vegetius Renatus—it holds the secret of our wealth for it contains the formula for Greek fire."

"Greek fire?" Stephen had asked, staring intently at the ochre colored vellum.

"It is the fire of the sun given to man, no water can put it out and it will cling to their death the poor souls who come in contact with it. Few know how to make it and even fewer know how to recognize its ingredients. Before your training is done you will know all its makings… hand me that flask…now watch carefully this is the final ingredient of Greek fire…remember tell no one of it," Gregory had cautioned him.

The days of perfection ended in the summer of his eleventh year, Stephen had just finished the orders for the day when the stranger arrived, coming right behind him and into the private workroom. No one ever arrived past the setting sun, the dangers of travel by night being too many to risk. It seemed the full moon and sparse street lanterns had provided him the advantage of travel that fateful night.

"Are you Arc the metal smyth?" The fierce looking stranger had asked.

"Who asks?" sneered the elder Arc, angry at the stranger's intrusion into his private sanctuary.

"Ælfric of Abingdom."

Ælfric stood nine heads high, with broad shoulders and a thick chest. His countenance was one of arrogant disapproval and his presence filled the room with a mixture of disgust and apprehension.

"Your reputation has traveled far and I have made haste to you to enjoin you to sell me one of your famous swords. No price will be considered too high," said Ælfric.

"I have taken your order and I will have one ready for you in a year, perhaps two, now leave," the senior Arc ordered, flicking his right hand at him.

Ælfric ignored the older man glancing around the sizeable room before spotting a large cloth over a nearby table. Quickly going to it he removed the fabric before Gregory could prevent him; revealing a beautiful treasure trove of weapons including a finely finished sword inscribed with the Latin words, Vivere commune est, sed non commune mereri.

"What is this inscription?" Ælfric asked.

"So you are both ignorant and arrogant," Gregory said, barely containing his anger, "It means—to live is common to all, but to be worthy of living is not—the words of Prudentius."

"I shall take this one then and save both you and me a year or two," Ælfric replied, with a touch of meanness added to his voice.

"It is not for sale, it is for my brother a Templar Knight who arrives soon, I suggest you leave me to my work."

"No, I will have this one and pay twice your price for the trouble. Your brother shall be paid for his delay and I will be on my way," he said, dropping a small bag upon the table, "there you will find 200 deniers, more than enough to compensate your time and your brother's delay."

The limits of his patience reached, Gregory drew his dagger, and pounced upon Ælfric. Ælfric deflected the blade with his mailed forearm and then struck him with his fist breaking his jaw. The old bull staggered back and was set to charge again when Ælfric kicked him backwards, causing Gregory to tumble and strike his head against an anvil, breaking his skull open. Stephen watching from the corner grabbed his loaded crossbow and pointed it at Ælfric. But, his rigid body held the crossbow with trembling hands, unable to fire in his fear. Frozen to the corner, he stared at Ælfric with wide eyes, as his father's blood rushed from his wound and spread across the floor towards him.

"There are many sheep in the world. Now, you find you are one of them. The masters in need of them are many, you shall have no trouble finding yourself another, peasant," said Ælfric, staring the boy down.

"He was my father," Stephen screamed, tears streaming from his eyes.

"That is perhaps regrettable, but he attacked me unfairly, I had no choice but to defend myself," Ælfric replied. Picking up the bag of money he began to leave with the sword.

"Now you steal your price and what was never meant for you, I shall see you die," Stephen cried out.

"Unlikely, but perhaps I do owe you something. Here is enough for his burial. He now has no need of anything more," Ælfric said, as he condescendingly scattered some coins at Stephen's feet, leaving him sobbing in the corner, his head now down, hiding his shame as his grief grew.

~

As the memory of his father's end and his failure faded, Stephen found himself at the waters edge, the time evaporated—and his new journey set to begin. William ordered the knights to build a fire in order to signal Gaius, but Stephen approached William explaining there was no need, for he could signal him without it.

"What magic would you employ for this Stephen?"

"The magic of my father," Stephen said, producing a palm sized, polished bowl of bronze so smooth that one could see the details of their eyes.

"How is this to be used," William asked.

"The power lies in its ability to channel the sun, watch."

Stephen proceeded to direct the mirror towards the sun casting its light so powerfully that even in the daylight its beam could be seen to light the ground. The knights drew close to watch this magic.

"Gregory made this?" William asked.

"Well, he formed the shape and inscribed the engraving of the map of the Mediterranean on its back and I polished its internal surface until I could see myself," Stephen explained.

"I can see Gregory has made you a Byzantine wizard, go then and guide Gaius to us."

~

Gaius paced the deck in search of a sign from William. He could see the outlines of Acre and knew that William would be waiting somewhere near shore. *Where was his signal of fire?*

"There," Gaius' son exclaimed, "That spark, it twinkles like a star."

Gaius looked at the spot and could see the twinkle, bright as a star, but far too small for a fire. *What trick does William employ now, no doubt some enchantment from his brother Gregory,* Gaius thought.

"Make for the star, it is no doubt our friend William," Gaius ordered.

They turned the Genoese designed galley toward the false blaze and headed in. The galley was twenty years old, kept sound and sturdy through the care and direction of Gaius—the Sea King—William's nickname for him. He met William acting as pilot for Lionheart in the third Crusade. Now, in his fifties, the leathered skin of the old man still held the shape of a thin younger man. Raised as a fisherman, no one knew the Mediterranean better than him. He had traveled its length and breadth more times than he could be remember. He lived for the sea and he believed it would no doubt take him when his time had finished.

~

"It is good to see you my friend, it seems that the sea has left you the same these last five years," William shouted to Gaius as he drew the galley close to shore.

"It is my ten sons who keep me erect and well."

"Come ashore, we have much to discuss, my brothers will load the supplies," William directed.

With the galley secured, Gaius and William sat at the shores edge and observed the men making preparations for their travel while they spoke.

"William slow their pace, we will not leave until near sunset when the winds can move us offshore more easily. Tired men make poor sailors and worse company." William gave the orders and the two men resumed their talk.

"Why have you summoned me, the message was most urgent and I made haste as you instructed."

"War brews in Rome and I wish to stop it, failing that, I hope to prevent the Templar's involvement in it. I needed the fastest passage to Naples in order to accomplish it. Which is why I sent my best rider to you."

"Well this can be done, but the pirates do not sleep now, if we are to escape their eyes our passage must cling to the coast and it will slow our journey."

"We must risk the pirates, as I cannot add time and lose the opportunity to prevent this tragedy from unfolding."

"I will risk anything you ask William, but allow me to take some coast and swing across the sea at my choosing. Would not our death provide the greatest delay?"

"Yes, you are of course right, Gaius, I will not ask you to invite trouble. But, a little risk is in order or I may be too late to accomplish anything."

"Then we shall pray for good fortune and see if the Gods answer. Now, tell me the news from afar. How does your brother fair? My time from him has been too long."

"Gregory fell to an assassin a mere year ago. His wife begged that I take their son as my own in that time of distress. It is the boy who travels with us this day," William said, motioning to Stephen, "I took him on as squire, but intend on returning him to his mother on this trip. I have not yet told him of these intentions. I fear he will take such ill news as his failure. But, it is not his failure that prompts me to such action. Stephen is bright, but I feel he is ill suited to follow my road of blood."

"This news makes my heart heavy, Gregory was a friend," Gaius said, pulling a dagger from a sheath and handing it to William, "This was given to me by your brother."

"I would know it without your voice to the matter," William said, holding the finely hewn dagger up to the air to examine the golden oak hilted blade, "it is among my brother's best work."

"It saved my son's life and will save more should we find battle in our future," said Gaius, adding, "So the child falls far from Gregory's tree?"

"In matters of the mind Stephen is everything that was his father. He sees the unseen and seems to have knowledge beyond his years. He is skilled with all manner of weapons, but I see no warrior in him. He has a gentle and good soul."

"The world is filled with those who can kill, would the world not be better served with men of no malice," asked Gaius.

"Perhaps. He is an attentive student as well, should you wish to teach him something of the sea. He will no doubt enjoy a rest from me."

"And, Gregory's assassin, have you found him?"

"My Templar brothers are searching, but no word has returned of his whereabouts. I assure you his days living free from my wrath are numbered. I know his name and sword. And, Stephen knows well his face."

Taking back his blade from William, Gaius said, "I will happily join my blade with yours to end this cur's life."

"Just get me to Naples soon. I suspect the list of those wanting him dead will be long. Assassins rarely make many friends. My only hope is that my blade reaches him first." William said, moving to join the others loading the boat.

From the shores of many lands, the Mediterranean seems a calm sea, but Gaius knew this to be far from the truth and was in constant observation of her subtle and changing face knowing if he mistook any of her bad moods it would prove fatal. As the sun moved past the zenith, the wind began to slowly shift behind them pushing now off shore, Gaius gave the order to board. William, four knights, six of Gaius' sons employed as oarsmen, and Stephen were now taken aboard and the trip to Naples began in earnest. With luck and a steady wind the trip would take no more than thirty days. He would lead them along the coast of the Christian Territory, move around Cyprus near the Kingdom of Armenia, slip past the barren coast of the Seljuks of Rum and finally into the open water of the Mediterranean towards the isle of Crete, from there they would cross the Adriatic sea to their final destination, Naples in the Kingdom of Sicily.

The Mediterranean at the mouth of the Aegean Sea would prove most challenging for Gaius because the Bedouin pirates were now powerful foes on the seas between the old and new worlds. Constantinople's economic power had created the desire for her golden and silken treasures to flow towards: Rome, the Franks of Europe and even the edges of the old western empire. Constantinople attracted pilgrims, students and for the educated, the lure of administration jobs. It was an open and mixed society and created more opportunities than any other city in the Byzantine Empire. All of this caused the development of the sea-lanes to carry her astounding wealth over the Mediterranean and with it—the rise of piracy. The Bedouin Pirates were especially dangerous, preferring to kill all that could not be ransomed easily. No target seemed beneath their view for any vessel could be used to support their aims. Gaius would have to live up to his title as sea king and guide his small group over an angry and hostile Mediterranean in a ship thirty feet long, with no marine armaments, and no support other than what was brought aboard. Gaius felt a chill and covered himself. He suddenly felt small and alone. Gaius repositioned his hands on the tiller, gave the order for the rowers to begin their task and said a prayer, not to Christ his lord, but to an ancient God of his country, Greece: Poseidon, "I beg of you, add your strength to my arm, so I will not fail these fine men." He studied the horizon, as the ship left the shores of Acre, looking for any sign that he had been heard. But, all he could see were clouds forming in the distance.

The Blood of the Shroud

Constantinople, Holy Center of the Christian Empire – 1203

TWO - SILENCE, SECLUSION, HUNGER AND VIGILANCE.

Muhammad al-Hassar could barely control his apprehension as he watched Ibn al-Arabi meditate calmly at the bottom of the bathhouse pool. He had been under the cool bluish water for more time than would be required to consume a large meal and still he remained submerged with no signs of movement or distress. He wanted to drag him out but Hassar was deadly afraid of water of any depth. Hassar ruminated as he watched him. *Why had Arabi dragged them from Mecca to be in the center of the Christian world now?* Danger was fermenting here like old fruit and it could be smelled in every corner of this metropolis. Visions, it was always visions with Ibn al-Arabi, he hated visions, while he knew them to be true or at least believed them to be true in the case of the great mystic-warrior Ibn al-Arabi, he still hated them. Visions had taken them halfway across the known world and now they were on the move again but this time to be among the infidels. Al-Hassar worried for their safety.

Ibn al-Arabi returned from the other plane to find his body submerged in liquid. He liked the feeling of weightlessness, silence, seclusion, and the connection to the universe brought to him by the water. His lungs began to ache and reminded him that he was not a fish but merely a man underwater. He unworriedly unfolded himself and returned to the surface to engage the agitated Hassar, "Worry not my friend, all is right."

"All is not right," protested the large round figure of Hassar, "we are in the middle of an infidel stronghold for untold reasons…"

"Not untold my friend, simply embedded in a riddle I have yet to solve, fret not for I shall uncover soon what it all means."

The riddle that Ibn al-Arabi spoke of was at the center of their journey to Constantinople. The three prophets, Jesus, Moses and Muhammad, met al-Arabi during one of his journeys to the other side and had told him to make the trip to Constantinople, once there he was to help the wolf-on-the-crest, the boy craftsman and the bride of Christ. None of it made sense to Arabi at the time, but the prophets would say no more and so Arabi traveled with his trusted assistant Hassar to Constantinople to do what was required of him. And, while Hassar protested at every turn towards the infidel's capital he would not leave his friend's side no matter what dangers were before them.

They had no trouble entering the metropolis, all scholars were embraced by Constantinople—it was after all the most cosmopolitan and modern city in the world. It housed treasures from both east and west and invited knowledge to its gates without hesitation and regardless of its origin. It was the center of the Byzantine Empire and valued thought above all. They had found suitable lodging at the Forum Bovis near the Harbor of Eleutherion and waited. Ibn al-Arabi's books on law that he had penned when he was sixteen under a pseudonym were in great demand here in Constantinople and it was with no trouble that he soon found a merchant at the forum interested in all of them. This sale gave Arabi a tidy pension for their journey. However, he had no need for the money immediately placing the sum and all his financial dealings into the hands of his trusted friend Hassar as he had always done.

They had been in the city for a month when news of the attack and sacking of Zara by Christian Crusaders reached Constantinople and to their ears. It shocked everyone from those in the highest levels of the administration to the peasants on the streets. The Venetians under the guidance of their old blind Doge had tricked the Crusaders into recapturing Zara for them, plunging the empire into crisis. *If Christian knights could savagely attack a Christian city, what would happen next? Who was safe?* Arabi contemplated this news with great interest and was certain that the matter had to be part of his mystery and the reason he was there.

Ibn al-Arabi spent the morning hours writing and meditating taking his first small meal around noon in the courtyard of the Forum Bovis, while his friend Hassar made inquiries and did research for him around the city. Arabi sought any news that would bring him closer to solving his riddle. *Who or what was the wolf-on-the-crest, a place, a person, or a thing? No one knew of a boy craftsman in the area. It seemed preposterous when he asked, how could a boy master a craft—a talented apprentice perhaps,* he thought. The bride of Christ was obvious to him, a nun, but in a city of thousands of nuns, how could she be found? He consulted maps of the city to see if any areas were known as the wolf-on-the-crest, or if perhaps an area outside the city was referenced in this manner, but nothing appeared and no one knew of such things. As his questions grew, but not his answers, Arabi thought it best to let the riddle unfold itself to him and so he put the matter to rest.

Hassar's inquiries caused the gossip of Ibn al-Arabi's arrival to slowly find its way into the compound of the emperor and to the ears of the emperor's Islamic mathematician Nur. Nur who was greatly enthralled with Ibn al-Arabi's spiritual writings invited him to visit the palace compound so they could talk. Arabi took this as a sign and agreed to the visit immediately; hoping that in the confines of Constantinople's political power the answers he was seeking would be revealed. At minimum he hoped he would be allowed to visit the royal library to search for his answers. Nur's envoy, Kragan, arrived by royal coach with instructions to return only when Ibn al-Arabi was ready no matter how long that should take. After writing a short note of instructions on a clay tablet to Hassar, Arabi was ready for his journey to the palace much to the relief of Kragan, a strange, thin man with glaring eyes of blue gray that gave one the ill feeling that they were soon to be someone's snack. The coach was a small covered wagon guided by a coachman, pulled by two white mares and escorted by two immense warriors. Arabi wondered why two huge warriors from the emperor's private guard were necessary for such a journey and asked Kragan. Kragan mumbled a vague reply that was both meaningless and meandering but Arabi allowed his answer to stand unchallenged. All in the envoy's group eyed the pauper looking Ibn al-Arabi with distaste. However, Arabi's powerful, and muscular dancer's body and his charismatic presence demanded respect by all and his peculiar escort said nothing. Arabi attempted conversation with Kragan but found he could not be drawn in. Whether orders or disinterest tightened his tongue he could not be certain. However, it left Arabi distrustful and with little to do but watch the scenery pass as the mares ambled back to the palace through the tight streets and alleys of Constantinople.

The city beyond the walls of the Forum Bovis was not heavily populated and they soon found themselves in the countryside that separated the palace from the citizens. When they had reached an open and uninhabited area of the city the coach was suddenly pulled to a stop by the coachman and Kragan hesitantly said he needed to relieve himself. The guards dismounted and walked slowly to each side of the wagon. With a quick grasp of Arabi's arm the larger of the two warriors quickly pulled Arabi from the wagon's interior. All were surprised when Arabi did not tumble to the ground in a heap as expected but had used the warrior's force to spring himself outward above the behemoth twisting and turning his body. Arabi even when he was in the deepest of thoughts was always keenly aware of his surroundings and was ready with his counter move long before the giant had grabbed his arm.

Slow and hulking in his eyes, his adversaries advanced towards him like dust in the air. As he twisted in the air like an eagle in flight he judged the distance from his landing spot to the warrior now behind him and once his feet had hit the ground he immediately sprung into a backwards handspring twisting once so as to face the warrior and then with a short dash towards him, placed his feet into the joins of the warrior's thigh and torso, pushing himself upward into the air removing the warrior's helmet in a single fluid motion. Arching his body backwards arms overhead with hands full of helmet, he fell to the ground using the force of his swinging arms and the fall to break the warrior's nose with his own helmet. The warrior stood dazed with his nose barely attached to his face. Once Arabi had returned firmly to earth he pulled the warrior's sword from its sheath and sheared off the warrior's right hand that was closing in on him. As the severed right hand fell to the ground he used the hilt of the warrior's own weapon to strike him against the side of his head causing him to fall into a bleeding mass at his feet. The coachman's brain had now activated enough to attempt a leap at Arabi. However, Arabi had only to point the sword at him impaling him as he fell. The second warrior had now rounded the coach and Arabi found himself unable to remove the sword from the dead coachman. He swiftly turned to face the second man unarmed and unafraid. The attacking warrior sensing victory over the unarmed Arabi lifted his sword high above his head in order to deliver a single killing blow but severely misjudged Arabi as an opponent. Arabi dived towards him, tumbling like a ball, passing the giant to his right, grabbing and using the warrior's right leg to swing behind him and then reached up between his legs with his free hand to grab his testicles and pull. The warrior shrieked and lost control of his sword causing him to slice deep into his own leg.

Ibn al-Arabi now turned his attention to Kragan who was running wildly from him. Arabi wishing to quickly end this farce of competition grabbed the nearest hand-sized rock and threw it at his head bringing him down immediately. Arabi went to him and asked, "What is the meaning of this attack against me?"

The frightened and bleeding Kragan replied, "Nur had bragged of your eminence in the Muslim world and we thought that such a renowned man as yourself would fetch a substantial fortune from your Muslim brothers."

"This stupidity for money," Arabi said in disgust, "in the future you will find less hazard in the things you fear than in the things you covet," and with that he left Kragan with his wounded, lifeless gang and made for the palace on foot.

Arabi had traveled hundreds of miles by foot in the past and the journey to the palace in this manner caused him no concern. He made it to the palace walls the next day, forced to sleep unprotected in the open air only one night. It took some time before the guards were able to get word to Nur, so Arabi debated scripture with the amiable and conversant guard who stood over the southern entrance to the palace compound. Nur arrived some enjoyable hours later befuddled by the conditions of Arabi's arrival. "Where is the envoy Kragan?" he asked.

"Kragan thought he might wear the skin of a lion, but discovered he was more suited to the covering of a rabbit," Arabi replied, much to the confusion of Nur.

"No matter," said the perplexed Nur, "let me take you to the bathhouse as you look more like the earth than is acceptable in these confines."

They made their way to the imperial bathhouse and Arabi washed himself while Nur fetched garments more suitable for the visiting scholar. Afterwards, Nur suggested a meal in the gardens outside the Blachernae Church. Arabi while used to the regimen of a stoic felt in this instance sustenance would be beneficial given the events of the past day and so they dined on dates, bread and white mashed beans in the splendor of the gardens. "The Church of Mary holds the shroud of Christ should you like to see it," Nur said, in an indifferent manner. The words struck Arabi and dropping his bread he said, "Yes, this would be most beneficial to me," feeling compelled to do this immediately. But, before they could make their way inside, Kragan's voice was heard, "That is him, the one who attacked us, seize him." Kragan in his haste to quickly convict Arabi had left too much space between his knights and Arabi, forgetting his foe's speed. To Arabi it was evident the likelihood of his success over the twelve guards before him would be most unlikely and he chose to take flight through the doors of the nearby church latching the great wooden doors behind him. It became immediately evident to Arabi that his flowing scholarly gown would not do in the chase and quickly removed it, tying it around him in the fashion of a groin cloth. Free to move, he quickly made haste to the center of the church where a great baptismal bath stood. It was an enormous pool covered by an ornate brass lid. He quickly slid the top to the side and climbed into the cool pool, took one large breath, reset the lid into position, and then sank to the bottom to wait. Soon he could hear the guards enter and rustle about in an attempt to find him, but to no avail. Most left with Kragan, but one remained hesitant and certain that Arabi could not have escaped undetected and continued a slow search of the altar. Arabi entered a trance leaving only traces of his mind so he could remain undetected by thought or motion and waited for the knight to lose interest.

The search of the altar proved useless and just when he was about to join the others the knight spied the baptismal bath, *impossible*, he thought, but decided to explore the interior for assurance. He placed his sword within reach on the marble table next to the bath and slowly moved the brass lid. In the darkness of the church the bath water appeared black forcing the knight to move the lid until the opening was large enough for a man to enter. He decided to probe the bottom of the bath with his sword but before he was able to grab it Arabi sprung from the water, placing his hands over his face while burrowing his thumbs into the knight's eyes. The knight attempted to pull back and release Arabi's grip with his own hands but only succeeded in pulling Arabi from the bath falling backwards down the steps while Arabi continued to dig his thumbs into his eyes bursting his right eye first and then his left. Now completely blinded he let him go. The guard screamed in agony as Arabi made his way from the church.

Nur, confused and dazed, was still outside when he escaped from the interior of the church and asked, "What has happened?"

"A great difference of opinion it would seem," answered Arabi, "I must go."

"You will not escape, everyone is looking for you. Come with me I will hide you!"

"This task must be accomplished alone as I will not endanger you. Please do nothing, I have no fear and you should have none for me," Arabi said, running off, leaving the frightened Nur where he stood.

The Blood of the Shroud

Mediterranean Sea – 1203

THREE - FOR IT IS BY FIRE THAT EVERYONE SHALL BE SALTED.

The moon hung high over the Mediterranean, held by some unseen line, the nearby shore a brush stroke of blue and black. Gerald stood watch. The rustling sail and the water lapping the sides of the Osculum Pacis—the kiss of peace—was all that could be heard aboard the galley. Gaius sat near the tied tiller half asleep but balanced. The current moved them slowly northwest. And, William dreamt.

Christ lay dead before him. He cried. He touched the shroud and felt his tears leave. The wail of a thousand people and the kisses of a million angels was heard and felt. He knew everything; he knew nothing. Christ was gone. Only the shroud remained.

William awoke fitful to the unmarked morning, the orange edge of the sun barely above the azure horizon; pushing the blackness of the heavens back to its beginning. He reached over the side and washed his face with the dampness of the Mediterranean and rose. He walked along the deck gently touching the men awake. The wind would soon begin and a repast was in order. One of Gaius' sons started a fire under the gimbaled cauldron. Shortly stale bread dipped in fatty fish soup was passed to the men and they ate in silence.

After their morning meal Gaius called for William and Gerald.

"Have you seen it?" Gaius asked.

"The ship," said Gerald.

"Yes, we must soon break from this eastern shore and cross the mouth of the Aegean and those who follow us are unlikely to be our allies."

"Pirates?" asked William.

"Perhaps or something equally as distasteful," replied Gaius, "the vessel is too large to be fishermen. We could continue up shore pretending to fish and hope they move off, but the Aegean Sea can be more unpredictable than the Mediterranean and we could find ourselves fighting the winds or worse, costing us weeks in travel."

"What is your thinking?" William asked.

"I believe we should put every man at oar, round Rhodes quickly and then make for Crete. If they catch us there, we can swiftly set upon the shore as defense. Our vessel can make it through the breakwaters; theirs would have far more difficulty and possibly run aground making it nearly impossible for them to leave easily again."

"Then Crete shall be our shield," ordered William.

With this simple plan now spoken, Gaius made preparations for their sprint to Crete. He would lead them north around the isle of Rhodes holding tight to the shore, and then attempt their run to Crete through the small islands that floated between them. Gaius guessed their position somewhere off the southwestern region of the Byzantine Empire. Putting them a day or two at the most from the shoreline of Rhodes. He stayed bonded to the tiller throughout the day. The ship changed course moving towards the center of the Mediterranean at mid-day, and he thought, *I will take this as good fortune wrapped in thorns.*

The day passed quickly and the oarsmen took their rest for the night. The stars rose. After evening meal Gaius tied the tiller again and then took from a small pouch, a modest well-worn board with a knotted cord at its center. Stephen watched attentively. The board seemed familiar to him with its many inscribed symbols on its face. Gaius held the cord tight with his teeth, drawing the board in and out from his face and then steadied it. He counted the knots between his face and the board and repeated the action five times. Stephen knew this device. Then the name of it came to him, "Is that an al-kamal?" Gaius looked down at the young boy and said, "Yes, it is a kamal. I once showed your father how to use this very one." Then it occurred to Stephen from where he knew this apparatus. It was from a drawing his father had made on one of the many boards he used for notes in his workshop. "You can find where we are at sea!" Stephen exclaimed. Gaius replied in a cautious tone, "I can only find where I have been with any accuracy. It is useless in the day or cloudy night. I need that bright star and my experience to give me guidance," and then he pointed to the North Star and demonstrated to Stephen the kamal's method. After that, they sat and covered themselves in cloth and talk.

"Gaius, when did you meet my father?"

"I was pilot for King Richard's fleet in the crusade against Saladin in 1191. Your father provided war counsel to Richard and your uncle, the Wolf of Acre, was with those at the front, along the shore, with his Templar brothers." "Why is he called the Wolf?" Stephen asked. "A few days before the battle of Arsuf, Saladin's forces attacked his line. Leading the charge for Saladin's army was the astonishing Ayaz al-Tawil. A giant over eleven heads high carrying a massive spear, he plowed everyone aside like small children and charged down on William who had fallen from his mount in the pitched battle. William stood his ground as the titan charged towards him. Ayaz's spear was so massive that even a large man could not place his hand completely around it. It was a small tree carried by a leviathan. William, in what seemed a fit of madness to his brothers around him, sheathed his sword and axe behind him as Ayaz cleaved his way towards him. Just when it seemed that Ayaz would impale and split him open, William quickly dashed to Ayaz's left and then leapt up grabbing the spear, pulling it from him. Once it was free from his grip William swung the massive spear at the side of the stallion tearing its flesh from its side, dropping both Ayaz and his horse in one sinuous motion. Then five Templars in unison pounced upon Ayaz killing him in an instant. The battle raged for another three hours. William fought barely ten paces from the fallen giant through it all. When the battle was done William said a prayer over the legendary warrior and personally delivered his body to the camp of Saladin. Taken by his charity and bravery Saladin offered William drink and let him return unharmed even though it was well known that Saladin feared all Templar Knights and would kill them instantly if caught. Richard upon hearing of William's victory over Ayaz named him the Wolf. When Richard returned to France he ordered a special Templar tunic for William bearing on its back a large embroidered wolf on the crest of a mountain. After the crusade when William was given his command at Acre he became known as the Wolf of Acre." Stephen grew silent and fell into his thoughts.

The night was uneventful and the morning returned unhurriedly. Stephen awoke to find the men already at work and decided to explore the galley in detail this day. His father's words came to him, ... *creation favors the organized Stephen, know the details of your equipment,* which meant knowing your surroundings, supplies at hand and the possibilities for invention they provided. Stephen quickly ate some dried fish and hard bread and then went about the task of memorizing everything aboard the galley. To his knowledge only his father had exceeded his ability to memorize things. He had been trained to remember every object and its location in his father's workshop at an early age. He took note of every liquid, powder, stone, tool, weapon, rope, fabric, container and edible aboard the ship. He tested himself throughout the process until he could recite every object and its location with ease. He then set out to create as many useful combinations out of the materials at hand as he had been taught. By this exercise he realized he could create three new weapons, an alternate sail, a crude fresh water collection device, a chair, a small table, dozens of marking devices for writing and drawing, and some fish hooks. He then wrote what he had memorized on the deck to seal this information into his memory forever. This made the day shrivel past him.

Signs of the tailing ship vanished and the crew began to relax. They were well within view of Rhodes now and would round her eastern side by noon tomorrow at the latest. All seemed well aboard the boat and Gaius rested most of the oarsmen and relied primarily on the sail to make progress, knowing they would need all the men well rested if their suspected adversaries should return. It was during this time that William and Gerald noted Stephen's occupation of the day with definite interest.

"William where does this peculiar responsibility of Stephen's come from?" Gerald asked.

"He occupies himself with a strange game of my brother's invention no doubt, though I know of no use for it, nor even how it is played."

"Do you not find this unusual recitation a bit alarming? It is as if the boy is possessed," said Gerald.

William laughed.

"You have forgotten my brother's preoccupation with the...what was it...the internal substance of a thing! He believed that a thing possessed a hidden element that could only be revealed through careful measurement and meditation. It is some part of that exercise no doubt that Stephen mimics. Remember no matter what madness this is, Gregory was a resourceful man of the highest order and perhaps Stephen shares his gift."

"Perhaps, but he would do well not to display it beyond his close friends," Gerald replied.

That night under the stars Stephen and Gaius talked again of things of the mind. Gaius had also observed Stephen's exploration and inquired to its meaning.

"What did your search of the Osculum Paci bring?"

"I have discovered many things that could be. I was moved by truth of my father's wisdom that time and opportunity wait for no one. He taught me that circumstances never adapt to one's whims and to succeed at war you must adapt yourself to the occasion."

"What manner are these things that could be?" Gaius asked, skeptically.

"Aboard this vessel are the makings of a catapult for one."

"A catapult!?!" Gaius said, incredulously.

"Yes, all the materials are here, they are just hidden in other forms. The oars are levers, the railing a fulcrum, the ropes can be used for assembly, the cauldron can be used for the cradle and clay pots for the Greek fire."

"Greek fire, you can make Greek fire, here and now?" Gaius said, stunned at this revelation.

"Well, yes…not without some delay…but, yes I can make Greek fire with what I have brought in my bag and what you have aboard."

"Does William know this?" Gaius asked.

"I have only discovered it this day and you are the first to know."

Gaius quickly left and returned with William, "The boy says he can make Greek fire, is this true?" William did not know the extent of Stephen's wisdom. He was aware that his brother Gregory could produce the fire-of-the-sun and that it was possible that the knowledge could have been passed to the young Stephen.

"Is this true Stephen, can you make the fire?"

Stephen now without hesitation replied, "Yes, but its production would require two more men under my direction and a day to prepare the materials properly and an hour to heat it once the mixture was made in order for it to ignite. But why would we want to set ourselves on fire?"

"Not us Stephen, not us," his uncle replied already absorbed in thought by this news.

The Blood of the Shroud

"Stephen how much could you make?"

"I could create enough to fill the clay pot that holds the oil." Stephen referred to a pot that was the size of a large man's belly used to hold the cooking oil. William knew well what that could do. While it would not sink the ship that might still be lurking, it would certainly warn them off if it could be delivered to them.

"Gaius can you spare Gerald and myself from tomorrow's activities?" asked William.

"You intend to prepare an offering of warning no doubt," replied Gaius.

"Yes, a gift should we need it. We would still need a method to hand it to them."

Still incredulous at what he had heard from the young boy, Gaius said, "Well that will require little effort as Stephen can give you a catapult as well."

"A catapult," the astonished William exclaimed while taking in the young man in new light. Then they spent another three hours discussing in detail the manner and method of Stephen's catapult and fire.

While the two men led by the young boy created an additional arsenal for the Osculum Paci, Gaius was vigilant in his inspection of the weather the next day. It was changing fast. He knew the signs. Fog was coming. This would slow their pace to a crawl and strip him of a way to guide them safely. It was imperative that they make it to the north shores of Rhodes this day. The steady wind and Gaius' calm hand guided them quickly to the eastern edge of Rhodes, but then their luck turned. The fog began to form in late afternoon. The water seemed to give up the spirits of the dead as the fog formed, its shapes and density giving the appearance of wraiths floating and conversing. Gaius while brave was a superstitious man and this added to his apprehension. He considered this as an evil omen. Soon the density made it impossible for them to progress further and Gaius dropped anchor.

For three days the fog remained around them like a wall causing the men to grow anxious and quarrelsome. Fresh water aboard the galley was now in short supply and Gaius needed to bring them to shore to resupply. The murkiness hung around them like a blanket making safe passage impossible to guarantee. The fog hampered the development of Stephen's Greek fire, as he could not expose his ingredients to the continued dampness. These developments worsened William's mood. He needed to be in Naples pleading his case before his Templar Master, Philippe de Plessiez, soon, not caged by mist in the Mediterranean. And so, he pushed for Gaius to have the men row them from the mist not even knowing if this was possible.

"We must move from this prison of vapor, Gaius," said William.

"It is dangerous, we could find ourselves moving into shore and the rocks with little time to prepare."

"If it were any other man I would not ask, but I have supreme faith in you my friend to prevent that from happening."

And so Gaius, shielded only by experience, ordered his sons to row forward, towards an indefinite future. Gaius kept the men quiet and the pace slow. Stopping frequently so that he could listen to everything, his ears providing the only vision available to them. In this way they crept forward through this murky and damp purgatory. On the fifth day the fog retreated slightly at mid-day bringing some bright relief to the men only to have it leave quickly again. However, through it all Gaius' experienced hand kept them from harm. Finally, on the twelfth day they broke through the fog and into the blue skies of the Mediterranean. With this clarity came some difficult news; Gaius no longer knew exactly where they were. With their rowing and the current they had passed Rhodes and in some miraculous manner made it through the small islands that surrounded it without running aground. They were in the middle of the Mediterranean somewhere and he had no idea where. His instincts told him that Greece lay somewhere to the north and Crete to the south. He felt that they could not have gone further, as their pace had been too slow.

Everyone aboard the Osculum Paci also was aware that the surroundings were unfamiliar as not a shore was in view. So all looked to Gaius for guidance. William broke the silence first, "Well, Gaius you have done well. We are free from our imprisonment. Do you have any idea where our tunnel has taken us?"

"Only that Greece should lay north and Crete to the south."

"Then it should be a simple matter to travel north and find familiar shores to guide us."

Gerald pointing to the east cutting their discussion short, "The hounds are here." All turned in the direction of Gerald's outstretched arm. None required his bright vision now as the vessel was clearly in view and less than a half a day behind.

"She is a cog, clearly she chases us," noted Gaius, "If we are caught we will stand little chance against her. She will tower over us."

"There is one bright spot she has no oars," said William, "If she stops to engage us and we can disable her some, we will be able to move off by oar before she can start."

"There are many ifs in your idea William," said the unconvinced Gaius.

William called out to his nephew, "Stephen how much longer to complete the fire?"

"I have a day of grinding and mixing," he replied.

"You have less than a third to make it ready and will that catapult of yours work?"

"We have yet to test it, but it is based on simple mechanics and should deliver our gift at least three boat lengths."

"We can no longer test as it will give our pursuers knowledge of our power," said William, "I must trust in my brother that he has taught you well."

"He has," Stephen replied. But, he was not sure. This was beyond his calculations to deduce. The accuracy of any catapult without a test was impossible to judge. Especially since this one's power was to be derived by four running men jumping overboard to raise the levers. The whole matter was worrisome to Stephen and the beauty of his idealized workroom faded in the glaring certainty of battle. Here was no place for an untested idea. The men he loved would unquestionably die should he fail to deliver his promise. Both fire and catapult would need to work perfectly if they were to succeed. His father's words came to him, ... *the apprehension of failure is often as good as the anticipation of reward in stimulating a person to their best...*

Gaius set all available oarsmen to their tasks and set the sail high in hopes of stealing time for them to make their preparations. William's idea was to continue their charade as fishermen and ordered the knights to strip and hide their weapons and clothing but make them ready for instant use. Stephen continued with the mixture for Greek fire. Even with the mixture prepared properly he was reliant on the heating process to ignite the fusion of materials. If it did not get to the proper temperature it would do little more than coat the mad dogs pursuing them. And there was the matter of its delivery; while he was sure that he could deliver it three boat lengths, as the cog grew closer he realized how much it towered above them. It was not distance he needed but height to clear her railings. He recalculated and came to the chilling conclusion that the hounds would be nearly able to jump aboard before he could guarantee that the fire would reach their deck.

He called for William and worriedly explained his concerns. "Uncle I have started the heating process on the fire, but it is the catapult that concerns me. We must be well within the range of her archers for me to deliver it. Also, we must wait for the fire to come alive before I can trigger our men to leap over the sides to pull the catapult to life." William looked at the small boy and a kindness fell upon his voice as he said to

Stephen, "Wisdom and bravery are the elements of greatness Stephen, I have great faith in you, fear not, it will end as it is ordained."

William met with Gerald and Gaius and discussed their options. "Stephen must have time to fulfill the details of the fire. The hounds will be able to see our preparations clearly before we are able to deliver our cargo to them. The crudeness of the design might confuse them if we act our parts clearly. Gaius there is also the matter of the Osculum Paci's position, she will need to be guided with our side facing our enemies and we will need to be nearly at rest to have opportunity for a clear and accurate shot at her deck." Gaius looked back upon the catapult of oars and rope. "I will have to turn and make for the hounds to guarantee our position or the dogs could fire upon our stern before I have time to place us into position," the doubtful Gaius said, "That will mean we will be without sail and stand naked before our enemies for some amount of time. You do realize that even if Stephen delivers the fire perfectly we could face twenty archers with nothing more than our faith to defend ourselves?"

"Yes, I believe you perceive it exactly as it is Gaius," then with a touch of wit to his tone William added, "Then we will need to provide another galley of faith at our side."

William arranged with Stephen a signal for the fire's readiness. Stephen would need two estimates for their plan to succeed. He would need to estimate the point in which to turn their galley towards the hounds allowing enough extra time for the fire to reach the proper temperature before they reached them, too much heat and the pot would explode on the deck of the Osculum Paci and burn them all to death, too little heat and the mixture would fall upon the deck of the hounds useless. He would also have to guide Gaius on how close they would have to be in order to clear the railings of the cog. There would also be the need to judge the exact moment to order the men over the sides using their weight to pull the arms of the crude catapult up. This was dependent on them moving in unison and out from the boat rather than down. To add force to their exertion he had to use the mast hoist leaving them temporarily without sail power. Once the trap was set they would have to bring the men back aboard quickly and have the oarsmen begin to row away from the enemy while arrows were most likely being shot at them. Adding to his anxiety was that he had never really used Greek fire. He knew everything by formula perfectly, but he had never really set it off. He knew the signs of its readiness, but had never experienced it first hand. He was working completely by training alone.

The hounds were bent on catching them as all their sails were now in use. They were also judging the moment. Gaius estimated their speed at two knots and once they turned it would become three with Osculum Paci's speed added to the angry dogs. *Just a matter of moments before they were side by side,* he thought. Stephen gave the signal and Gaius turned their craft. The hounds seeing this shortened their sails and reduced their speed. Stephen energetically watched the mixture and the distance between the vessels in a stoic mindful manner. Gaius slowed the oarsmen's pace to keep time with Stephen's requirements and the two vessels approached each other.

The men of the Osculum Paci were silent attempting to act the part of fishermen feigning ignorance of the approaching ship. The knights had stowed their shields under soft cover in easy reach. The ships grew closer. Soon, it became clear that Bedouin pirates were indeed pursuing them. Their dress and manner gave them away. Gaius waved in a friendly manner towards them. They held their swords high in reply. There would be little time for pleasantries it would seem. Gaius knew while the pirates had no fear of battle they would prefer to take them prisoner and secure their galley unharmed. There was little value in dead slaves and the galley could be used or sold easily. They would give some quarter but only if they were convinced that the crew of the Osculum Paci would give up easily.

Seconds before the moment of action Stephen realized that the mixture needed more time and signaled William over to him. "I need more time, it is not ready." William said nothing and moved towards Gaius. "Can we be slowed?" "It matters not our speed, we are seconds from their side." "Delay us somehow Gaius." While Gaius could speak in the tongue of the Bedouin's his accent would not allow him to pass as friend in deep conversation. He shouted a greeting. This had no effect on the pirates and they ignored him. Their archers were now evident on deck and it would be only moments before they let loose a volley to express their strength over them. Gaius looked desperately at Stephen in hopes that he was ready. Still, no sign was forth coming. Moments were all that was left before both ships were side by side. Stephen looked down at the crock frantically. The Bedouin archers began to pull back their long bows in preparation. Gaius waved a flag of cloths to serve as notice of surrender while the Bedouin commander of the cog eyed them suspiciously.

Stephen stared directly at the small opening for the fire's signal. The thick mixture did not steam easily but once it had, mere seconds were left to deploy it. Gaius waved his rags frantically attempting to gain the moments needed to unleash their weapon, with his other hand resting on the tiller; shouting simultaneously at the pirates that they were unarmed. The men of the Osculum Paci stood frozen in a timeless embrace with their destiny. Three of the Bedouin archers let go of their pointed reply. Stephen saw the sign of readiness in the crock and immediately shouted to the weight-of-men to move. The catapult was sprung and the secondary arm of chain at the end of the oars spun quickly letting the vessel fly towards their enemy. As it flew, Stephen could see immediately that the crock would harmlessly pass over the Bedouins. His body began to shake with fear and then he heard his father's voice, *start with the vision of the end, for what you see can be.* He looked down at his loaded crossbow fitted with the igniting quarrel and picked it up to fire. Letting his vision guide his arm and eye, he traced the path of the crock to its final destination with his sights. A Bedouin arrow creased his right arm, but he moved not, now obsessed by his vision. He pressed upon the trigger and the quarrel swiftly left the guides of the crossbow, ignited and made for the crock not yet above the Bedouin's ship. Another volley of arrows reached the Osculum Paci killing one of Gaius' sons instantly and wounding another. William was pierced in the shoulder as he raised the men who had acted as weights but made no show of the pain, continuing in his task to save the men. Gerald in the same moment signaled the knights to erect their shields for defense. Gaius watched in rapt attention at the quarrel's fiery flight. At his angle it seemed impossible that the quarrel would strike the crock. But it did. The impact of the flaming bolt caused the crock to explode and fire rained upon the Bedouin's ship causing one sail to catch fire instantly. The pirates found themselves under a maelstrom of flames and they became like agitated wasps, wildly swinging their arms, causing more injury amongst themselves. Gaius took no delay in this confusion, as some experienced archers, unfazed by the flames, continued to fire upon them. The oarsmen of the Osculum Paci needed little prodding and were at their task quickly. Gaius swung the ship to make their profile narrow to the archers and they limped away from the conflagration as fast as possible.

Gerald quickly pulled apart the catapult's lines to make the sail ready again and soon wind added to their power and the distance from the enemy grew steadily larger. The comfort of dusk arrived soon afterwards and the men of the Osculum Paci looked back at the glow of the enemy ship. The knights tended to each other's wounds and when all were cared for they rested. Stephen insisted that he be treated last, enjoying the look of the cut upon his arm. William treated his wound and said, "This will scar cleanly the arrow was sharp." But, Stephen did not hear him, watching with delight the line of blood from his wound drip to the deck, as William sewed his cut shut.

Gaius washed his dead son that night with the tears of the Mediterranean, holding his own for later. All aboard allowed him clear space not daring to intrude on his solemn moment. He lingered at his son's face and kissed him upon the lips remembering him as a child. His eyes welled with tears, but he would not let one through. Once his son was cleaned he lifted him gently and placed him on a clean white linen shroud, wrapped him and tied up the bundle that was his son, tightly. Gaius then prayed.

The next morning Gaius declared they must go to Athens so that he could transport his dead son to his mother. No one aboard the Osculum Paci objected.

FOUR – THE THREE GIFTS OF EMPIRES—CONQUEST, SLAUGHTER AND PLUNDER.

"Do they not know I alone speak to God?" Innocent the third angrily exclaimed, while his out-stretched right arm swept his desk clean of the many gold and silver jeweled objects upon it.

Abbott Martin bowed in fear at the great man's anger and timidly replied, "It is the doing of the old blind doge of Venice he is undoubtedly possessed by the Devil."

"And what of my knights, are they also possessed by the Devil? They are under my holy orders to attack Egypt not the Christians of Zara," screamed the Pope, "and now my crusaders head for the center of the empire: Constantinople!"

Ælfric of Abingdom sat cloaked by the darkness of the room's corner bored by the angry rhetoric of the Pope, and said squarely, "Perhaps it is time for the center of Christian power to return to its proper place—Rome."

Innocent's eyes angrily narrowed and he nearly excoriated his personal henchman, but stopped to weigh the strength of Ælfric's idea.

"Would it not better serve Christians everywhere for Constantinople to be reduced so that you may regain your rightful and complete rule over all Christendom as ordained by God? Have they not flaunted your rule with their complete disregard of your authority?" said Ælfric, now standing in the center of the chamber, placing himself in the stream of light from the window above, giving him the glow of holy authority.

"How do you mean?" the Pope harshly questioned.

"Well for one, why do all the relics of Christ stay with them and not you? Is it not you who converses with our Father? Who better to safeguard Christ's memory?"

"You are right of course, but what is to be done now?" asked the Pope, losing some of the potency of his anger.

"It is a small matter for me to retrieve what is rightfully yours while the city falls under the temporary domain of your Crusaders. Is not the Abbot an expert in such matters, could he not supply me with the tidings necessary for me to safeguard these holy antiquities back to you, your eminence?"

The Pope contemplated this carefully and then replied, "Better yet, he will join you to ensure that everything is precisely identified and returned to me."

"But, your holiness I would only slow Ælfric in this quest, I..."

"Silence Abbot Martin. You will go as I have decided!" and with that, the Pope gestured for both to leave with a quick wave of his right hand.

Abbot Martin turned and fell on one of the plates that had been swept to the floor and crashed to his knees. The Pope turned his way and gave him the eye used for the soon-to-be-dead. The Abbot quickly righted himself and left the room with Ælfric. Once they were free of the Pope's ears Ælfric promptly said to the Abbot, "I shall have half of the gold you have retrieved from the floor."

"What do you mean, do you label me a thief?" the overly righteous Abbot declared. Ælfric spun around immediately and boxed him in his right ear with an open hand, "Take me not for a fool or I shall delight in feeding you to the hogs! Your ruse may succeed with the Pope, but not with me. I will have all of what you have secured from your journey to the floor now!" The Abbot still holding his throbbing ear reached into the pouch of his robe and timidly handed the towering warrior the golden-jeweled challis he had stolen from the Pope. "We go for great treasure in Constantinople I will have my due," Ælfric ordered and moved on down the hall away from the Abbot. The Abbot Martin lingered behind using his throbbing ear as excuse and reached once more into his robe retrieving a few small silver coins to inspect for value.

"You may keep the coins as a reminder of what I see," Ælfric shouted back to the astounded Abbot.

Ælfric moved out into the afternoon sun squinting. The guards threw themselves into full attention as he moved past them. Ælfric ordered his waiting squire to retrieve his horse and waited. Now he had holy authority to plunder anything he wished. This journey would be his final campaign as the riches of Constantinople rivaled everything the old Roman Empire had once been. He would swim in a sea of gold after this and all that he need do is bring back some faded and torn relics supposedly touched by Christ. He believed in none of it. *The righteous sheep unable to find their own way succumb easily to the rants of superstitious prophets; I cannot bear the stench of their ignorance of what is real in this world,* he thought.

Abbot Martin ventured into the Pope's private kitchen, bribed the cooks with some of his new wealth and helped himself to freshly slaughtered and roasted meats, berries, nuts, fresh bread and wine. Nothing would be missed in a kitchen that overflowed with a cornucopia of delicacies for a single man. He squealed softly to himself as the flavors passed over his tongue and down his throat. He dipped his bread into fresh cream and contemplated this journey and how to outfox his newly minted partner and rival for Constantinople's riches. *How had this happened,* he thought. *I prefer my thieving to take place closer to the safety of home.* "Ælfric, bah," he whispered to himself, "May he choke and die on hard bread." His ear still smarted from the blow inflicted by Ælfric and his wicked thoughts gave him comfort. *Perhaps this is not all bad. I may make use of this oaf of iron and use him as he thinks to use me. He needs my wisdom as much as I need his arm.* He reached for more wine and sank deeply into his thoughts.

The Blood of the Shroud

Constantinople – 1203

FIVE – THE ROSE OF GOD.

She stared at her reflection in the bowl of water. She saw the loveliness of her face. All admired her long auburn hair that graced the curves of her flawless cheeks. God had given her an uncommon exquisiteness. She was a rare flower untouched and perfectly shaped in a field of weeds. It was as if all that was given to her was extracted from the many around her, so that by comparison she rose above them. It made her desired.

Everything she beheld in the mirror-of-liquid appalled her. "Why have you cursed me God?" Christina uttered, "Why have you made me the object of so many desires unwanted?" She picked up the nearby knife and held it to her face and contemplated the first cut. She thought of Psalms, *Lord…many are they that rise up against me.* She twisted the knife against her face, drawing a pinprick of blood, but could not plunge it in. She sobbed and pleaded with God for escape from her torment, throwing the knife to the floor and then tossing herself upon the bed, writhing from the anguish of her fate.

"Christina come now, we eat," said her mother from other side of the door, "leave your prayers we have much to discuss tonight."

"Leave me be," Christina whimpered in return.

"Come now, you are to be wed and your protestations will not delay it," her father ordered.

"No, I will not, leave me be! You may force this wedding upon me but I will not come. Leave me!"

She cried again and would answer to no more of their pleadings and so after some time they quieted and left her alone to sleep.

When she awoke the sun was already high in the sky and she stood to admire its effect upon the countryside through the single small window her room afforded. She noticed the small tray upon her side table filled with food and drink. She tried her door. It was locked as usual from the outside. No longer trusted by her parents to remain since her last escape. She contemplated starvation but was too hungry to carry the sin further and reached for the fruit. It was sweet and she contemplated its appearance. *Perfect. If God has created perfection, it is for a purpose, what is mine?* She finished and fell to her knees to pray. She would remain this way for several hours hoping to be answered by her true love Christ.

Benozzo was a rotund man with a ruddy, severely pocked face, long beard and stringy hair. Adding to his appearance was his disgusting personality, which alone would have been excuse enough to avoid his presence. However, his wealth forced the false admiring of those who wished to share in his affluence. He was a successful exporter of Constantinople's finest goods to the western empire. So all the producers of wares catered to his many desires in an effort to expand their trade. Benozzo yearned for the striking Christina as his bride. Her parents the cloth makers desired greater wealth. The union would provide them clear access to Benozzo. It was not chance that guided the gluttonous Benozzo's attention to Christina but the careful scheming of her parents that successfully created the intended union between the two. Christina's attractiveness was so desirable that it served as dowry enough for the wealthy Benozzo, even causing him to guarantee a mercantile contract with her parents once the wedding was made. That to was the planning of her parents, whose shrewdness ensured numerous affluent suitors were available for Christina. In order to create a bidding war for her supposed affections. It was only Christina herself that posed any threat to their future prosperity. Beyond the constant attacks upon her virginity by unwanted suitors and Christina's wish to show her devotion to Christ by remaining chaste, there was the grave matter of her wounding the first suitor arranged by her parents. It was only by careful arrangement that the news of her attack remained from Benozzo's ears. Their scheming had effectively twisted a date for the wedding and a dinner for a public declaration by Benozzo. It had only required the services of an herbalist to sufficiently drug Christina into near stupor for them to succeed through that night. Now only weeks separated them from their desires. After it was done, Benozzo could do with Christina as he desired and in any manner he wished. It would be his right. They would have their contract.

Christina's father Leofrick was a slight man with no remarkable features other than his lack of chin and hair giving one the distinct impression of a vulture. Perhaps it was the humor of God that his features should match his attitude. For Leofrick was good only at stealing fortune rather than creating it. His own business as a cloth maker was really a forced inheritance left to him by his father-in-law, who he had drowned in a tub of entrails to secure his future. God had also seen to it that Leofrick would be perfectly matched with a bride of suitable temperament. It was after all, his wife Matilda who strongly urged Leofrick's indiscretion in the matter of her father. There was little in the way of love between Matilda and Leofrick, both preferring the pleasure of affluence to affection. Had not their combined talents for thievery and murder so perfectly intersected, one would have surely killed the other on their wedding night.

Christina was not the product of their union, but the daughter of Matilda's stunning sister Arabella. Arabella was the favorite of her father and he lavished never-ending praise and fortune upon her. In contrast, Matilda was treated like an unwanted guest in her own home. Matilda having nothing but envy and contempt for her blessed, and much loved, younger sister sought to ruin her after her father's forced demise. Left without inheritance Matilda felt assured Arabella's life would crumble under the weight of existence. But it was not to be. Even without dowry, Arabella's loveliness provided ample suitors to her door and she was soon wed to a successful carpenter named Barda. Arabella's pregnancy came soon after and this event seemed to magnify her beauty and joyful personality in Matilda's eyes. This infuriated Matilda severely and murderous aspiration rose within her again. However, much to the satisfaction of Matilda, Arabella died with the birth of her only daughter Christina. This event left Arabella's husband, Barda, so tormented that he took his life the next morning leaving the poor Christina unexpectedly in the hands of Matilda and Leofrick.

At first Matilda and Leofrick were completely dismayed at the prospect of feeding another mouth and contemplated discarding her in the nearby woods like rubbish until Matilda noticed the striking resemblance Christina had to her sister and thought perhaps a beautiful minion in their service would enhance their prospects later on. But, almost at once it became apparent that Christina was unusual, showing strong signs of devotion by holding conversations with God at the top of her voice at the age of three. Only the mocking of her captor-parents silenced her habit, but not her faith. As Christina grew so did her piety. Once Matilda realized that Christina would provide the larcenous pair with no benefit she sought to kill her in her sleep. As Matilda's hand encircled the throat of the young Christina she was stricken by an unknown malady and bedridden for a month. From then on Leofrick and Matilda schemed on what should be done with Christina but dared not harm her out of fearful superstition. When she turned thirteen Christina's beauty enthralled all that encountered her. And, her captor-parents realized the true potential of her birth and sought to capitalize on her indirectly through marriage. This proved to be far more difficult than first imagined by the pair, as Christina had no desire to be wed. Her desires were to join the monastery of Cluny and serve her life in the devotion of Christ. This was at direct odds with the peculating pair's plans for her, forcing them to use drugs and imprisonment to ensure their purpose.

These were the conditions surrounding Christina when Benozzo arrived unexpectedly one night knocking with his iron-ended cane. The thunderous noise from Benozzo's hand seemed to portend events out of the control of the maniacal pair. At first they thought to avoid the uninitiated appointment with the intended quarry of their plotting. However, the hastily whispered strategy between them found no avenue of escape and they let him in.

"Oh Benozzo, how excellent it is that you should drop by now. We were just commenting on how blessed Christina will be to have you as husband," said Leofrick.

"Yes, yes, of course," Benozzo said, weakly, adding, "I have only this moment to inform you of my travels, so I came tonight. Zara has been attacked by Innocent's crusaders and I must travel to see the results of these action on my fortunes since I have much invested there."

"Will this have much consequence on your business?" Matilda said quickly, fearing her future prospects were fading with this news.

"I need to see the affect of this action on the greater aspects of my business to know. It requires my hand, which brings me to my visit tonight. I wish to take Christina with me to Zara and wed her there, as my stay may be extended and it would not do to miss my own wedding."

This curve was not to the liking of the depraved pair and they cultivated a disconcerting silence in the room. Benozzo broke the mood sensing their disagreement.

"Perhaps it's our future contractual arrangements that you worry over. Fear not, I am ready to transact such business now. All the necessary documents have been made ready for your signing should my preparations in these matters be to your satisfaction."

Leofrick sensing the need to dodge this point returned with, "No, my dear Benozzo we are simply distraught that we will not be able to attend your nuptials as our business is here and requires our constant attention." In the back of Leofrick's mind was the matter of Christina who had not been prepared for leaving tonight and would undoubtedly cause trouble should she be forced to leave right then.

"But perhaps we can arrange things here so that we may bring Christina to you ourselves in three weeks time and still be part of the festivities," Leofrick said, hoping to regain control of the circumstances.

Matilda now sensing the direction of her husband's plotting added, "Yes, I cannot stand the thought of seeing my only daughter wed in strange lands without my support. It is simply impossible."

Benozzo contemplated this and finally said, "What have you to drink?" Not answering Matilda rushed off to find their best wine.

"Sit, sit Benozzo you must be tired. Perhaps this is best, we will have time to contemplate your documents and my wife will get her wish to see her only daughter married to such a fine man as yourself."

Matilda returned and poured a large drink into the cup set before Benozzo. He drank and grabbed the flask roughly from Matilda pouring himself an equally large second cup, downing it quickly. Benozzo ruminated on the crafty pairs words as he drank and thought, *so these carrion beetles will not give up their treasure thinking me a fool*, and then spoke to them in his kindest manner.

"Perhaps you are right, I will not burden you with these matters tonight. In fact I shall send my man Boethius to bring you ample funds for the journey and I will have him craft the arrangements of your travel to me. I will happily pay all your expenses, after all we are to be related now."

"Oh, that will be splendid, thank you Benozzo you are indeed as great as your reputation," Matilda replied with joy, gleeful at the aspect of his words, sensing no danger in them.

My reputation is one to cause fear and trembling in those who know me, you old sow, he thought, but answered, "It is nothing, now that concludes my business and I will bid you a fine night." And then, Benozzo left, leaving the pair in a glow of corrupt pleasure.

Boethius waited by the wagon for the return of Benozzo, bored. He spotted a snake slithering just beyond the path's edge and quickly threw his wrist dagger piercing the center of the serpent's head. He ambled to it slowly and looked down upon the dying reptile to inspect its agony, enjoying the manifestation of the pain he had inflicted upon the poor serpentine beast. But, his introspective enjoyment of torture was cut short by the return of Benozzo.

"Let's go," Benozzo said, curtly.

"No girl?"

"No, you will have to attend to that after I have gone and then bring her to me. Kill the old fool and disfigure the old sow so she will act as warning to those who intend to use me. The pair thinks of me a fool as if I would not know the intentions of my intended partners even before meeting them. Do they think my wealth is the gift of God? I am God here and they will soon have proof of it."

Boethius delighted in his master's words. Since arriving in Constantinople he had little opportunity to enjoy his trade. His mind began to work upon the details of his future work with much delight as they made their way to the harbor.

Athens – 1204

Six – Character fashions fate.

Gaius buried his son in the shadow of the Parthenon. The sun was bright, the sky cloudless. It was a perfect day made overcast by the departure of his oldest son, Donus. The mourners wailed. The men were dispirited by the countenance of his loss as they watched the body lowered into the ground. William stood near his friend Gaius providing indiscernible but needed support. All the men shoveled the earth in unison over the lifeless shrouded form in silent homage. When it was done Gaius was first to speak.

"He was in the flower of his youth, let us drink fine wine this day, so that we may remember his fragrance."

They returned to Gaius' home to find it filled with drink and splendid food. If he mourned, he did not show it—preferring to embrace life right then. The saddened men took to his efforts and regained some of their camaraderie. The drink seemed sweet. As the liquid warmed them they opened up to give praise to the fallen with stories of his youth and humor. And, laughter was exchanged briefly for the grief they all felt that night.

The next day William with Gaius, acting as guide, sought out news from the merchants of Athens in the town's square. Their delay with the fog and pirates had cost them time and William was anxious for any news of the newest crusade. The attack on Zara was the gossip of the day but most knew little of substance relying instead on rumor for their accounts, which when taken in whole seemed unreliable and useless. However, one merchant knew of an old acquaintance of Gaius named Eudoxius who had recently returned from the Dalmatia region near Zara and suggested that perhaps he could provide the knowledge they required. Gaius knew this fur trader Eudoxius well enough, having provided him transport on more than one occasion. When they found him he was engaged in preparations for another journey. Eudoxius was a short, well built man with a cropped beard and short hair in the manner of the ancient Greeks having taken his look from the many statues that remained in view throughout Athens.

"Eudoxius you look well. The years have been kind to you," said Gaius. Eudoxius looked up from his packing and stared at him for some moments before replying. "Ohh, Gaius is that you? You have changed much in my eyes since I saw you last," he replied, "Has life treated you well?"

"Like all, life has taken some from me but in whole, given me more than perhaps any man deserves. I have friends and family and who has right to ask for more?" replied Gaius.

"Indeed you are right to think this way," the trader said, "Have you sought me out or has chance once again played its curious game upon us?"

"No, I have sought you out for news for my friend William here who has need of information about the crusaders who have taken Zara."

Eudoxius eyeing the commanding Templar said, "I bid you well William, what little I know you may have. I made it to the fringes of Zara the day before the attack began. The forces of Innocent were many thousand strong and I observed from a distant hilltop the attack first hand. Ships with banners displayed were many and fair. They first used a ram against the chain that protected the harbor breaking it with some effort. But after that, they crushed the defenders of the city with little force and sacked the town of its most precious relics, quickly making the city their own. They were moved by hundreds of ships under Venetian colors. After many nights I hid my furs and ventured into the town to see if any trade was possible. Zara was largely unharmed but much had been removed of value. Trade seemed unlikely in these circumstances and I hoped perhaps informal honesty could serve me in some manner later. So I found a place of drink in hopes of hearing dialogue from lips loosened by wine. I was rewarded. The crusaders had been promised ships for their Egyptian campaign by the Venetians, but were unable to meet the price when they arrived. In exchange for their transport they had agreed to reclaim Zara for them. But now the forces somehow find themselves under the command of the son of the deposed emperor of Constantinople, Alexius IV, and plan to make their way to take Constantinople as well."

"Are you sure of this?" William said, aghast.

"I have no want to mislead you, my preparations are not to hunt but to take shelter. No major city along the path to Constantinople is safe now. You Templar above all should know well the temptations of wealth among the misguided warriors of Rome. If they feel they have any holy sanction they will not rest until everything in their path is blighted by their presence."

"Did the Venetian ships leave before you?"

"Only a few small Venetian ships headed out from the harbor, but I could not tell their direction. Most of the crusaders were still too engaged in their drunken thievery to leave before I left," replied Eudoxius.

"How many days have past since your visit to Zara?" William asked.

"Twenty sunsets distance me from my past at Zara," the trapper replied. William and Gaius looked at each other, thanked Eudoxius and left.

~

The home of Gaius had taken on the manner of an inn with the Templars and his sons now home. Food and drink seemed endless and the men were enjoying the rest. Stephen however wasted no time rebuilding his supplies and searching out arrows suitable for modification as quarrels for his crossbow. He had succeeded in replacing five quarrels but his coveted igniting quarrel would require more time and supplies than were available to him right then. He had cleaned his crossbow of the effects of the sea-salt-air and it was now in perfect form again. With his large leather shoulder bag resupplied he turned his attention to his Templar brothers. For them he re-edged each of their swords more from his habit of purpose than need. When William returned he was applying the finishing touches to William's axe. Even with William directly above, Stephen did not pause, locked into a concentration of character reserved for someone far older.

"Stephen, I have need for you."

Stephen finished the stroke of his stone upon the edge of the axe and then looked up at his uncle surprised, "You have returned uncle, have you news?"

"Yes Stephen, I have much to report, find Gerald and bring him for we must talk now!" The young boy responded quickly, without word and raced to find his uncle's friend.

Gaius, Gerald, Stephen and William gathered around a small fire ring that was made near the rough portico of wood at the rear of Gaius' home. It served as a meeting place for Gaius and his sons after meals and before morning work. Now it would serve as forum for William's discussion.

"My worst fears have been realized. The forces of Innocent have been corrupted and have attacked the Christians of Zara. Whether this is the Pope's aspiration or that of the Venetians whose colors they now fly; I am unsure. If our reports are true they intend on moving and taking the great knot of the empire."

"Not Constantinople," Gerald exclaimed.

"Yes, and I fear we are too late to stop them for the ships may have sailed from Zara, leaving us no time," William explained, "My dreams have foretold of this moment. For many weeks I have dreamt of Christ and his shroud. I believe he commands me to take action at Constantinople and save it from the hands of the tainted."

"Surely our lord does not command you to go alone, while we are not many, five Templars can dissuade or overpower three times our number," Gerald said.

"You are right my friend, but I wish you to continue the journey to Philippe de Plessiez and secure as many Templars as you can and meet us at Constantinople. If I can succeed in securing the shroud it will take many more to hold it," William replied.

"It is madness even for the Wolf of Acre to go alone," Gerald returned.

"He will not be alone, I will go with him," Stephen declared firmly.

All eyes turned to the young boy in a matched look of disbelief.

"You?" Gaius questioned.

"Yes, I am good in all manner of things and I have earned my place with him," Stephen said, with an assurance born from the facts of action. The men looked at each other but none could find reasonable quarrel with his assertion and let his idea stand.

The men talked well into the night making plans for travel and immediate arrangements for supplies. Gerald was to take the Osculum Paci guided by Gaius' sons as soon as it was fitted; and Gaius, Stephen and William would take a smaller vessel across the Aegean Sea to Gallipoli the gate to the Marmara Sea—the door to Constantinople. In the smaller vessel they hoped to pass any Crusaders they met unnoticed or unwanted. The smaller vessel would need to rely primarily on wind for passage but Gaius was confident under his guidance the journey could be made safe and fast. At least to Constantinople, their return he feared would require more providence than planning.

The next morning the men met and ate in near silence exchanging words with a warrior's brevity. And then, Gaius, Stephen and William

The Blood of the Shroud

left Athens with the breath of the Aegean Sea at their backs and headed for Constantinople.

~

The sea bore the marks of God's handwriting in glimpses of white and viridian. Stephen stood to the fore of the small boat gazing over the wide expanse of moving colors in deep thought. Milan and Acre seemed so long ago now. Even his youth was removed from him. In its place somehow the unexpected mantle-of-man had been placed around his shoulders. He looked at the scar upon his right arm and wondered how many more he would be allowed to bear before his meeting with Christ. In this modern age of war he was now required to be one of its warriors. He felt to his essence the purpose of this quest. Whether God or the dreams of a man sanctioned this trial, made no difference to him. Its purpose for him was plain. Success in this life meant living. He could not simply hide in the shadows of faith and his workroom. To be alive meant risking something. Right or wrong he believed Christ commanded that; and would call him to the birthplace-of-his-soul, when his task was done here on earth. He thought of Isaiah, ...*for they shall eat the fruit of their doings.* It was time for him to do, so that he could taste his life.

William examined his axe. The finish on its edge was superb, an instrument of ends in his expert hands. He thought of its past. Death is committed to the memories of knights by slashes of fear. The scars they raise are never removed. Enshrined in a secret tomb that all Templars know they would join in time. He believed he should be worthy of the fallen, for was he not the dead living a daydream of life? To him killing required reverence for what he had taken. He was a holy man who tried to civilize a perilous endeavor. The spirit of Christ alone sustained him in this cruelest of professions. This was his duty, his unyielding thing to bear. With each death he found it harder to find his way back to the light of life. He knew not the limits of this journey; only what he would have to give to accomplish it.

Gaius glanced at the two men with a respect borne of shared experience. Should he face Armageddon, these two would be fine companions in the expression of it. He shifted the sail to catch the wind at a more suitable angle and studied the skyline behind them as he turned the craft. The appearance of shapes on the horizon behind them concerned him. He thought for a moment perhaps his old eyes were deceiving him. *No, they are ships,* he thought, *perhaps hidden before this time by the many small islands that dot the Aegean.* He called out to William and Stephen.

"Someone is behind us."

The pair looked up and studied the distance.

"I count four, perhaps five ships," Stephen said.

"If it's the Crusaders it is not the main force. Eudoxius said the army at Zara was carried by hundreds of Venetian vessels. That would mean that the force would be as large as twenty thousand or more. To take Constantinople it will require at least that many," William declared.

"If it is them, we can do nothing now but lead them there," Gaius said.

The distance to the gate of the Marmara Sea that was home to Constantinople was not great but their reliance on sail alone put strains on maintaining a direct path. They would be at minimum two days ahead of their chasers should the winds remain in their favor. The race to the Sea of Marmara turned more serious with the sighting and they worked through the nights to remain ahead of followers by day. Gaius calculated that they were close to the inlet of the Marmara Sea. And, finally the large islands of Lemnos and Imbros that marked the direction to the Dardanelles inlet and the Sea of Marmara just beyond it appeared before them the next day.

As they entered the channel they looked behind them one last time but could no longer see their pursuers. The passage through the narrow Dardanelles channel was eerily devoid of all inhabitants and they quietly passed into the open waters of the Marmara. Their path now required no navigation as Constantinople rested on the left of them, along the northern coast of the sea. They encountered another small craft the second day in the great sea heading west. They attempted to make contact, but were waived off frantically at the sight of William wearing his Templar tunic. On the morning of the third day, the great city of Constantinople came into view. And, with her gaze now back upon them, the realization that they were not alone made knots of their bellies. The Venetian fleet had arrived well before them, over 400 ships strong. Their arrival went completely unnoticed in the pandemonium of the crusaders as they prepared themselves for battle. The entire fleet was there but not yet in place to wage war. Even the greatness of this fleet would have no impact on the great sea walls of Constantinople. They would have to enter the Golden Horn and attack the city from the northeast where the estuary shores allowed for landings and the walls were most vulnerable. Based on the mass of ships before them the chain across the Golden Horn still held. *Hopefully, they had time to reach the palace grounds and take the shroud before the crusaders attacked,* thought William.

"We must take to the shore on the west before the city begins. We will have no chance at entering the Golden Horn with this many vessels before us. Our best prospect is to cross from the west through the fertile plains of Thrace and enter the city from the north through the land walls of Theodosius," William said, "They will be lightly guarded since they now expect a sea attack."

"Guarded or not the walls are thick and the entrances not many," Gaius replied.

"We will not use the entrances, we will pass through the aqueducts," declared William.

"William, on foot that is a several day walk to the palace at the north!"

"Gaius, if I should need to overcome every obstacle before I meet it, surely I will fail here. Make for land and allow me to fail in the attempt, not with my answers for they are becoming in short supply."

Gaius groaned and said, "Yes, let us fail in this mad attempt. Go prepare yourselves while I find you a safe shore."

Gaius turned the vessel and headed west along the shore until he found a suitable spot for a beach landing and dropped anchor.

"Why have you stopped Gaius?" William asked.

"I need the wind to shift before we make our attempt. Also, we should make some arrangements for our next meeting. I will wait four days near this shore. If you have not returned I will attempt to enter at the Harbor of Eleutherion. I once knew the harbor master there and will seek his help should I need to search for you."

"It is too perilous, if the days pass beyond four, return to Athens and your family."

"Now is it I who must overcome your obstacles?" Gaius said, smiling.

"The Harbor of Eleutherion?" William replied, annoyed by the sound of his own reasoning.

The landing took place at dusk. They watched in silence as Gaius made his way back to the open sea through the breaking waves. William and Stephen then headed to the edge of the nearby woods and made a small fire on the beach. "We will leave before dawn Stephen, eat some and take your sleep. I will watch and wake you when your time has come." William waited until the moon was hung high in the sky before waking the boy and then taking rest himself.

~

The dawn was full of dew and soft crashing waves when Stephen awakened William.

"Uncle I have laid out a small meal for us, let us eat and begin our journey."

They ate quickly and then began their walk towards the city's north wall. When the sun was halfway to its zenith they spotted a small village outside the city walls. William knew of it.

"That is the industrial quarter. We should walk there and perhaps we can purchase horses," William said.

They marched on and reached the village soon after. It was abandoned. They walked in silence and came upon a young girl, dirty and ragged sitting on a log.

"Where are the others?" Stephen asked.

"Run, mountains, trees, behind walls, scared big boats."

"Why did you not go?"

"Momo bad, inside, want me help. No help. Momo sleep, hot."

"We will look, perhaps we can help," Stephen replied.

William did not hear the sound; he felt it. A resonance that brought with it warning: the heavy misstep in anticipation, the silent rejoin of a man's intent, a noose brushed against, an adversary's grip made stronger against the hilt, the anxious breath released too soon. He pulled his Gladius dagger free from its sheath—a handcrafted jewel modeled after a Roman artifact Gregory had purchased in Rome and improved upon. It was a foot and a half long, with a polished razor sharp edge and a small hand guard above a sharkskin-covered hilt. It was a light and swift weapon and in close quarters provided William with his most effective defense from malice.

"Stephen, stay with the girl I will look."

William made for the small straw and wood, door-less hut. He paused for an imperceptible second before entering and then stabbed through the left edge of the outside wall, piercing muscle and slicing bone. From a hiding place on the opposite side of the lane a screaming villain came with an axe and William in his sights. The girl started to run, but Stephen grabbed her from behind and held her fast. William turned to meet his attacker and saw his opponent's failure immediately. The inexperienced die in battle not for lack of skill but from an inability to keep their eyes open at the crucial moment of contact, giving an adversary advantage. His attacker now in good position and with ample speed closed his eyes seeing only the start of his delivery. In that briefest of moments William was able to avoid the villain's axe and slice off the hand that carried it, causing the hand and axe to drop together. William plunged his sword through stomach of his opponent as the villain regained his vision—seeing his end quite clearly.

The hidden man in the hut staggered out and fell moaning to the ground. William walked to him, crouched down and spoke softly, "Your end may take hours unless I finish what you have started. What is your wish?"

The fallen man looked up spitting blood and said, "Now!"

William then plunged his sword through the robber's heart and held it, praying silently for the man's soul, until his end came. William turned back to the other man and the whispered cry from his axe-wielding foe yielded only, "spare me," before he closed his eyes for his last time.

Stephen held the girl firm as she sobbed, frightened of the men before her.

"No hurt, bad man tell me do, say give me food, no hurt me."

"Stephen leave her be, we must go. Her fate is in Christ's hands now."

Stephen released her and she ran off screaming and crying to no one.

"How did you know?" Stephen asked.

"Experience born from death," he replied and they began to walk again.

They arrived at the edge of the village and could see the main entrance to the city from the west—the great inset in the wall of Theodosius with large wooden doors, known as the Golden Gate. It was closed and above it hundreds of warriors guarded it. Ahead of the great defensive walls of Theodosius was a dry brick-lined moat that formed the first line of protection, beyond that laid a wide flat terrace of earth and finally the massive impenetrable walls. Guarded properly these measures were impossible to breach by any force. The dry ditch struck William odd. *Why have they not filled the moat yet? Is it overconfidence or mistaken strategy that they leave it dry? Do they expect an attack only from the Golden Horn?*

Turning to Stephen, William ordered, "We must travel quickly through the fields and find a hole in the warriors on the wall while the moat remains waterless. If they fill it we will be much tasked to cross it."

They moved quickly using the tall grasses to cover their movements and after three hours succeeded in finding a large hole in the defenders along the top of the walls.

"We will wait until dark then make our way to the wall and then follow its face until we find a suitable opening," said William.

The wait until dusk seemed immeasurably long, especially since their silence was required for security. Finally, the sun firmly passed the horizon dragging the cover of black sky over them. Then under a still moonless night, William pulled at Stephen's sleeve and they crept towards the dry moat. The moat had appeared shallow from the distance but when they reached the edge they realized the great depth facing them. The angle to both sides was also considerable. What little light that was available at the top disappeared as they looked into the depths of the channel. It would be no easy task to climb up or down and remain noiseless through it all. Although, the guards were not many, they were alert and walking the length of the wall at regular intervals. William pulled on his riding gloves and mimed for Stephen to do the same. With their gloves secure they began to make their way down the jagged face of the trench. The two scurried slowly to the bottom. Stephen slipped once and nearly fell to a certain and painful landing, but regained his balance with the aid of William's quick hands. Time became uncertain as they crossed into the darkness. Their arrival at the bed of the man-made river cast them into a pit of blindness. The distance across was equal to the height of the sides and made more treacherous as the bricks were cast upon the floor in a chaotic manner, making walking upon them seem impossible in pitch-black darkness. With their feet they began to cautiously feel their way across.

When they reached the middle of the moat—the murmur began. *The sound of the wind through tall grasses,* Stephen thought. But, it grew more intense and distorted itself into something different. *The ocean waves upon the shore, carried by the breeze perhaps.*

"Run, the moat fills!" William sang out.

Now they had no time to feel their way along the uneven bottom. Stephen immediately took to bouncing from one brick to another, not allowing time for his weight to fully rest on any surface—springing like a deer under hunt. How William was fairing he could not judge in the blackness. The sound of the water was now a torrent in his ears. But, it had not reached them yet. William was first to contact the other side and climbed a few feet and waited for the younger man to reach him. He looked towards the sound and could see the furious face of the water coming at them fast.

"Hurry!" William commanded.

Stephen could move no faster, but moved towards the sound of his uncle's voice instinctively. Unknowingly in the darkness, only one leap remained between him and his uncle when he felt the mist of water upon his face. He leapt one more time and in the air found the hand of his uncle on him—pulling him upwards. The water pressed at their legs and they fought their way up to the edge, as the water rose quickly higher. They climbed like men chased by fire and finally reached the top greatly winded. Without resting, William rose and hoisted Stephen to his feet dragging the young man to the great wall. When they reached it, they rested in the darkness, listening for the cry of detection their shouts were sure to bring.

Constantinople – 1204

Seven – All shall quake before them.

Alexius III, the current Emperor of Constantinople had blinded, deposed, and thrown into prison—his brother—Issac II, the former emperor, throwing the empire into political chaos and unwittingly providing the Venetians an excuse to attack their chief rival for financial dominance of the empire.

The leader of Venice, the Doge Enrico Dandolo, was in his eighties and appeared feeble to all that met him. He had carefully cultivated this facade over many years and enhanced it by pretending blindness when negotiating. He was far from feeble, holding the sharpest financial mind in the empire. The power of Venice was a manifestation of it. But, his empire had reached the limits of his considerable talents; the Doge Dandolo knew that in order for his financial kingdom to emerge from the shadow of Constantinople—it would need to be destroyed. That required what he did not have, an army. He had slowly built up his empire through trade, not wishing to waste his talents and money cultivating a large expensive military force—something he thought was better leased than owned. And, he wanted to distance his beloved Venice from the repercussions a war would undoubtedly incur.

Unexpectedly, Innocent's crusade provided the means he was looking for. From the beginning the Doge worked endlessly with his court to manipulate the crusaders. He promised the crusaders transport for

33,000 men at the nominal price of 85,000 marks insuring that no city could outbid him for the contract. He added to this free transport and lodging for all the crusaders on his island, St. Nicholas, while the ships were built. But, while Boniface of Monferrat, the military leader of the crusaders negotiated with him, the Doge had his spies seed distrust and animosity amongst the crusaders with cunning rumor. Keeping the crusaders from acting in unison—distracting them from raising the required funds for his ships. In order to diminish Boniface's military authority once the campaign began, he then pledged an additional fifty-armed-war-galleys commanded by his loyal generals. To the crusaders he seemed a saint above reproach and the deal was struck by the weight of their support over the nagging doubts of Boniface.

Soon the Doge Dandolo had his wish and the crusaders were stranded, surrounded by water and unable to meet the price now owed to him. Supplies for the crusaders stay, while adequate, were maintained at a subsistence level, in order to intensify their anxiety. The knights bound by their strict code of honor found themselves now owing money they could not pay and no way to raise it. The Doge was now ready to execute the beginning of his plan.

Zara was a test of his control over the crusaders. His city, Zara, had been lost to the Hungarians and he wanted it back. So Enrico made a simple proposition to the crusaders, attack the city of Zara, return it to his control and they would share equally in any treasure that was taken. The only issue that brought with it some moral consequence for the crusaders was that Zara was a Christian city and under the protection of the Pope. It was no surprise to the Doge that a few days without water and food on St. Nicholas made the crusaders amiable to his wishes. He knew that morals were the provenance of the well fed.

So when Issac II's son, Alexius IV appeared at his court, the Doge was completely delighted. Alexius gave him everything he desired and at no cost, offering even to pay the crusaders the 200,000 marks they needed to finance their entire crusade in Egypt. Most of which would be paid to his treasury for their supplies. All the crusaders need do was return the rightful ruler to the thrown—Alexius' father. He now had military might and a moral cause. He could not have designed a better plan to usurp Boniface's crusaders for a second time. Zara had required skillful manipulation, this required nothing but his blessing and the support of his military envoy to ensure his interests were carried out.

The plan to reseat the aging Issac II was not without its critics and some of the crusaders abandoned the main force and headed to the holy land in protest. But with Boniface at his side the Doge was able to craft a plan to destroy the great Constantinople under the guise of rectifying a grave injustice. And so, a force-of-honor, twenty-five-thousand-strong, remained on Venetians ships and headed to the center of the empire.

The city of Constantinople was protected by massive walls at its north and along the sea to the west and south. Boniface thought these impenetrable and no attack was planned against them. He knew to succeed he would need to own the Golden Horn. Three great rivers created the natural harbor known as the Golden Horn. It ran along the northeastern side of Constantinople. But the harbor was hard to protect. Defensive walls could not be adequately formed at her shores leaving the city vulnerable from this side. So a great chain was made to protect this inlet from intruders. The massive black chain had taken more than five years to create and the combined talents of 76 blacksmiths. Each link was more than two feet long weighing 300 pounds each and the entire chain had more than seven hundred links. It required more than one thousand men to deploy it across the Golden Horn killing 50 in the task. On the east side, in the town of Galata, one small castle held the responsibility to raise and lower the great chain for Constantinople. It was one of their great engineering feats. It had successfully protected the city for hundreds of years. But, under the leadership of Boniface of Monferrat it had taken only five hours for the crusaders to defeat the garrison at the Tower of Galata and gain control of the gate to the Golden Horn.

The Byzantines attempted to retake the tower from the invaders the next day, but by then Boniface's force on the shore were more than 20,000 strong and the defenders were thrown back with little effort, forced to retreat back across the inlet and inside the city walls. With the tower fully in the control of Boniface the great chain was lowered and the invading fleet moved into the Golden Horn. The fleet of Constantinople that rested on the other side of the chain lay dying from the neglect of arrogance. Its decline was the process of many years of disregard by bureaucrats unaccustomed to war. As the Venetian fleet passed not a single Byzantine vessel moved from the docks to engage them. The guards on the walls of Constantinople watched in horror as the invading force took position for their siege of the great city. Fear swept across the town as the news of Boniface's success in the Golden Horn was traded among them. The citizens trembled. Emperor Alexius III trembled with them and then abandoned all, by escaping in the night, through the Harbor of Eleutherion with his favorite daughter Irene, close members of his court and what treasure could be carried.

However, the Venetian leader's good mood on entering the Golden Horn was lost with the news that the royal court had released Issac II from prison and reseated him as emperor the day after Alexius III's departure, thus losing their advantage of purpose and the reason to wage war against the celebrated city. With Issac II restored to the throne the supposed purpose of the attack was complete. They were livid. The Doge had only pledged support for the young Alexius IV and the restoration of his father to gain control of the city. His intention had been to strip the city of its wealth and power through battle. The Doge had planned on a fight—not an unintentional victory.

~

Boniface of Monferrat, aboard his flagship, sat in a great chair, contemplating the news of Issac II. He was no closer to funding his crusade than when it started four years ago. Why had he listened to the Venetians? Those serpents kept encircling his throat every time he spoke with them. Against his better judgment he allowed the Venetians to release Alexius IV to join his father as co-emperor against his promise that the 200,000 marks would be paid to him. Boniface thought a ransom paid by the emperor for the son would provide better insurance. Now he had to wait. He was tired of waiting. His squire interrupted his thoughts.

"Sire, Ælfric of Abingdom wishes an audience."

"Who?"

"He comes directly from Pope Innocent and wishes to speak with you."

"The Pope has an envoy here? Why am I not told of these things," he wanted to kill something, "Let him enter!"

Ælfric entered the room unfazed by the other's status and neglected to bow.

"Why have you come? I have many pressing matters and have no time right now," said Boniface.

"Only to aid you sire," Ælfric unctuously replied.

"How?"

"This matter of the funds for the crusade," said Ælfric.

"What do you know of this?"

"Only that the Venetians are stagnating this simple matter with their bickering and demands. This is a simple matter made complicated by competing interests."

"I already know this, how is this of help to me?"

"Then let me be clear, now that the Venetians in their limited wisdom have decided to free Alexius IV, instead of ransoming him, it is unlikely that he will have much interest to strip what is left of the royal treasury to finance your adventure. My spies in the city have already informed me that Alexius has left the city on tour of the territory of Thrace under the guise of collecting funds for you."

"I also know this, as it is my guard that protects him," Boniface replied.

"It is not funds he seeks to collect, but time. Time that you do not have. Already, many of your ships are planning to leave you now."

"Impossible, how can you know this?"

"My eyes are everywhere. Have you forgotten the origin of your journey? Did you think Innocent such a fool he would not place many loyal to him amongst your crusaders? One thousand of my men are aboard your ships already. I could order the entire Venetian fleet burned at dusk just to show those fools who is really in power."

"You would not dare!"

"I dare what I wish, but that does not serve my purpose right now," replied Ælfric.

"Then what is it that you wish?"

"War and conquest. I want Constantinople reduced to rubble."

"It is impossible now, we have no reason. The crusaders would reject this."

"Not if I give them good reason," Ælfric said, looking out the porthole at the city of Constantinople.

"What reason?"

"Get me and my men inside the city and I will incite the populace against the crusaders. Once they attack us, you will have your reason."

"What can I give to Issac II to allow you in?" Boniface asked.

"Tell him that you have uncovered a plot to kill him by those in his court."

"But, they have just freed him, why would he believe that?" Boniface replied.

"Simple, tell him it is the Venetians who have bribed them. I assure you the blind emperor will trust the great Boniface of Monferrat over

The Blood of the Shroud

his court. Did they raise a hand in his defense when he was imprisoned? He has no love or trust for them. With his son gone he will have no one but you to turn to. Tell him you are sending your best knights to protect him. Tell him I will come as your envoy to speak with him. Tell him anything you like, but get me in and you will have the money for your crusade. I will know what to say and do once I am there." Ælfric answered firmly, his hand teasing the hilt of his stolen sword.

Boniface thought for a moment, "If I do this, how do I know you will not betray me?"

"My betrayal? Is it not the Venetians you should worry about? Do you not think it strange that first you and your crusaders attack Zara for the benefit of the Doge, corrupting your cause, and now find yourself in Constantinople? Do you see Egypt more clearly from here? Grant me this small favor and you shall be free of these treacherous Venetians."

"I give you your entrance into the city and you will give me my cause?" Boniface asked.

"You give me entrance and I will give you the city to do as you wish!" replied Ælfric.

Boniface hesitated and then said, "I pledge it will be done then. I will send my squire to you when it is made ready."

As Ælfric left, Boniface realized he still did not know what this envoy's purpose had been. *Sent by Innocent, for what purpose? Why had he not been informed?* But, his hesitation slowly vanished as he rationalized that Ælfric had obviously been sent to protect the interests of Innocent's crusade. That had to be it.

Boniface's squire waited on deck for the return of Ælfric. He felt a hand on his shoulder and turned stunned to find Ælfric behind him, "…How?"

"Most men spend their lives sleeping while they are awake. Worry not, you have served me well and have nothing to fear. Boniface will send you to me when my demands of him are done. Use any excuse to alert my second here on the flagship and he will know what to do with the information. Tell him I head to the Harbor of Eleutherion to wait," and with that Ælfric turned to go.

"My money?" questioned the squire.

He turned back and looked down on the squire with flinty eyes, "Ahh—you are indeed brave to ask. I will give you something far greater."

"What is it?" the squire eagerly asked.

"Your life. How well will you fare if Boniface knows you have betrayed him? Remember my dictates or you shall soon find yourself at Boniface's mercy. If I remember correctly he favors the thumb-screws at first..." Ælfric said, his voice trailing off as he walked away.

The half-finished task is rarely useful in the hands of others, Ælfric thought. *I will educate Boniface like his treacherous squire. Let them understand the brilliance of my victory at the end. Even this close, everything that is—is not yet. The power of a storm cannot be felt just as the clouds form.*

Abbot Martin met Ælfric when he returned to his vessel.

"Do we return home now?"

"Home?" Ælfric said, "We have only begun here. We head for the Harbor of Eleutherion."

"The harbor? But, Issac has been returned to the throne. What more can be accomplished now?"

Ælfric stopped, and stared irritably at the Abbot.

"You begin to feel as a lodestone on my back. Do you think the fortunes of a feeble emperor would affect me in the least? He is merely another pawn to be moved at my discretion. The path to my desires is of no consequence; a favorable ending always shines like gold. I will have what I seek. Should you delay me further with your useless prattle I will be forced to drop you over the side and take delight in your sinking. Now ready yourself, we leave soon."

The Blood of the Shroud

Ælfric gave the Abbot his back and headed to his quarters ruminating on how he would later kill him.

The Abbot chafed by his remarks thought, *how dare he speak to me in that manner, he is not the only one who plots. We shall see what the end brings and for whom.*

~

Boniface was a man of honor and kept his word to Ælfric; within two days Ælfric had his audience with Issac approved. Ælfric entered at the Harbor of Eleutherion and secured entrance to fifty of his finest knights, which included ten of his private guard. 950 warriors remained aboard and waited. Upon his signal forty would secure the entrance to the city and allow the balance of his men safe passage into its heart. From there they would find their targets and await the commands of Ælfric. They were promised mayhem, drink and half of what they could carry as reward. The Pope had provided three ships for Ælfric's quest. Ælfric planned for two of them to be laden with the Pope's treasure and the last one would carry the price for his service.

Ælfric and Abbot Martin rode in near silence on the road to the palace, with ten of Ælfric's private guards protecting them. Even with a royal invite the tension felt throughout the city demanded additional caution. The journey to the palace from the harbor would require less than a day on horseback and so they rode at an easy pace. As they entered the largely barren Fourth Hill region, they were met by fifty of the emperor's famous Varangian guard, which immediately surrounded them. Maxentius the constable of the guards spoke first.

"Which among you is Ælfric?"

"I am," came the answer from the middle of the group. The Varangian's reply came quickly in the form of crossbow-bolts, killing him instantly. Abbot Martin uttered loudly, "Na…" and then quickly silenced himself. Ælfric's men drew their swords but were held back with Maxentius' words.

"Hold your swords or you shall join him, we wish not to kill Christian knights under orders, sheath your swords! The plot is finished; your assassin-leader is dead—your time is done here. We will take two of you, as hostage and the balance will be escorted back to your ships unharmed. Once you have left, we will release your companions."

Ælfric's men sheathed their swords slowly, saying nothing.

"I will take your silence as agreement. Tell the Venetians their treachery has failed here." Maxentius motioned for his guards to take the two riding at the front as hostage and the balance were cut off like sheep to be guided by forty men back to the harbor.

Ælfric gazed back on his ever-loyal second, Bryce, bloodied, dead and twisted upon the ground—but showed only stoic resolve, thinking on how best to exact revenge on the fool who betrayed him. The group split and ten now guided Ælfric and the Abbot towards the palace. Ælfric took in his captors with an eye for escape. Only one archer remained in their group. The guards now complacent at their easy success had sheathed their swords and began to talk amongst themselves, trading useless chatter.

Maxentius rode to him and demanded, "Your sword knight, it will be returned when you are fixed to leave."

Ælfric contemplated action, but decided for now it would be better to act the part of the fox than that of the lion and handed his sword casually to Maxentius. Ælfric took in the Varangian guard. *They are soft, like women dressed for court, riding horses meant for leisure. Still, even the small dog can draw blood,* he thought. Having assessed them, Ælfric turned his attention to the countryside. Only one small grove of trees, down the hill on his left could provide him any cover, beyond that everything was open. He would stand little chance against all of them along this trail. But, he saw his opportunity; the crest of the hill would present itself in a little while. The trail at the peak was bordered with large rocks on both sides and the first group led by Maxentius would need to narrow to pass over it. With half of the group over it he would have a few moments to engage the riders behind him. He needed to improve his odds—*six or seven to one would do,* he thought. Five riders were before the Abbot and him and five rode aft. The archer with a crossbow rode to the back of the Abbot and over his right shoulder. The rider behind him was animatedly engaged in conversation with the knights behind him. To succeed, he needed the archer eliminated first. For that he would use the Abbot as distraction. As the last of the first group rounded the crest Ælfric calculated his actions.

He threw the first of his two small wrist daggers into the haunches of the Abbot's horse, causing the horse to bolt and run into the guards ahead—scattering them over the hill. His second dagger was thrown at the archer's exposed neck taking him down. He turned his horse quickly and trampled the man, crushing his head under hoof. He then turned his concentration to the four before him; he needed a weapon. The rider who had been behind him was young and surprised by his action. He turned into him slamming his war-horse into his. The young knight attempted to pull his sword but Ælfric slammed his head backwards with his mail-covered forearm causing the knight to lose his grip. Ælfric gained control of the sword and pulled it free from the rider with his left hand.

Now ignoring the young, unarmed and unbalanced knight, he could hear the men over the crest reassembling while he rode forward and took off the head of another struggling to remove his sword from its sheath. Only two of consequence remained on his side of the hill, but he could hear that they would soon be joined by the others and quickly made for the closest warrior. The knight was ready and appeared fearless at his attack—the element of surprise now gone. It mattered not to Ælfric. The warrior took a high approach with his sword, intending to slice Ælfric's right shoulder and arm. But, Ælfric pulled his horse in front and to the right of him and went down the hill before his opponent could strike, causing him to block the warrior to his right, as he attempted to turn his horse in chase.

Now only five were after him, two missing apparently in a chase for the Abbot. Ælfric knew the Abbot would provide nothing more than amusement and his only chance was in the small grove of trees down the hill before all were after him. He needed to split the five in order to defeat them all. He could tell that some of the riders were unaccustomed to their steeds. A mistake he would capitalize on. His mighty stallion, Cometas, raised by him from birth, ran under him, field tested and true under any conditions. They would have a difficult time keeping pace and would fare worse should they choose to follow him directly. He raced down the craggy hill. He could hear the first of the riders tumble with horse, taking another warrior with him. *Foolish exuberance,* he thought, now they are three. He made it to the base of the hill and raced for the trees. His pursuers were undaunted, now moved by humiliation and the desire for revenge. As he passed the first tree he could hear the riders split around the grove to encircle him. He decided to engage the rider moving on his left. The bright sun and cover of trees gave him a few moments of invisibility and his opponent could only hear his hoof beats come towards him, until he engaged him. Their swords struck with the bright tone of metal as they rode past each other. He turned to see the warrior ready himself for another charge. The others were now in view and racing towards them both. Ælfric charged with his sword low and to his back. His opponent held his high. They made a mad dash for each other. All that separated them was thirty feet. At twenty, the steeds were at full gallop and only seconds remained from contact. Ælfric leaned forward, arm back and waited. Waiting for the precise moment when his sword's tip could crease the neck of the horse and still be used as defense, if the horse did not drop or rear from his cut. He moved Cometas slightly to his left and quickly pulled his sword forward; the horseflesh sliced easily as Ælfric rode swiftly past, causing the horse and rider to fall to his right dislodging the rider who broke his neck as he struck the ground. Ælfric continued riding fast, moving back into the trees.

The two that followed were closing fast upon him. He hoped now that anger had replaced all sense in them. He had noticed a tree had fallen across the path and an alternate run had formed around it. The tree on its side peaked at the height of a man and over the years a thorny bush had grown into it, turning the trunk into a wall. His stallion was used to the weight of war-armor weighing several times the weight of a man. Now, unladen by it, he was sure that Cometas could jump the height and span of it. It would save only moments, but he hoped that the younger of the two knights would follow in an effort to prove his worth. Ælfric knew he had little chance.

He galloped on. Within mere feet of the obstacle he put his weight to the balls of his feet and moved slightly out of the saddle with a straight back and leaned forward. He gave the mane of Cometas a firm and full grip and they went into the air. He stayed in position as his stallion adjusted his legs, to clear the trunk, landing firmly on his trailing foreleg followed closely by his leading leg. Cometas made it all look effortless. Ælfric listened carefully and could hear one knight speed up. He would attempt what seemed easy. His horse balked at the jump, casting the rider off and forward into the tangle of growth. Ælfric heard him strike the trunk with a deadening thud. *Broken ribs,* Ælfric surmised. He slowed his stallion and turned the powerful beast to face the last opponent. The knight rounded the obstacle and was surprised to find Ælfric calmly waiting for him. He stopped quickly unsure of what he was to accomplish now that the chase had finished.

"Are you not ready?" Ælfric teased.

The knight adjusted himself in his saddle nervously, but said nothing weighing his options.

"I assure you your death will be quick, but not painless."

The knight stared at him for a moment, then turned and galloped off.

Ælfric, got down from his mount, moved to the front of his horse, kissed Cometas' nose and patted him gently, "You have done well Cometas, just one more thing before we go." He moved to the horse's rear and swatted him to move him off at a gentle gallop down the path.

He walked around the wall-of-tree and found the foolish knight tangled, but alive in the bramble. Grasping a leg firmly, he dragged him out. The young warrior moaned.

"We will now see your true worth," Ælfric said, to the confused and injured young man. Making him rise, he pushed him forward to the center of the path and then waited.

"Why do you wait, kill me, I am ready," the young warrior spoke tentatively.

"But I am not," Ælfric replied, pummeling the boy's head with the hilt of his blade, dropping him to his knees.

Soon, the hoofs of others grew apparent. In rode Maxentius followed by the Abbot and two Knights.

"Free him and I will let you live."

"Drop your swords or watch me remove his head," Ælfric returned.

"Do so and you will die soon after!" Maxentius cautioned.

"You were ten and now you are three—by now you should know I do not die easily. My patience is at its end. Drop your swords and you will be free to tend to your wounded and I will take my leave and return to my ships."

Maxentius looked at Ælfric distastefully, but could see no purpose to more deaths and ordered his men to unarm themselves.

"Move away now and leave the Abbot," ordered Ælfric.

Once Maxentius and his men were far from sight he whistled for his stallion Cometas to return. He retrieved his sword, sheathed it, then mounted Cometas and turned to the Abbot.

　　　　　　　　The Blood of the Shroud

"Are you well?"

"Yes, it is a wonder they did not kill me," the Abbot said, nervously.

"Yes, a wonder indeed. We will wait a few hours and then enter the palace compound under the cover of night," said Ælfric.

"How can we continue now, your men are under guard to the ships, your plan has failed," said the Abbot.

"Nothing has failed. My men are already acting on my orders; did you think I would place all my faith in a single course? Prudence demands preparation. Look towards the city. The first fiery plumes of my commands rise up. Within hours the city will be ablaze. The gates of the harbor are burning and soon hundreds of my men will enter and create a chaos even Satan could not have dreamt of. The emperor will assume they are under attack and order his defenses. His vaulted Varangian guard is now split and the palace under protected because of it. Everything is as it should be. In just a few hours I will have the shroud and my ships laden with gold and silver."

And, with it all, your head in a jeweled box Abbot, for your treachery here today, Ælfric thought, *soon, very soon, it will be done.*

Constantinople – 1204

Eight – For love is as strong as death.

Leofrick hurriedly packed as Matilda raced to each of their hiding spots to remove the entirety of their treasury. Christina locked in her room could hear the pair fretting.

"Hurry, Benozzo's servant will be here any moment, what is his name?" Leofrick commanded.

"Whose name?" Matilda replied, too occupied in her hunting to listen to the chatter of her husband's conversation.

"The servant!"

"What servant?"

Leofrick stopped in a murderous manner and turned to locate his wife.

"Benozzo's servant you idiot!"

This caught Matilda's attention and she turned and threw a nearby pot at her husband's head and screamed.

"Boethius, you old fool. It is a wonder that you can find your hole in the morning," and then she returned to her mad scramble.

The knock on the door stopped them both and Matilda yelled at Leofrick.

"See to the door."

"Where are the servants?"

"They ran off hours ago with your memory. Get the door while I hide our money. Have him wait outside so we can finish in private."

Leofrick moved off angrily to get some satisfaction by venting at Benozzo's servant. He opened the small-gated-peep-door and saw the bored Boethius waiting.

"You must wait, we are not ready."

"Benozzo has sent you something you must see at once," replied Boethius.

"What is it?" the suspicious Leofrick asked.

"I cannot tell. It is in this small chest I have brought for you."

Leofrick at first thought to wait until they were finished packing, but curiosity got the better of him and he opened the door slightly to peek at the chest. It required two hands for Boethius to hold and he seemed to be under stress by its weight. Curiosity bent judgment and he opened the door fully to retrieve the box, greedily grasping it with both hands, jerking it from Boethius. Once fully in his hands, he felt Boethius' concealed dagger enter the right side of his throat and quickly cross to the left. He tried to cry out, but could only gurgle blood through the new slit in his throat. As Leofrick dropped to the floor, Boethius grabbed the empty box from his dying hands in an effort to minimize the noise of his death. Leofrick could still see Boethius faintly, as he walked over him, entering his home, while he frantically tried to warn Matilda: the darkness-of-death stealing his vision.

Maltida was still in a mad rush as Boethius entered the back room and sat calmly upon a stool to watch her. She finally noticed him and screamed at him.

"I told Leofrick to have you wait outside," then noticing that Leofrick was missing added, "Where is Leofrick?"

"He is gone," Boethius said, wearily.

"Gone, gone where?"

"Where he can escape the nagging of his repulsive wife."

"How dare you, I shall have you flogged when we reach Benozzo's side."

"Please keep your threats coming, it will make it all the more enjoyable for me when I silence you forever."

Matilda suddenly frightened at his words called out.

"Leofrick come quick."

"I should think poor Leofrick out of earshot of your screeching now," Boethius said, motioning behind him with his still bloodied dagger. Turning the dagger back towards her, he pointed it to the bag Maltida had filled and said, "What is that you have there, gold and silver?"

Maltida gravely frightened by the sight attempted to run from the room, but Boethius quickly rose and tripped her. Matilda went flying into the frame of the opening, smacking her head against the wide beam knocking her unconscious. Christina listened to the activity in the other room in horror. She could hear Boethius drag Matilda to the table and place her on it. Sounds of rustling and objects kicked aside came at her in a terrifying way. The ripping of fabric and then silence gave way to unknown time. It seemed as if hours had passed before the sound of splashing was heard and the sputtering of Matilda as she gasped for breathe. She screamed and Christina could hear Boethius ask, "Where is the key to the room?"

"What room?" Matilda replied in panic and then screamed out in complete anguish as Boethius replied, "Enough of your games witch, Christina's room." Another anguished scream came from Matilda and a breathless reply, "The bag." Christina heard footsteps and more things being cast to the floor and finally, "Ahh... yes...good." "Is this all your money? Still you attempt to evade my questions," and with that, more tortured screams came from Matilda.

"Yes, yes, that is all, please no more."

"Good."

More screams came and then Matilda said, in a breathless manner, "I have told you all."

"Have you?" asked Boethius, grinning with the blood of Matilda smeared across his face.

Christina sobbed uncontrollably as the shrieks from Matilda went on, broken only by her pleadings for mercy. She sank to her knees and attempted to pray through the agony of sounds. The torturous cries from Matilda went on until late afternoon and then suddenly stopped. The relief from her silence was replaced with abject fear of what stood beyond the closed door. She wiped her tears and trembled as she heard the lock on her room being released. She grabbed and clutched a large wooden candlestick for defense. The door swung wide open and she could see the battered and partially flayed nude body of Matilda lying on the table—she screamed, dropping the candlestick to cover her eyes and then fainted.

~

When Christina awoke she found herself tied and gagged, covered by wool and hay, lying in the back of a wagon and she could hear muffled voices.

"Here is my pass to enter with the seal of the emperor, Alexius III."

"He is no longer emperor, Issac has returned to the throne, this pass is worthless."

"You are right. Perhaps if I pay a small tiding to the new emperor you can see that I am allowed in."

Christina could hear the rustling of cloth and the tinkling of coins.

"Yes, I will give this to him when I see him, pass now, but make no trouble for me or I will see you hanged."

"Yes, of course, I have brief business here and will be gone soon, worry not."

The wagon moved on and Christina began to tug at her bonds in hopes of freeing herself. Her mind frantically searching for answers, *I am in the palace compound. Why have I been brought here?* Her bonds were too tight and she ceased her struggle. Finally, the wagon stopped and she heard more muffled conversations.

"I need you to hold her here so I can secure our passage out. No one is to see her."

"Passage will be difficult, the siege has begun, the city burns."

"I saw the flames, just hold her, I will find a way out."

The conversation was replaced by rustling and finally her being uncovered by two burly robed men. She feigned sleep. It was dark and through her half closed eyes she could make out nothing but a dimly lit doorway. She was dragged from the wagon and thrown over one man and carried inside, taken down a hall, placed on a small bed, untied and then locked in the room. When the door closed she was in complete darkness, but relieved that the men were gone. As her eyes adjusted, she could begin to see that the stars were dimly lighting the room through a small high window. She glanced around and discovered a small cross upon the opposite wall. Dropping to her knees, afraid, she began to pray to Christ, "Save me from this demon Satan has sent for me…" The distant shouts of men, still too far away to be understood, interrupted her soft words. And, for a brief moment the faint whiff of fire glided under her nose. A sound like distant thunder arose and she trembled. It has begun. Armageddon!

The room began to glow around her as a wave of calm spread over her like summer sun. Confused she looked around but could not find the source. It was everywhere and nowhere. The words, first faint as from a distant shore, grew closer, "…Christina, be of good comfort, it is I, be not afraid." Christina shivered—it was Christ! He that she loved above all was here. She could feel his touch upon her, making her quake with longing. He spoke to her with a commanding tenderness, "Soon they which are sown of good ground will come to you. I will send you as sheep in the midst of wolves; take no thought of how or what ye shall do: for it will be given to you by me in that same hour. Let your light shine before these men, for they will have need of it." The light began to dim and Christina called out, "Please wait," but the room returned to darkness, leaving her confused and worried. She wanted no part of any of this. Getting upon the bed drained, she closed her eyes and fell into a deep fitful sleep.

~

An eruption woke her. She looked out the window to see the moon near its zenith. People shouting and running could be clearly heard. The ground rumbled repeatedly from distant impacts. Shouts, combined with screams, mimicked the noises of animals in heat. She drew in a shallow breath and held it. Frightened and shaking again, she prayed for protection. She heard sounds in the hall, outside her door and the rustling of keys. In tones too low to recognize a conversation ensued, turning to argument and then fighting. Loud crashing and guttural sounds were mixed with groans. Someone fell. Then silence. The jingling of keys began again. In hopes of escaping her fate she moved backwards to the corner furthest from the door. A key made fast to the keyway and the heavy door slowly opened, bringing with it the warm light from a single candle. It was Boethius. She shrieked and looked to arm herself, but nothing appeared. The light magnified the distortions of his hideous grimace and he crept forward clutching his side with his free hand. He made two short halting steps towards her and then fell. The candle dropped with him and was extinguished, plunging her into complete darkness. She screamed and wanted to run but could see no exit. She felt the wall and moved slowly along it to the door. Finally, when it seemed that the door had vanished, she grasped it. She crept around it and felt along its face to find the hall. Just as she was to leave, a hand grasped her ankle and she screamed again. She turned and kicked, matching foot with what she assumed was face, heard a crack and then a groan. Boethius released her and said quietly as if talking to someone else, "Why was my heart always bitter?" And without seeing him, she felt him die and grew strangely sorrowful at the passing of the beast.

D.B. Sanders

85

She stood for a moment allowing her eyes to adjust to the darkness but all remained without form and she decided to allow her hands to guide her to freedom. She moved slowly down the hall feeling the rough wall with one hand, while the other remained outstretched before her, to prevent collision with some unseen obstacle. Her foot touched something soft and wet; she gasped and moved on without inquiry—not wishing to understand her discovery. She traveled down one hall to a corner, then made a turn to her right and traveled perhaps a hundred feet when an old man on her right spoke—startling her.

"Are you lost?"

His tone was friendly and she answered.

"Yes, can you help me?"

Quoting scripture the disembodied voice said, "Everyone that asketh, receiveth. Stay, I will come to you. You have nothing to fear, it is quite safe here."

She heard him move towards her briskly and then gently touch her arm.

"Come, come sit here."

"I must go."

"Go where? Our world burns tonight. It will be safer here for now, sit."

"Can you see?" Christina said, confused at the speed the man was able to travel in the blackness.

"My eyes no longer serve me. But here I need them not, for this place is my home and I have traveled it I think many years more than your age. Come sit, I will pour you wine and you can tell me how you have come to arrive at Blachernae.

"I am at the church?"

"Poor child you are indeed confused, yes Blachernae Church." Excuse my poor manners I am Paternus. And you are?"

"Christina."

He poured her wine and then sat. Christina drank from the cup and felt its warmth inside her.

"Christina, why are you here?"

"I was brought here against my will to wed a man named Benozzo. But the man who took me is dead now. I am free, but now trapped by the circumstances here."

"Trapped? Where would you wish to be tonight?" Asked the incredulous Paternus.

Christina paused and then said, "Christ visited me this night and told me I was to go forth for him."

Paternus hesitated and then said, "Ahh, Christ. We live in the age of visitations and yet he completely ignores me. No doubt the sins of my past," he took a large gulp of wine and refilled his wood cup.

"What can this blind old monk do for you child?"

"Guide me to a door to the outside, I must go."

"Have you not heard me? Are you not frightened of what lay outside that door?"

"Very!"

"Perhaps you should give up this quest. Your Christ may have only been a dream, a mere thing from your fears. Why would he ask so much from a girl so young?"

"No, it was he, I know not why he commands me, only that I must do this thing!" Christina protested.

"You could die! Demons dressed as Knights roam our world tonight, cherishing mayhem over life. Are you not afraid?" Paternus said, sternly.

"Yes, gravely, but I must do what my love commands. He will protect me."

Paternus relented, quoting from Esther, "Who knows whether you have not come to the kingdom, for such a time as this? I will help you Christina as you no doubt would venture forth without it." Paternus got up and Christina could hear him gather some things, he then came next to her and touched her with a cloth.

"Here, put this on. It is a monk's robe. It will keep you warm if nothing else. I have placed some bread and cheese in this bag for you, take it, perhaps I am your sign from Christ. But, if not, hopefully he will take notice of my good works today."

Christina dressed and then the old blind monk guided her quickly through the maze of blackness until they reached a door that would lead her outside.

"Are you sure Christina, you are welcome here."

Frightened at the tempest beyond the door, Christina replied in her bravest voice, "Yes," and pushed open the door and plunged into the madness before her. Standing on the path beyond the door, she turned to thank the monk one last time, but was greeted by a blank wall with neither monk nor door in sight.

The Blood of the Shroud

Constantinople – 1204

Nine – Strength made perfect in weakness.

Stephen hugged the rough land walls of Theodosius in anticipation of their imminent discovery. None came.

"We must hurry," whispered William, "We must travel fast before the moon rises, stay as close as you can to the wall."

They moved, not quite at a run, along the wall, stopping only to listen for guards above them. When they reached the Lycos River, that provided the city with its water, the full moon had crested the horizon and began to feed the blackness a rich blue light. Drenched in a heavy sweat, under their heavy wool and iron mail, the two surveyed the river. It was a small waterway but it would impede their travel. A small tunnel guided the river through the great walls. Stephen began to disrobe.

"What are you doing?" William said, softly.

"I need to see into that tunnel," Stephen replied.

William began to protest, but thought better of it and allowed Stephen to proceed with his plan. The water was cold and Stephen began to have doubts about the feasibility of accomplishing anything, but continued into the cold river and headed into the indefinite darkness. Sinking to his waist he stayed close to the right edge and was able to find ground to walk upon. The water began to feel as flames as the coldness wrapped around his body. Twenty feet in he came to an iron gate meant to prevent passage into the great city. He pulled on it at different sections and discovered that a lower bar had rusted through and believed it could be torn free with the aid of William's strength. He inspected more bars and discovered that three more were in the same condition, allowing enough space for a man to crawl through. He returned to William to report his discovery and found him gazing out towards the north.

"What do you see?" Stephen asked.

"The crusaders have made camp to the north. You can see the flicker of their campfires. Time is now our enemy. What have you learned?"

"We can enter on this side but what lies beyond is unknown. We could be trapped once we reach the far side and would have to return. What shall we do?"

William thought for a moment and then spoke.

"I believe that once we reach the other side you will present us with more of your wisdom. Let us move."

William quickly disrobed and used their cloaks to make bundles of their gear. Carrying them on their shoulders the two entered and returned to the Lycos river gate. With the great strength of William the bars were twisted enough to pass beneath them and the two crossed to the other side. The tunnel echoed and magnified every sound so they traveled in silence. They had only gone halfway when William whispered, "Stop!" The water felt as ice and Stephen desperately wanted to keep moving, but stood still as the feeling to his legs was lost.

"Do you hear them?" William asked.

"No," Stephen said, straining to hear something over the echo of babbling water.

"Four men, perhaps more are ahead, move slowly and watch for signs," William said, as he moved closer.

They crept forward ten more feet and they could begin to see the end of the tunnel. The moon was higher now and had enlivened the landscape before them in a blue spotlight. A few more feet and a fire became evident. William made out six men with horses, all on the north side of the river, a mere forty feet from the opening.

"Stay to the north side of the tunnel, they will not be able to see us from there," William cautioned.

They slowly moved forward and a small bank began to form at the edge but was muddy and too difficult to walk along. Soon they were at the edge of the tunnel and William peered out to inspect the guards more closely. The guards were engaged in an animated conversation amongst themselves completely ignoring their duty. The wall on the north had several small bushes and William estimated that they would provide enough cover for them to dress and rearm themselves. William pulled at Stephen and they made their way up the bank as silently as possible. Every sound seemed magnified in Stephen's mind and he kept his eyes riveted to the guards to his right. But, the guards were now occupying themselves with wine and laughter. The bushes lay only a few feet from the opening and they made the small journey in a few heartbeats. Stephen's legs were completely numb and he was now moving as an old man might. William recognized his condition and immediately began to rub the young man's legs vigorously to renew them. Stephen thought, *what drives him, his legs can feel no different than mine?* Stephen motioned that he was fine and William began to dress, with Stephen following his actions. The scratchy and heavy wool now seemed a great comfort to him. William turned to the younger man and asked, "Can you kill two of them quickly?" Stephen hesitated, "…kill?" William said, sternly, "With your crossbow, can you kill two of them swiftly?" Stephen had understood the question when first asked, but it was the realization that he would need to take a life directly that gave him pause. This time the deaths of others would not be indirect. He would stand-alone when these men were killed—their blood would cling to him for all eternity.

"Yes," he replied apprehensively.

"Make yourself ready then. I need you to kill at least two by the fire. I will give you fair warning."

Stephen's hands trembled, but his experience allowed the crossbow to be quickly readied for action. He then placed a second quarrel by his side for rapid reloading and started to pray for forgiveness, silently.

William watched the group carefully. The men urged on by the liquid amusement grew louder; finally one felt the need for privacy, to relieve himself, and walked towards the wall looking for a suitable spot, so that he could act as fountain. He began to drain as William crept behind him with dagger in hand. The drunken guard was completely unaware as William dragged his dagger around his throat, holding him tight, and then laying him at his feet silently. No one at the campfire noticed the passing of the man's life, a mere forty feet away. William returned to Stephen.

"Once they notice his delay, they will send at least one to look for him. Should there be two, shoot when I have finished the first," William said. Motioning to the fire with his gloved hand he added, "Kill the one who stands near the horses first. Most of their weapons are near their mounts and his body will act as a wall. Next, kill the one who makes the best time towards us. Do you understand?"

"Yes," Stephen answered, understanding all too clearly the deadly task that he was to bear. There would be piles of dead before this night was over and he would be the cause of many of them; in this he was certain. He gripped the crossbow tighter in an effort to still his shaking hands and waited for his moment to come.

"Nicholas, you drunkard, where have you gone?" one of the men near the fire shouted.

"He has fallen, no doubt asleep, go get him!" another of the group replied.

"Why me?"

"Bahhh, stop complaining, you son of a goat, I will go and help you with him. I need to relieve myself anyway."

"Nicholas, Nicholas," the two shouted as they lumbered towards the wall.

William waited. The two men found their dead companion and began to gently kick him.

"Nicholas wake up," shouted one of the men.

The other realizing that something was wrong reached down to pull at his friend when William made his move. Acting like his moniker, he swiftly covered the ten feet in near silence armed with his two favorite weapons: axe and sword. Driving the axe through the nearest man's skull, the man dropped to the ground screaming, clutching his head with the axe still embedded. Stephen watching in breathless anticipation as the first man went down in a crumpled mass of blood. Stephen turned his attention to the campfire and took aim at the large bearded man by the horses, felling him without effort, with a piercing shot to his stomach. Now everyone was alarmed. William thrust his sword through the side of the second man, who screamed in agony loudly. Two guards remained fixed at the campfire hesitant; knowing an archer with a crossbow was in the darkness. Then gaining the courage of fleas, the two started to run off. William put his foot on the back of the man with the axe protruding from his skull and pulled it free. Stephen reloaded and took aim at the fleeing men, taking another down as easily as his first. William ran after the last man until he was just a few yards away and then let his axe fly into the man's back, causing him to tumble forward in misery. William continued to move upon him, finishing him with sword through the back of his neck.

"Retrieve your quarrels, we will need them again." William shouted to Stephen.

Stephen went first to the large man by the horses and was surprised to find him still alive, clutching his stomach in great pain.

"Do your duty assassin," the man screamed looking up at the younger man.

Stephen froze. William came from behind and thrust his sword into the man's neck. The man gurgled an obscenity at the two before dying. Stephen threw up. William allowed him time and then said sternly, "A wound like that would take hours or perhaps days to kill. We are not torturers, but warriors. It is a kindness to end that suffering. It is our duty. Now retrieve your quarrels."

Stephen wiped the spittle from his lips and looked down on the dead man. His eyes remained open and fixed on him as he reached down to twist the quarrel from him. The sound of ripping flesh sickened him again and the grim reality of battle sunk deep into his belly. He went to the second man to repeat the terrible task of retrieval. He was glad to find him dead and still. William checked the others and quickly finished those that clung to life. William took from two the cloaks that identified them as Varangian guards and tossed one to Stephen.

"Put that on, it may buy us passage into the palace compound."

William arranged the dead men around the campfire, posing them together as if alive and then inspected the steeds for suitable mounts for their passage to the palace. They mounted and pointed the horses north.

"Should the guards look down from the wall, all will look right, at least till morning," William said, as they rode off. Stephen looked back at the campfire and thought, *what a grim mockery of life the posed dead made.*

Their arrival at the palace compound was met by pandemonium and they entered easily. Many were fleeing, as the city to the south now was burning fiercely; driving those living in the palace compound into panic. Disguised as Varangian guards the watchmen at the gate gave them only cursory glances and waved them on.

"Attack from the Golden Horn is imminent," William said.

They rode quickly through the compound looking for the Blachernae Church. It had been years since William had been to the church and now in the dark, with the confusion around them, it was difficult for him to get his bearings.

"We must ask someone for its location," said William.

Stephen looked around and saw a once proud young mother with a child huddled up against a wall and called down to them.

"Can you direct me to Blachernae?"

The mother looked frightened and confused.

"How can one of the Varangian not know the church of the shroud?"

Stephen dismounted and came closer to them.

"I am here to protect the shroud, but I am now lost in the moment. Can you help me?"

She looked into his eyes, peering for truth and replied, "It lies just beyond that building," pointing south with her finely covered but dirty outstretched arm, "A beautiful garden stands to its front. It cannot be missed. You have come to save the shroud, but who will come to save us, who…?"

Stephen could find no suitable answer for her, turned without answering and went back to William.

"We are near."

They rode to the front of the church and tied the horses. The great doors were ajar and William drew his sword. They entered quietly and could hear whispered voices echo back to them.

"Have you found it Abbot?"

"The light is bad, bring that torch closer. It should be here, near the altar. Perhaps it has already been moved."

"We are not alone," whispered William, "Stay close. Is your crossbow at ready?"

"Yes." The ground shook and Stephen asked, "What was that?"

"A bad neighbor," William said, referring to a catapult now in use, "It has started. Make haste."

The two moved along the aisle on the left, up to the altar, using the darkness and colonnade for cover, until they could move no closer without revealing themselves.

"Hurry Abbot we are not alone, the rats have come. Show yourself," Ælfric commanded turning and looking to his left.

The building shook from impact freeing bricks and glass from the walls. Ælfric drew his sword and Stephen saw the mark of Gregory upon it.

"It is he."

"Who?" William asked.

Stephen ignored William and took aim. Ælfric heard the latch and put the torch in front of him and then moved quickly from the spot tossing it towards the sound, blinding Stephen. Stephen fired, but it was too late, Ælfric was gone.

The Abbot sensed his time had finally come. The shroud and its location were well known to him. He had hoped for violent distraction in order to flee with it, leaving Ælfric to deal with matters of death and mayhem. He grasped the chest and was surprised by its weight. *No matter,* he thought, *it is a short journey to the horses.*

The candles throughout the church provided enough light for William to see the Abbot moving quickly towards the rear of the church.

"Stephen, after him."

"But…," was all that Stephen could mutter before William screamed, "Now!" Forcing him after the Abbot. As Stephen turned to give chase William heard the whisper of a blade making its way towards the young man. He turned, pushing Stephen out of the way, meeting the blade with his, diverting the deathblow with the flat of his blade. The push was hard, causing Stephen to fall to the marble floor with a loud thud.

"You are no Varangian guard," Ælfric said, in an almost reverent way.

William pulled himself into the dim light of the nave cutting his cloak at the shoulder and tossing it off to the side revealing the red cross of a Templar Knight.

"And, you are no Templar, drop your sword now and I will allow you life," William replied.

"I will enjoy cutting off those arrogant words when I remove your tongue, Templar." Ælfric said, thrusting his sword forward but found it easily avoided by William with parry and movement.

"Did you train with children?" William retorted.

Ælfric quickly thrust his sword forward again; turning his blade tip up with such speed he sliced into William's cheek and grinned back his reply.

"No, with demons."

William astounded at the man's speed found himself pushed backwards towards the altar with a series of parries and thrusts in combinations giving credence to the idea that Ælfric consorted with Satan's minions. But, he took no more cuts and gave one in return upon Ælfric's forward leg. Ælfric gave him a stern look and then intensified his attack in silence. His moves were so deftly made that it was all that William could do to hold him back. Stephen watching from the floor was torn between helping William and chasing after the Abbot, who now possessed the shroud. The rear door slammed shut, punctuating the Abbot's escape and forcing his decision. He had lost his grip on the crossbow in the fall and he was delayed further, searching for it in the dim light. Finally, his hand touched upon the handle and he pulled it towards him. He gave a thought to fire at Ælfric, but had no time to load and catch the Abbot. Now, only four shots remained. He turned with regret and ran towards the rear door as the swords of clashing titans rang in his ears.

The building shook again and bits of the ceiling fell near them. Ælfric stared at William.

"The Venetians grow impatient, I must cut your lesson short," and then launched into another series of rapid combinations that kept William from an opening.

"You are well trained Templar, but your end is near."

"Many have made that claim, yet I live."

Ælfric danced to the side and back contemplating his final moves. The building shook and flames rained down upon them both. William needed his axe behind him, and used the moment to move behind the large marble altar for space and time. Again, the building was struck bringing a massive portion of the ceiling directly at William. William looked up and could hear the words of Ælfric as he watched the mass fall quickly towards him.

"God has decided to judge you this day, Templar."

Ælfric turned and ran to the exit as he heard the falling mass crush the Templar where he stood.

Constantinople – 1204

TEN – NO TWO OFFER THE SAME PRAYERS.

Women and children ran past her screaming. Old men pulled carts loaded with everything they owned. Some could not move and cried, head in hands. Others, in panic, ran for short distances in one direction and then turned and ran back, unsure which course brought safety. The depraved attackers engaged in rape and murder and laughed while they did it. Fiery bundles rained down around them, setting buildings and people on fire. Some chose to die while others bravely fought for life.

Christina, in this confusion, could not bring forth any firm emotion to bear on the wickedness before her. She walked calmly through it all, observing the madness with a detached demeanor: the mix of fear, horror and determination so twisted up inside her. The world froze for her and she could see clearly the individual elements of this terror. In this fixed view of the madness around her, only one motion drew her complete attention—a fat robed man carrying an exquisite chest to a horse. He frantically attempted to hoist it to the back of the animal, but he was too short to arrange the matter and finally set the chest down on the ground. He stood and stared at the chest for a moment and then flung it open removing a cloth from its interior. Christina even at a distance knew the elegance of a fine fabric. *This is a mere rag; hardly worth the effort to store in such a fine chest,* she thought. The fat man grasped it in his hands and began to shove it into a leather bag tied to the horse's saddle. He had succeeded in forcing most of it in, when he looked up suddenly, stared at the sky for a moment and then fell over, covering his eyes, screaming, until he fell unconscious.

Christina felt compelled to give him aid and ran to him. At his side, she uncovered her head to have a better look at the man and realized by his hair he was a man of the church. She felt his face, he was bitterly cold and she presumed him dead. The suddenness of his passing confused her.

Stephen burst through the rear door of the church to see the Abbot lying upon the ground with a beautiful auburn hair, girl kneeling above him. *Had she killed him?* He screamed for her to stop, but she panicked and mounted the Abbot's horse riding off to the north. The cloth dangled from her leather bag. *She has the shroud,* he thought. With no time to get his horse he ran after her on foot. He felt helpless to stop her and then heard a girl shriek from around the building. He ran faster and as he rounded the corner he could see three men with poles surrounding and taunting her. They could not reach her easily for fear of being trampled. But also, she could not escape, as the men had boxed her into a corner. Stephen stopped and loaded his crossbow quickly as the standoff continued. With his crossbow ready, he approached the men and shouted.

"Let her be!"

The men turned briefly and glanced at the younger man before returning to their mischief.

"She is ours, find yourself another," they shouted and then they went on with their taunting and jeering of Christina.

"Leave her be or die tonight," Stephen commanded loudly.

"Keep her pinned as I swat this fly," the oldest of the three, armed with pole and sword told the others. He turned to meet the younger man face on and was kissed on his forehead with Stephen's quarrel immediately. His companions faced him and said in unison, "He killed Theon," but hesitated in attacking Stephen.

Christina seeing an opportunity to run, charged her steed at the one on her right, felling him, and then made her escape, leaving her rescuer behind. She had traveled thirty yards and was around another building, when she suddenly pulled her horse to a stop. *Keep going, this stranger means nothing.* But, her conscience nagged her and she turned her steed and decided to return to the scene of danger.

Stephen dropped his crossbow and made a dash for the opponent still standing. The villain smiled and thought, *what a fool,* and readied his pole. Stephen ran forward and then jumped, twisting his body completely around, arm outstretched, dagger in hand, letting it fly, adding so much force to the delivery that the man was knocked over when it struck him in the throat. The last man, forced to the ground by Christina's horse, finally fearful pushed himself up and ran off.

Christina had rounded the corner in time to see the grace of Stephen as he twisted in the air, only to be horrified by the results of his magnificence. She watched in terror as he walked calmly to a man with an arrow protruding from his head. He attempted to twist it from the dead man. It seemed to her as if he manipulated some grotesque puppet at the end of a stick. With no luck in freeing the arrow from the man's skull he moved to the second man, placing his foot on the man's shoulder and pulling a dagger from his throat. The dying man's blood spurted high. She felt faint and turned away, as tears rolled down her face. She thought to run again, but the boy saw her and cried out.

"Please, wait."

She hesitated, but held her ground nervously, as the boy ran towards her.

"You carry what I have come to save," said, the breathless Stephen.

"Save, save what?"

"That in your bag," Stephen said, motioning to the satchel on her horse with his hand.

"The rag?"

"Not a rag, the shroud."

"What shroud, what madness do you speak?"

"Not what, but whose? You carry the shroud of Christ."

Christina glared at him, *the shroud of Christ?* None of this made sense to her. *This was the one, sown of good ground, a boy, a killer?* Her thoughts were interrupted by a large group of shouting men, who were just entering the courtyard from the west. There was no time to decide what was right or wrong.

"Get beside me, we must leave," Christina said, offering her hand.

Stephen leapt and with the aid of her smooth hand was set behind her. Christina quickly turned the horse and they made haste through the back corridors of the palace compound until they found an opening through one wall that had been ripped open by something fierce.

"Go that way," Stephen commanded, with an outstretched arm pointing the direction.

"Do you think because you sit with me you have become my owner?" she replied angrily, "I have just freed myself from one pair and have no intention of gaining another in this life. I will go where I choose, as the reins of my life are in my hands, not yours."

"I can save us, I am with friends," replied Stephen, greatly perplexed at her attitude.

"Save us, thousands have taken the town, do you plan to kill them all?" Stephen could offer no adequate reply and chose to remain silent in hopes of reducing the fire inside her. *Besides,* he thought, *we are at least outside the palace walls and away from immediate danger.* He desperately wanted to return for William, but this vixen he thought could not be controlled and he would not leave the shroud in her unstable hands.

Christina's attitude began to soften as they rode quickly from the palace compound. As the foothills of the region known as the sixth hill appeared she realized she did not have a plan, other than to flee.

"Where are these friends?" she asked, tentatively.

"My friend Gaius has a boat to the west of the village outside the walls near the Golden Gate. My uncle William, a Templar will meet us there. Do you know of it?"

"Yes, I know of it," Christina answered softly and with trepidation, thinking: *my home is there and in it, my dead parents lay rotting.* She shuttered at the thought of even being close to her home. *But, this was at least a plan, a direction to travel.*

Christina guided the horse west, using the walls of Theodosius as a compass. They rode in silence each absorbed in thought. Stephen could smell the sweetness of her hair as it flowed across his face. In the blue moonlight, she appeared as perfectly sculpted marble. *To look upon her was to be transported to a more peaceful world,* he mused.

~

Ælfric burst through the door to see the Abbot lying on the ground. He shook him, but he was slow to wake. So he left him where he lay and looked around. To his right ran the young squire chasing the Abbot's horse ridden by a girl. He whistled for Cometas to come from his hiding place. The streets were now filling with looters, so he rode with sword in hand. The foolish attempted to dismount him. The lucky ones were left behind, missing only a hand or an arm. They caused him no real danger, but delayed him in his search. He rounded one corner to see two men outstretched and dead. He would have ignored them had he not seen the quarrel protruding from one man's skull. He dismounted to examine the scene. A looter thinking he would have Ælfric's horse for himself, pounced upon him, and ended up impaled with an arm removed, just to warn the others watching. The gang of thieves around him ignored him and returned to their private duties of carnage and rape.

The area bore signs only significant to Ælfric, a horse cornered, a private battle and two leave to the west, riding one horse. With his understanding firm, Ælfric began his pursuit again. Ælfric thought, *who are these Templars who dare steal the shroud from me? Is it more valuable than I have been led to believe? If so, why send a single Templar to retrieve it? And, who is this girl that travels with them?* It perplexed him. He had no use for puzzles. *Regardless of their intent, their plan is a failure, the Templar is dead and only his squire and the girl remain. Soon enough, they will all regret crossing my path.*

The palace compound was now alive with attacking crusaders and some streets filled beyond capacity, blocking Ælfric's ability to pass. He would need to find a way out soon or be so ensnarled in the mayhem, that the children and shroud would escape his grasp. He turned down a small alley and headed for the southern wall. Reaching the wall he traveled to the left and found his exit, quickly making his escape, to the open countryside, just in time to see the pair half way up the sixth hill.

~

Stephen turned and looked back to see a lone horseman exit the wall and turn towards them, at a gallop.

"Someone is after us," he said.

Christina stopped the horse and turned to gain a look.

"How do you know he is after us?"

"We saw no one at our exit, yet this man gallops towards us, after exiting at the same spot. I see no reason for chance to have played a hand in this. Please, let us make haste if only to rid me of my doubts," said Stephen.

Christina thought for a moment and then without word kicked into the steed to put him at speed. As they crested the hilltop, they both turned and could clearly see that the man behind them had gained on them. She bolted over the side and raced down the hill. It became evident that he would catch them, as the countryside offered no real cover. Christina now was fearful, as Stephen's words rang with more truth.

"What can we do, there is no place to hide," Christina asked.

"The Lycos River is just ahead. Make for where it leaves the wall. It passes through a tunnel large enough for us to pass safely through," Stephen replied.

At the base of the hill they could see the rider change his direction and come more directly at them. *We will be through the tunnel before he can reach us,* Stephen hoped.

Stephen could feel the night giving up its hold on Constantinople. *Soon dawn would be here.* As they reached the tunnel opening, Christina screamed, and pulled the horse to an abrupt stop, nearly casting Stephen off. William's macabre arrangement of dead guards was now overrun with a murder of crows, busily digging into the wounds for morsels of flesh while others dined with glee, on the eyes of the men. *What madness has overtaken our world,* Christina thought.

"We must go now," Stephen urged.

He got off and grabbed the reins from her loosened hands and led her into the tunnel as she buried her head into her hands, sobbing. At the tunnel's entrance he quickly made a bundle of his things and tied them to the horse and led Christina still on horseback into the tunnel. Christina's sobbing turned into a choir of women in agony as the tunnel echoed her pain. Stephen was relieved when the passage to the other side was done. At the tunnel bars Stephen spoke to her in soft, soothing, tones.

"You must get down, we can go no further by horse."

But, she could give no response.

"Please, we must go now!" Stephen said, with greater urgency.

Finally, she held her crying some and looked down upon him, helpless to move until he offered her his hand.

"Take my hand, we must crawl under the gate here, we will be in the village soon."

Christina placed her hand in his and slipped into the cold water without reaction. Stephen helped her remove her bulky robe so she could fit through the bars.

"Take a deep breath and crawl through here," Stephen instructed.

Christina moved slowly, but did as she was told. The cold water awakened her and she stared at him through the bars from the other side, finally speaking.

"Are you really the one?"

"One, one of what?" Stephen said, not understanding her question.

But, she did not reply, instead turning to make her way up the bank.

Stephen wedged their bundles into the bars and passed beneath them, and once he was through retrieved them and followed her up the southern bank. The sky was now painted fresh with the hint of day. As he exited the water he could see the neatness of her curvaceous figure against this new brightness. The damp dress clung to her shape giving him unexpected excitement. He turned quickly, to refresh her privacy, as his outstretched hand held the robe for her.

"You should put this on, it is cold," he said.

She turned to look at him and was surprised to find him hiding his gaze. She had become accustomed to the uninvited and unwanted attention her looks bought her. She had concluded long ago that men were incapable of any other reaction in her presence. She took the robe from him, but delayed in putting it on, to test her observation. When time adequate for her dressing had past, Stephen turned to find her still inadequately covered and turned quickly again.

"Uhh…is something wrong with the robe?" Stephen said, hesitantly, realizing he did not know her name.

With her suspicions of his manner confirmed, she put the robe on and answered.

"No, it is fine. If your stutter betrays a need for my name it is Christina."

Stephen not wishing to turn again until confirmation had been given of her dress asked,

"You are dressed then…Christina?"

"You seek to hide yours then," Christina asked.

"Hide? My name, no, uh, Stephen. I am Stephen…Arc."

"You sound unsure, Stephen…Arc," she said, teasingly, but then remembered their circumstances and ended her game, "We should go."

Remaining silent, she walked past him and headed west. Relieved, he followed her.

"We should be at the village before the sun is hot," Stephen said.

He caught her thin smile as she passed and thought it curious; *at least her tears have dried.*

The village, there is only one village outside the walls, Ælfric thought, as he stared approvingly at Christina through the bars. He whispered, "Cometas let us prepare their welcome."

Constantinople – 1204

ELEVEN - TO SAVE THAT WHICH WAS LOST.

William dropped to his knees, and rolled to his right, moving under the large marble table as the lethal mass fell towards him. The ferocity of the fiery debris meant nothing to this massive monument to God and it exploded on impact raining fire and wreckage everywhere. Choking smoke began to dance around him. Looking for a safe opening in the rubble, a small breach presented itself near his feet. He twisted himself beneath the table and began to push the flaming embers back with his axe until he was able to crawl through. As William fought his way through the opening, his tunic caught fire, forcing him into a struggle with the flames now rapidly moving up his side. He rolled across the marble floor and extinguished the blaze. Partially burnt, soot covered and weary from his battle with Ælfric, William took strength from his resolve to save the shroud, in order to continue.

He eyed the destruction around him. The roof displayed a gaping wound and the wooden portions of the altar were now on fire. The conditions inside this crucible of faith emphasized his need to leave. He made his way to the front of the church to regain his horse, but the steeds were gone. *Stephen would not have taken both,* he thought, *he is on foot.* He could hear screams coming from the streets and made his way to the back of the church to survey the scene. The palace compound was in a state of pandemonium and he pulled his long sword and axe to attention.

A passing villain thought him unaware and attempted to impale him with a pole-axe only to be rewarded with his own death, a few moments later. He moved on and came across the Abbot seated on the stone steps, dazed and unaware of his approach. He grabbed him by his neck and demanded, "Where is the boy?"

Still too stunned to comprehend the threat William posed, he looked into his face and replied, "What has happened?"

"The boy and the one who was with you, where have they gone?"

The Abbot looked around utterly confused and gave up only one word as a question.

"Ælfric?"

Here was a name William remembered.

"Who?"

The Abbot awakened to his danger and looked directly into the Templar's steely face replying, "Ælfric of Abingdom."

Gregory's assassin is here, William thought, peering deeply into the Abbot's face demanding, "Does he have the shroud?"

This question stabbed at the Abbot and he retreated to the limits of William's grip.

"Please, I have nothing, I want nothing, please."

William could see he would get nothing more useful from this fearful fool and cast him off angrily without another word. *What trickery of fate brings this Ælfric of Abingdom to me and why does he seek the shroud? If the Abbot is without it, then Stephen must have it and if so, Ælfric is in pursuit! Stephen will make his way to Gaius,* William reasoned. He looked around and realized that he would need to battle his way from this compound if he did not find a better path. He turned and decided the alleys would provide the least resistance. Most would avoid them, given they were the estates-of-choice for refuse. Twenty steps in William began to think less of his decision. His every step carried with it feces, the smell of urine and fermenting waste. He moved forth as swiftly as his slimy footing would allow. The large piles could not be avoided and in the darkness he soon found himself ankle deep in God's worst creation. He exited the first long alley into a large-torch-lit-courtyard meant for merchants, now in the process of being ransacked by the invaders. His first thought was to retreat back into the alley, but he was immediately engaged by a sizeable man to his right, forcing him towards the center. Between the clashing blows he surveyed the courtyard. He was surrounded on all sides by three levels of walls and four small openings. Twelve crusaders were engaged nearby in all types of mayhem and two had turned to join their companion to defeat him. The three took turns in their attack on him, making a game of it. William was unafraid but realized if more entered the fray it would be unlikely for him to survive. He killed one quickly and the remaining two called for more help. William made a twisting-slashing attack to distance the attackers from him, hoping to create an opening for his exit. But, the attackers gave him little quarter and moved quickly back towards him.

Ibn al-Arabi watched from the highest wall, the attack on the Templar. *The odds are too great, even for this skillful Templar; he will die soon,* he thought. As William turned his back to Arabi the embroidered emblem of the wolf-on-the-crest came into the light. *The Wolf!* Arabi ran along the edge of the wall to his left and quickly leapt turning once in the air to land on the lower wall, remaining only long enough to gain contact and then sprang again to the lowest wall. He ran along the edge to place himself nearest to William and then leapt to the ground behind him, to face two of William's attackers unarmed. The surprise of Arabi's unexpected entry caused the attacking crusaders behind William to move backwards, allowing Arabi to move forward, deflecting the closest attacker's sword with the palm of his hand, giving him the space necessary to break the man's knee with a kicking blow. As the

The Blood of the Shroud

man crumpled, Arabi relieved him of his sword and launched into an attack on the other warrior. William deep into the threat of his own extinction could only partially grasp the significance of Arabi's surprise arrival. If he were an ally or just a victim of circumstances would require friendlier surroundings for him to determine. For now, he was content that someone fought with him. The fight allowed no time for discussion between William and his new ally and each carried the battle logically forward, sensing no need to discuss logistics. William invigorated by the stranger's arrival renewed the battle wasting no effort to kill the two before him and then rushed the three approaching, forcing them into a corner and causing them to ensnare themselves with their own efforts to kill him. Arabi having wounded another pushed him into the oncoming attackers, causing them to tumble forward. Wasting no time, he severely wounded all on the ground before returning to each separately to finish them. He searched the dead for weapons and pulled from them two daggers that he kept. William relieved of a battle on both sides turned the confusion of his attackers to his advantage and took off several limbs before ending their lives. The addition of Arabi to his fight reduced the matter to minutes and the courtyard was transformed into an arena of blood.

William turned to the smaller man and said, "I seek passage from this hell, do you know a way out?"

"Allah has given me some guidance, follow and I will show you what I have learned, Templar."

"William!"

"Arabi," he replied with a slight bow, "follow quickly, as time has become our enemy."

Arabi ran to the wall, leapt to some crates and jumped to the lowest wall astounding William by his speed and agility. William followed, but could not manage the maneuvers of his new companion. Climbing in a more deliberate fashion, he made the ledge with the aid of Arabi's hand.

"You would make a most difficult opponent I fear," William uttered softly to himself.

Arabi heard him and replied, "I would worry more at the difficultly of having a Muslim as your friend, William."

The pair ran along the wall past the courtyards and soon stood above a vacant lot. Arabi danced down some crates and barrels with William making an attempt to keep pace with him. They hugged a few building faces and came to large boulevard on the south end of the compound. Arabi turned to William and said, "We must cross here."

William viewed the street with a jaundiced eye. He had arrived in hell once more. Rape, murder, and plunder. No matter what sin he took in, the next seemed magnified in comparison.

"These men have no right to call themselves crusaders," William cursed.

Three men dragged a nun to the middle of the street with lecherous intent. William made a move to defend her, but Arabi held him back.

"There are too many here William. We will not defeat them all, if they all join together to fight us."

William thought to toss off the smaller man, but realized the folly of his idea and remained in the shadows to watch in horror as the nun was defiled.

"We need horses," Arabi said.

In this, William was in complete agreement and looked for an opportunity. Twenty feet away, two invaders on horseback, near a wall, watched in amusement at the men taking turns attacking the nun. William turned to Arabi and motioned towards the men.

"Can you take the man on the right?" Arabi replied without hesitation, "Ee," in the Arabic affirmative.

"Then we go," William commanded and the two rushed the horsemen.

The horsemen ignored them in the confusion, long enough for William and Arabi to span half the distance. Arabi pulled ahead of William running with the speed of a lion, daggers in hand. He passed the rider on the right and headed directly for the wall behind him. Seemingly walking upon its face he twisted and turned backwards enabling him to seat himself directly behind the rider, simultaneously plunging both of his daggers into the horseman's neck. The horseman's companion now alarmed had pulled his sword and was about to impale Arabi when he met William's axe with his head, throwing him off his mount and hard into the wall. Arabi pushed the dead man from the horse and moved forward to take the reins. William retrieved his axe and then took control of the second steed.

William, now ready to ride, looked upon the men with the nun. Having finished with their personal amusements, the men repeatedly stabbed her until she no longer screamed: much to their delight. Arabi saw the punishing look William gave the men and knew there would be no restraint he could place upon him this time. William rode to the men with his sword in hand and removed the hand of one man while slicing the face of a second, grinning man, in a continuous motion. The last man attempted to run and William gave chase knocking him to the ground, trampling the man to death with his steed. He turned back to rejoin Arabi and noticed the coward with the missing hand on his knees beside the dead nun and rode slowly towards him. The blood spurted uncontrollably from the man's arm as he cried in anguish. The coward looked up at William, as he rode slowly past, with terror in his eyes. William quoting from scripture said, "O death, where is your victory. O death, where is your sting," as the man finally crumpled before him, to die slowly in the blood of the nun.

In the chaos, no one gave William and Arabi more than passing thought as they rode off quickly to the west. William studied the smaller man as they rode. He did not dress as a Muslim. In fact, his dress was an indeterminate mix of finery and poverty combined. *What a curious fellow this Muslim,* he thought.

They galloped to the western wall and found a small gate thrown open and made their way from the palace compound. A few miles away they looked back to see it engulfed in flames and smoke. To the south the clouds above the city appeared dark.

"Where do you wish to go," Arabi asked.

"I must find…"

"A boy?" Arabi finished.

"How would you know of this?" the startled William asked.

"It was foretold to me. In a vision I was to help the wolf-on-a-crest, the boy craftsman, and the bride of Christ. Since the bride is still a mystery to me, I chose the boy."

William stared at him without speaking, *so this Muslim joins me by vision. Why would Christ send a Muslim to my aid?*

"I must get beyond the city walls to the west. A demon I fear hunts my nephew," William finally said in reply.

"May I suggest we travel near the northern wall and view the military gates for weakness? We must pass the wall at some point and perhaps fate will place us with opportunity," Arabi suggested.

"Your plan has merit. But let us ride fast. I have traded blows with this demon and Stephen will fall before him should I fail," William replied.

"You are no longer alone, William, for I will ride at your side to defeat this demon. We will not fail, we will save the boy."

William, with Arabi close behind, galloped towards the northwest to cross the walls of Theodosius again. But, doubts lingered within him. *There could be no assurance in this path or that of Stephen's. Too many obstacles lay before both of them. Had Stephen left the palace compound safely?* He prayed for guidance as he rode hard through the blue night.

With the fire of battle no longer flowing through him, he began to feel the aches of past wounds. William's shoulder was on fire, *the wound of the Bedouin arrow,* he thought. It had gnawed at him for more than a week, but he had tossed off the feeling like a bad memory. The flames were long gone from his leg but the burning remained. He had no time for pain. The ride pounded at him and he suddenly felt old. He needed some rest and food. But, he pushed on: *he would rest when Stephen was safe. Strange how warm the night is.* He rode faster to feel the cool air across his sweaty brow. *That is better.* A chill came over him for a moment. *It will be over soon, and then I can rest.* The road became difficult to manage and his steed slowed uncertain of his hand. He fell forward and rested against the horse. *Soon it will be done.* William was barely conscious and the horse stopped. In the distance he heard his name. *Had day broken, it is so hot.* And, then he heard nothing.

Constantinople – 1204

TWELVE - THE AFFLICTIONS OF THE RIGHTEOUS.

The large mottled spider of brown and beige crept along the top of the tall yellow grasses. Using his long legs to cling to the tips, he floated above the ground quickly and without effort. For reasons known only to him, he stopped to secure his web on a specially chosen blade. He seemed to pray for his good fortune, as his back legs rapidly twisted the silk around the tip. He was the master of this universe, a singular example of God's greatness. Prey larger than his might had broken parts of his silken entrapments, but caused him no consternation, skillfully repairing the sections with ease. He stopped and surveyed his small kingdom of heaven, with a steadfast unbreakable purpose, and was rewarded for his efforts with a large and tasty meal of flies. The spider's path crossed Stephen's eyes and went unnoticed by the young Templar. His blue eyes transfixed on the vacant village across the small open meadow.

"Why do we not go," whispered Christina into his ear.

"I distrust this place."

"Perhaps we can avoid it," Christina suggested.

"We need food and more water," he replied.

He wanted to go on alone, feeling protective of Christina. He could sense her dread grow as they moved closer to the village. The sun had grown hazy from the smoke of the fires raging in the great city to the east. The village colored by the murky-blue-grey-smoke appeared to promise new horrors. He vacillated between leaving her there and traveling with her at his side. Neither option provided him comfort.

"If you would feel safer, I can explore the village while you wait here," Stephen suggested with a kindness layered to his voice.

But, Christina wished for the safety of the promised boat.

"No, I want to go with you. I cannot wait here."

"Stay close then," Stephen cautioned.

Stephen looked at his crossbow and loaded his weapon as Christina watched with an attentive eye. *Three quarrels left, there will be no chance to make more; it will have to be enough,* he thought. With the crossbow loaded, he left the safety of the tall grasses to venture forth and discover what this day would bring. Only three hundred paces separated them from the first of the buildings.

"Where best to find food and water?" Stephen asked of her, as they reached the edge of the village.

"Follow me, the baker is close."

To their dismay they arrived to find a ransacked shack and a cold oven. Stephen explored the remnants with his careful eye and discovered a small bag of salt that he promptly stowed in his leather bag. His inspection of the oven fetched several partially burnt loafs of dark rye, hardened from time. Christina found no water, but instead a clay pot partially filled with curdled milk. Stephen retrieved some wooden plates, scattered on the ground, and dressed a small table for a meal. From the burnt loafs, he cut away the worst parts with his dagger. With the food prepared and before them, Christina offered grace.

"Give us our daily bread, forgive our debts, as we forgive our debtors. Lead us from temptation, deliver us from sin: for thine is the most perfect kingdom of power and glory, forever. Amen."

They dipped their bread into the soured milk to soften it and ate their beggar's meal to the cheerful chirping of nearby birds. Their hunger colored their food pleasantly and the meager meal cheered their spirits.

"We will be safe soon," promised Stephen, "Gaius is anchored nearby."

"What is it like?" Christina asked.

"It, you mean Gaius?"

"No, to be free to travel where you wish, to see the world, to do as you please."

"I have not been free to do any of those things," Stephen replied.

"But, you came here and killed those men..."

"I had not come to kill when this began. I was to rejoin my mother in Milan. To carry on my father's work, the killing...the killi—," but Stephen could not explain it to her and got up hurriedly.

"We should go now," he said, tartly.

"Can't we sit a bit longer?" Christina said, hoping to return to the mood of cheer.

"No, gather anything of use you can carry," Stephen ordered.

Stephen quickly gathered the shroud and his things and moved towards the door, paused and turned to Christina.

"Are there any horses here?"

"The blacksmith is our only hope," Christina replied softly, confused by the change in him.

"Take us there," Stephen said and then charged through the door.

Christina saddened at the lost moment, followed him and then took the lead through the village to the blacksmith's shop. It lay just beyond her own home and she attempted to avoid it, but was noticed by Stephen.

"Why did you turn away?"

"My parents are dead in there."

"The crusaders?"

"No, they lay dead for other reasons."

"Why?"

"It is a tale for another time, Stephen, far from here."

He noticed the mood in her face and replied.

"Of course, perhaps in better times."

They moved past her home and Stephen noticed the brown fabric, hanging from lines.

"What are those?"

"We made cloth, but those are just rags left to dry."

"I want them."

"Why, they are torn and stained," she asked.

"I don't know yet. What else is inside?"

"We have some tools, bags and things," Christina replied.

"I need to see."

"I cannot go in there."

"Wait here, I will have a look and return quickly," Stephen offered.

"Please, I beg of you, take the rags and leave the rest, please!"

Stephen could see the terror in her eyes and regretfully relented, taking only one large rag that he folded carefully, placing it into his bag, before moving on. Now close to their destination, they moved at a greater pace and arrived at the craftsman's shop, soon after. The blacksmith's shop had once been a well-stocked ironworks and stable, but now only showed the vestiges of what had been. "Check for the horse," Stephen ordered dismissively. Christina glared and he spoke less authoritatively, looking up at her pleadingly, "If it should please you." Her point made, Christina pushed through the door to the small stable to check for the animal. The stable was dark and reeked of manure. The horse moved excitedly, side to side, and Christina could tell that he was hungry. She looked around and found some feed and prepared a quick bucket for him. He charged her in his need, but was restrained by a rope that had torn into his neck. She spoke softly and held out the bucket to him, calming him, as he furiously fed on what was offered. Stephen worked his way through the shop. It had been picked over and little remained of use. But, to his delight, he discovered some sulfur and ground charcoal carefully packaged in tanned goatskin. Added to his treasures were some scraps of iron that he felt could provide later use and he stowed it all. He looked out the back window and discovered the bloated and decaying body of the blacksmith, dead from a wound to his head. He closed the wood shuttered window and decided not to share his discovery with Christina. Calling out to her he asked, "Is the horse there?"

"Yes, but he is not fit to ride, he has gone too long without food and water," she replied from the stable.

A crashing noise came from outside, freezing both of them in place. Stephen turned and went to the opening to see the same, dirty and ragged girl, who was part of the earlier ambush against him, running away and screaming to someone unseen.

"Heeeere, heere!"

Stephen went quickly to Christina, "We have been discovered." He looked around frantically and said, "Get the horse quickly; prepare him to ride." Stephen pushed aside the debris searching for rope. Christina soon called from the small stable.

"He is ready, but he will not ride far, he is too weak."

"Bring him."

She led him and Stephen took his reins and guided him to the back.

"Stay here."

"Why?" Christina asked while she followed him to the back of the ironworks to discover the body of the blacksmith for herself. She gasped and covered her eyes. Stephen tied the horse to a post and began to lift the dead man, but could not manage it.

"I need your help."

"I cannot," Christina answered, mortified.

"We have no time. I need your help, now!"

Christina moved towards him trembling. She reached under the dead man's arm and lifted, while Stephen did the same from the opposite side. They moved him to the horse and rested him against the post. Christina

The Blood of the Shroud

looked into the face of the dead man and was greeted by maggots feasting on his face. Her stomach turned and she lost her meal of sour milk and stale bread upon the dead man's chest. Stephen ignored her and positioned the horse against the man, "We need to lift him on to the horse now!" Christina pulled her arm across her mouth, to clean it, and steeled herself for her next effort. The blacksmith had been a thin man and the combined efforts of the pair were sufficient to hoist the man over the horse with his arms and legs dangling from opposite sides. Stephen said, "We need to make him look as if he is riding and alive," and pulled the man's right leg to the rear and over while Christina pulled at his shoulder until they had successfully manipulated the man into position. Stephen began to tie the man's arms around the horse's neck, and with them firmly secured, he finished the ruse by tying the man's feet to the stirrups.

"Now what?" Christina questioned.

"When I tell you, set the horse off, make him gallop."

"He is too weak."

"Prick him with this, hard, and he will run," Stephen said, as he handed his dagger to her.

Shock registered across her face, but Stephen had no time for her and went to retrieve his crossbow and look for their pursuer. Armed such, he went to the front of the ironworks. Through the slats of the walls he could see Ælfric riding fast towards them. He returned to Christina. "When I tell you, send the steed in that direction," motioning with his arm towards the west. He returned to his post and watched as Ælfric drew closer. Stephen contemplated his best shot. He wanted him dead, but could not risk Ælfric seeing their location if he should miss. They needed time to escape. He needed a safe shot, to wound him and warn him off. The time neared and he called out to Christina, "Are you ready?"

"Yes," she replied, with a weakened voice.

"It will be soon," he said.

The hoofs of Ælfric's steed grew louder and Stephen ran to the back and gave the command, "Now!" Christina pushed the blade into the haunches of the poor animal and he bolted in fear. Stephen positioned himself for his best shot and followed the steed running from them in his sights. Soon Ælfric entered his view and he changed his target. Ælfric exposed only a tiny portion of unprotected thigh above his knee and Stephen took aim at it. He drew in his breath and held it, aiming at a spot smaller than a man's hand and when he was sure where it would be, he let his quarrel find its mark. Christina watched with trepidation. She had seen the quarrel leave but could not follow it in the air. It had not reached the target when she felt Stephen's hand on her arm, "We must go, run!" They ran through the small building and exited through the front without looking back.

"Where are we going?" Christina breathless asked.

"To the seashore, run!"

Christina took the lead once she realized that Stephen was going in the wrong direction. The only cover at the seashore was the rocky area near the city walls and she guided them there, darting between the buildings, attempting to keep them from Ælfric's view. Christina discovered her first. Around a corner, a small body, lying in a crumpled mass, face down and still: a young girl, small and fragile.

"This girl chooses her friends poorly," Stephen retorted, recognizing her immediately.

"Why would you say such an awful thing? What makes you think she has ever had a choice in this life?"

Christina kneeled beside the girl and turned her over. A bloody gash, starting at her jaw, crossed her face and ended at her ear.

"He bad, I help, no give food, all bad to…" the girl said, before going unconscious.

"She is alive," Christina exclaimed, "we must help her."

"Help her; twice she tried to have me killed!" Stephen replied.

"Would you then become what chases us? Blessed are the merciful not the merciless. Help me with her!" Christina ordered. A nearby home presented their only option and Stephen and Christina carried the girl inside to lay her on a bed of dirty straw. "I need clean cloths and water, find some," said Christina. Stephen was exasperated with her, but complied after reloading his crossbow. The outside had grown dimmer and the waves of smog-like-smoke surrounded him. He looked around for signs of Ælfric, but he could not to be seen. He looked inside each of the nearest buildings and found the basics for care, a candle, honey, water, and some clean rags. He returned to find Christina having torn away parts of her dress, to clean the face of the young girl. She turned to him, "What did you find?" Stephen presented his finds on a nearby stool, separating the objects for her inspection.

"That will do very well, thank you." Christina said, as she went to work.

Stephen went to the window to stand watch as she worked on the young girl, now despondent at their discovery and delay.

"It is not too deep, she will live," Christina said, "The poor thing looks as if she has not eaten in weeks." Turning to him, she said, in her sweetest tones, "Stephen would you look again for more food?"

He turned to her and in the warm light of the candle she looked like an angel and he found that he could refuse her nothing and said, "Yes, of course, food."

The excuse for food would serve him well, he thought. He had to look for Ælfric. He was sure that he was wounded and he would rather face him now, with two quarrels left, than to be surprised at a later time. He retraced his steps and found a suitable corner to peer from. In the distance he could see Ælfric moving in the direction of the city, slowly. He followed him, by hiding between the buildings, careful to make no noise as he watched the fierce warrior make his way to Constantinople.

Satisfied that his pursuer had been thrown off, he resumed the task of finding food with greater enthusiasm. He stumbled across a finely appointed home of several rooms, and located some salted meat, wine, nuts and a few apples, overly ripe, but still edible. He continued in his quest and to his fortune was added a fine leather bag, a needle, and a small knife. He stowed it all and made his way back to Christina.

When he entered, Christina had just finished wrapping the girl's head.

"How is she?" he said, unsure of what tone he should take.

"I grew worried, you were gone so long. She will mend I think. Did you find any food?"

"A banquet, we will feed like kings."

The young girl awoke and asked for water. Christina took her the bag and poured what little was left into her mouth. The girl winched, as she swallowed.

"What is your name?" Stephen questioned, harshly.

"Stephen!" Christina scolded.

"Well, she has a name!"

"Appa," the girl uttered quietly.

"Rest now Appa, we will eat soon," Christina instructed.

Christina went to the table to prepare a meal for Appa and looked at Stephen squarely with a gentle smile.

"This is very fine Stephen, there is plenty for now and later."

"We must leave soon," Stephen, replied, "Gaius will leave shortly."

"Appa needs rest before she can travel."

"You do not understand, it is dangerous here—we must leave. Can we not leave her?"

"Stephen, she needs our care, she is a child, and her wounds must be dressed daily. Would you have me leave her to the unknown, to die?"

Stephen turned and walked out without answering her, storming through the door. *It will be better to search for more supplies than feel my anger grow,* he thought, *Gaius would remain one more day. It is obvious that Christina will not move without Appa, I need a way to move them both quickly.* He remained mired in his thoughts as he moved from building to building, gathering as he went. A piece of string, a small broken knife with a good handle, a wooden cup with a chipped edge, a thigh bone of a cow, a few dry herbs, and a couple of edible roots was all the ransacked homes would fetch. He had decided to return to Christina when the meagerness of his finds prompted him to explore one more home. It too was in complete disarray and the task of sorting through it all seemed tiring to him, then he spotted it. It sat in the corner, crafted from a walnut branch, delicately carved, dressed in carefully sewn scraps of fabric, and fitted with a helmet made from the shell of a walnut: a little knight. He straightened the little figure's costume with his finger and remembered his oath, the duty of Templars—the protection of widows and orphans. Renewed by its memory, he stowed the figure and returned to Christina and Appa.

He walked in to see the young girl eating mashed apples with honey. He moved closely to Appa and with an outstretched arm offered her the doll without word. Appa put her bowl down, licked the mash from her fingers and took the figure in her hand and stared into Stephen's eyes, not knowing what to say or do. She returned her gaze to the small figure and then held it to her breast and cried. Stephen confused turned to Christina and said, "Have I done wrong again?"

"No, nothing is wrong, sit, I will prepare you something to eat. Appa finish your meal, you need your rest," said Christina.

Christina served him salted meat, a few nuts and offered the wine to him. Remembering the wooden cup, he fetched it from his bag and poured himself a drink. Christina looked at him with a promising smile and said, "You have done so well for us, thank you Stephen."

"We must leave tomorrow," Stephen insisted once more.

"I know, eat now."

Christina joined him at the table, sitting on the bench next to him, their shoulders touching.

"How far must we go?"

"If we leave at dawn, we will arrive before noon. I will carry Appa on my back if she is too weak."

"Do you know who chases us?" Christina asked.

"Yes, the villain's name is Ælfric, he killed my father."

Christina wanted to probe more on this news, but the intensity of Stephen's mood silenced her and he continued unabated. "Fate has brought us together again. He is after the shroud for some reason. I have wounded him, but I do not believe it will be enough to stop him. This man is a talented and strong warrior and he will not give up easily. He has somehow escaped my uncle's clutches, so he is very dangerous. I wish William were here."

Perhaps he has killed him, Christina thought, not daring to utter those words to Stephen. Stephen finished his meal and prepared himself to sleep on the floor, but Christina pulled at him.

"The bed is large enough, we can all sleep there," she offered.

The girls fell asleep quickly, but Stephen could find no peace for his mind and remained restless through the night, finding sleep only for a few hours before the dawn broke. When he awoke, Appa was still asleep and beside him, but Christina was gone. He hurriedly looked around the building for her, but no trace could be found. He woke Appa gently and said, "I need you to stay here, Christina is gone. I need to find her."

"Back you come, for me," Appa said, with fear attached to her face.

"Yes, I promise I will return, stay, you are safe here." Stephen said and then turned and headed for the door. Appa started to cry frantically as he left her side.

"Why are you crying, are you hurting?" Stephen asked.

"You go, never come, no one come for Appa, me fear you no come more, Appa lone more, more lone now."

Appa's head fell into the bed and she sobbed uncontrollably. He knelt beside her and gripped her hand gently.

"Do not be frightened, I will come back, I promise you Appa, I will return for you. I just need to find Christina, something is wrong."

He whisked her tears aside gently. He reached for the figure of the knight and handed it to her.

"Rest now, I will return soon."

He left unsure of his promise to her. He had not lied. But, his future and his direction seemed uncertain. He checked his crossbow and moved out the door. He cried out for her, "Christina." Repeating her name as he walked from house to house. *Where has she gone? It is dangerous to be shouting.* He had traveled the distance of twelve buildings when he heard the sounds of splashing water from around one of them. He turned to discover her half-dressed, breasts exposed, bathing herself from a barrel of water.

"Are you mad?" Stephen said, too angry even to notice her nakedness at first, "I thought you were dead!"

"I needed more honey for Appa's wounds and discovered this water when I searched for it. I had to clean the filth off of me; it was just too much to bear. I am sorry. I have filled our bladders first, we have plenty to drink and I have found more food for our travel," she said quickly, in hopes of reducing his anger.

But now, the beauty of her breasts had transfixed him and he had only half heard her, before realizing he was staring and promptly turned.

"Dress now, we must leave, you have scared Appa terribly, we must return quickly."

When they strode through the doorway Appa arose and hurriedly passed Christina to hug Stephen.

"You come, you tell good, Appa no lone more."

As Christina walked from the two, she whispered to herself with a slight smile, finding scripture for the moment, "Cause me to hear thy loving kindness in the morning; for in thee I do trust..."

Stephen took to packing while Christina re-dressed Appa's wounds for the journey. As meager as his finds were, there still was too much to take and he pared down their load to the essentials. The shroud was rolled and tied, then placed carefully in one of the leather bags, separately. With the balance of his tools and supplies placed into the other. He modified a broken basket with leather straps to form a handle and placed the food into it. With his preparations completed, he turned to Christina.

"If you help me with Appa, she can ride my back," he offered.

"Appa walk now," announced Appa.

Christina said nothing, but nodded that it met with her approval. And, Appa raced forward and gathered the hand of Stephen, dragging him forward to indicate her readiness.

"Well, she seems fit enough," said Stephen.

"For now," Christina replied, "for now."

The trio marched from the house and while the morning was no brighter than the day before, their newfound camaraderie improved their spirits and they strode forward as if no danger would befall them. They seemed to move past the village quickly and soon the forest presented itself to them. As they moved into the depths of the green the air seemed cleaner. But, Appa's strength waned and Stephen had Christina hoist her upon his back.

"We will be there soon Appa," Stephen assured her, "Christina we need to get closer to the shore, can you lead us there?"

Christina took the lead and the group trudged along. They were deep into the forest when Christina suggested a short rest.

"We are not far from shore now. A small break perhaps, some food and drink."

Stephen feeling safer and hungry agreed.

"Yes, a short rest by the shade of that tree," motioning to a massive tree standing guard over a deer trail.

They sat resting against the trunk and ate as the birds chirped. Christina mashed bits of apple in her hand and fed Appa.

"Appa drink some wine, it will ease your pain," Christina said.

Appa choked it down, as best she could, and then Christina offered some to Stephen.

"Where will we go first," Christina asked.

"Well, we must find William first and then I imagine back to Milan or Acre—I haven't really had much time to think about it, with all that has happened. Everything has changed."

"Changed?"

"We have the shroud now, once we have William, we will have to decide where to take it, I imagine."

"I should like to see Milan, what is it like?"

"Milan is a grand city with open courtyards filled with fine friendly people. There are books. The food is good and the air clean. The people are busy in craft and trade flourishes there. It is most impressive."

"And Acre?"

"That place is a destination to pass through. A fortification. The sun can kill there and the food is at times foul. It is for the pilgrims, for rest and protection, nothing more."

"I should like to see it as well, one day. It must be wonderful to travel the world."

"My lady, there is nothing wonderful about suffering the whims of the sea and thieves. To journey far is dangerous."

"All the same, I should like to see these places you have described. I have been no further than that village all of my life. My books and my room have been my only world. Now I should like to see what is beyond the horizon. To smell the air in places I have only dreamed of."

"Well, you will get your wish soon, for at the shore awaits your passage to the world beyond your books."

Stephen stood and gathered his bags and crossbow. With Appa firmly on his back they moved towards the shore-of-dreams. Appa squirmed as Stephen moved forward.

"Appa what is wrong?"

"Head hurt."

"We will be there soon, then you can rest again for a long time."

"Sooooon, loooong time," Appa repeated softly, playing with the words.

Christina felt relaxed and wanted to talk.

"Stephen can you swim?"

"Yes, my uncle taught me. He thought it best that I be able to swim, ride, and fight. We drilled daily in each area, before our first meal. Though I am not a knight yet, just a squire."

"Can you teach me?"

"To fight?"

"Nooo, to swim, like a fish."

"I can only teach you to swim like me. Perhaps, after you have learned what I know you can ask the fishes to teach you what they know."

She picked up a small stone and tossed at his head, laughing.

Christina could make out bits of the shore ahead and said, "We are close to the water, look." Stephen looked up and a smile crossed his face, *soon we will be free of this horrid place.* They walked faster until they were at the edge of the forest overlooking the shore.

"Christina, stay here with Appa while I look for Gaius."

He trudged across the sandy dirt and made his way to the beach keeping a careful eye out for dangers. He looked to his left and could see the smoke still rising from the city, but the air here was clean and the beach uninhabited and inviting. As he entered the sand, he turned to check upon Christina and Appa. Christina waved to him and he returned her gesture in kind. As he crossed the sand, it dropped to the shore and he could not keep Christina in view. He looked out at the Marmara Sea. The winds had picked up and the water was choppy. But, Gaius could not be seen. He climbed a small dune to gain some height. Nothing. He looked back upon the forest. Stephen was sure that he was close to the landing site, but Gaius was not here. His mood soured. *He might have gone on to the city. Perhaps he was forced to leave or worse dead.* Dread filled his heart. *I will have to tell Christina, we need to return to the city. Appa is getting worse.* He looked out at the waves hoping some miracle would occur, that his friend Gaius would rise from the waves. *Night will be upon us, there is no use in fretting about this any more.* He turned from the beach and headed back.

When he arrived, Appa was lying on the ground with Christina beside her. Christina turned.

"Is he far? Appa is doing worse, she will not be able to travel much more, she needs to rest."

"I cannot find him," Stephen said, with a heavy heart.

"Did he leave us?" Christina asked horrified.

"No, he would not leave us. William and I made an agreement that he was to travel to the Harbor of Eleutherion if we did not return in three days."

"Then our delay has caused him to move from us."

"No, we are within the time. He may have been forced or grew impatient and went to seek us out. Darkness will come soon. We should find shelter and discuss our future under cover. Stay here I will look for something. Tend to Appa, I will not travel far."

He traveled back into the depths of the forest seeking some cover. His mood darkened the trail and the forest lost its enchantment. Luck had not completely left him though. He spied a fallen tree that had become overgrown. He pulled back some branches and sent some rabbits running, he took aim and brought one down. *At least we will eat something fresh tonight.* He gathered his kill and returned to the fallen tree. He pushed his way into the thick of it and trampled down the grasses. *It would serve to hide us at least.* He returned quickly to Christina and Appa.

"I have found us some shelter. It will serve as cover tonight and make the hardness of the ground softer."

They covered the distance to their new home quickly and Stephen prepared a fire ring outside their fortress of branches, to cook their meal. Christina made their hollow into a home by arranging the branches and grasses gracefully and soon the trio ate a meal of wine and rabbit inside the hollow. After the meal was done, Christina pulled out the dirty cloth for Appa to have a blanket and put the child to rest. Once Appa was asleep, Christina looked at Stephen and said, grimly, "We have to go back, do we not?"

"We will discuss it in the morning, rest now."

He returned to the fire ring and took to the task of cleaning his quarrel of the rabbit's blood and entrails, and finished by inspecting his crossbow for damage. When his chores-of-readiness were done he put out the fire and disguised their presence in the forest. Returning to the hollow, he moved next to Christina, to add warmth to her rest, and fell into a deep and deserved sleep beside her. Christina was awakened by the dampness of Appa's body. She felt her face and could feel the heat of illness come from her. The dawn was approaching. She looked at Stephen. He was deep in sleep and she decided not to disturb him. She thought the forest might provide the necessary herbs she needed for Appa's fever and went to seek them out without Stephen. She cautiously moved over him and pushed aside the branches to leave their hollow. Carefully covering the entrance again, she then went about her search. A chill fell over her and she pulled the dirty robe around her tightly. She would need to move off the trail to find what she needed. She knew the fever fighting plants grew upon wet hillsides; she would have just enough wine left to distill them, if they could be found. The dawn seemed to break slowly as she made her way up the shallow hillside searching the undergrowth carefully. She praised the lord as she found the plants in abundance hidden in a thorny thicket of a berry plant. She reached in to pull the leaves from the branches and became snagged by the thorns as she tried to remove her arm.

"Perhaps, I may be of help."

The words startled her and she twisted to see the imposing figure of Ælfric standing behind her. She pulled her arm from the bramble ripping the fabric of her robe and ran up the hill to be stopped by another rough looking warrior, who laughed at her.

"She is a beauty," he said, grabbing her roughly and stealing a sloppy kiss as he clutched her.

"Tie her and leave her be," ordered Ælfric, "I need her unharmed if she is to be of use."

The lecherous warrior threw her roughly to the ground to subdue her and pounced upon her, tying her quickly with rough ropes.

"Gag her, I cannot have her alerting the one I seek," Ælfric ordered.

Bound and gagged, Ælfric came to her and cut the robe from her to reveal her beauty.

"You will lead me to the boy or I will give you to my companions."

Christina shook her head and he slapped her hard, causing her to lose consciousness for a moment. When her vision returned Ælfric was squatting before her. He held her face in his rough gloved right hand.

"Let us begin again. I will find the boy without you, like I have found you. If you help me, I will let you both live. If not, my men will enjoy themselves for a time and then I will kill you, but perhaps not quickly. I want only the shroud, nothing more."

Christina stared into his steely gaze and slowly nodded. Ælfric released her gag and she shouted loudly, "Stephen!" Ælfric punched her hard in the stomach, taking the wind out of her and then dragged her down the hill by her hair.

"Shout once more and I will end your life with more pain than you have ever known." He dropped her and then kicked her once more to ensure her silence.

"Put her on my horse," he instructed the three men standing on the trail.

"He is nearby. He would not leave this angel."

With Christina mounted in front of him, he pulled his dagger and held it to her throat, ridding up the trail, away from Stephen and Appa, to Christina's relief. Ælfric suddenly stopped.

"She relaxes, she did not come from this way, turn back."

Christina's shout had startled Stephen awake. He looked around, but knew there was no place to hide in the hollow. *Christina is gone!* He jumped up and grabbed his crossbow and pushed past the branches. He could hear hooves, *three or four riders perhaps.* He placed his crossbow on the ground hiding it in the tall grasses. He returned to the hollow. Appa was awake, but weak, and he said to her firmly, "Appa I need you be very quiet, no matter what you hear, make no sound. I will return for you. I promise." The hooves slowed and he heard Ælfric's voice, "I have her boy and if you wish her no harm, show yourself. I know you are near, come out now or I will cut off her ears." Stephen crawled from the hollow and stood to face the four warriors. Ælfric stared at him with eyes of flint.

"I know you, boy."

"And, I you villain, Ælfric the assassin of Abingdom."

"You have been most clever boy, but now you are alone. I have killed your Knight," replied Ælfric.

"You lie!"

"Think what you will, boy."

"I am Stephen Arc, you will die badly, Ælfric."

"You Templars are prone to meaningless threats, but the time for words of malice are done, give me what I come for or see your beauty's eyes cut out."

Stephen glared at him for a moment and then looked into the eyes of Christina to reassure her. He crawled into the hollow, and with his finger to his lips he motioned for Appa to remain silent. Stephen rustled about a bit and then grabbed the leather bag, dragging it out of the hollow behind him. He stood clutching the bag, holding it in front of him.

"Let her be free!"

"The bag first."

Stephen threw it to him and Ælfric caught it with his dagger, flipping it open to inspect the cloth.

"Now let her go," Stephen demanded.

Ælfric turned to his warriors.

"I need to return to the city now. Ten gold pieces for the man who brings me the lad's head."

"What of the girl?" one warrior asked.

"I shall take her for the trouble this boy has caused me."

"Ælfric, you were born from Satan's goat," Stephen cried out as Ælfric turned and rode away with Christina.

As the hoof beats of Ælfric's horse grew faint, Stephen turned to face the warriors. The largest of them turned to the others and said, "Let us not fight amongst ourselves for the prize. Allow me to finish him and I shall share the reward, so we may get on with our pleasures of drinking and whoring. Give me some room, I will show you good sport as I hack away at him." The two moved their steeds back and dismounted to sit and enjoy the theatre of death. The brute tasked with his end, asked of Stephen, "Do you tremble and wish to cry, small one?" Stephen showed no fear, glared back at him and said nothing. His attitude unnerved the brute and he moved his horse further back to gain room for greater speed, wishing to punish Stephen all the more for his insolent attitude. Now in position the warrior shouted at him, "I shall remove your limbs while you live, before I cut off your head." He charged forward, with his sword at ready, galloping towards the unarmed boy as his companions drank wine from a flask, laughing and cheering him on.

THIRTEEN – THEY EAT THE BREAD OF WICKEDNESS AND DRINK THE WINE OF VIOLENCE.

"I was doing something important, but I cannot remember what it was," William said.

"You will, I promise," Helena said.

"You know?"

"Yes, my dear husband, I know everything from here."

"Well, tell me."

"I think you would rather have a kiss right now."

"Yes, a kiss would be better."

They kissed and their embrace seemed to last for weeks.

"See I told you," she said.

"I had forgotten the feel of your kiss, how full your lips are, the sweetness of it. How could I forget such a thing?"

"It's been a long time."

"Why can't I remember how long?"

"It is hard to remember things here, I promise everything will come back to you, don't worry. Try the grapes they are always wonderful."

William took the bunch from his wife's hand. He marveled at their perfection. He bit off a small group and the juice ran down his cheek. Helena laughed and then wiped his face with her soft hand.

"You are still such a child. I love you. But even so, you can't stay here. Not now." William looked into her golden-brown eyes confused.

"Why?"

"It is not time."

"I like it here," William said.

"Everyone likes it here, but still you must go soon."

"May I have another kiss?"

"Of course."

"I remember something."

"I know, it means you will be going soon."

"Go, when did I leave last?"

"You didn't, I did."

"You did?"

"Yes, I had to go."

"I remember crying."

"You will remember more later, but don't be sad. The time is close, I need to tell you something."

"What?"

"You will need the star."

"The star?"

"Yes, take the star with you."

"I don't understand."

"I know, goodbye my love."

"I don't want to go."

"I know, remember the star, " Helena said.

Suddenly, it was morning. *Where am I,* thought William. He called out, "Helena?" A man's voice answered him, "I know not of this Helena. Arabi will return soon. Perhaps, he can take you to her." William remembered, "No one can take me to her, she is dead. How long have I been here?" "A little over a day, Templar," Muhammad al-Hassar said, as he lit another candle. William started to rise, but Hassar stopped him,

"You were injured and fell unconscious, please rest, I can bring you anything you require. I am a friend of Ibn al-Arabi and now I am yours, call me Hassar." William was weak and fell back, "Some drink." "I will make some tea, it will give you strength." "Wine." "Tea first, then I shall fetch you some wine. Are you hungry?" William thought for a moment, "Yes, I seem to be hungry." "I will bring food as well, rest now. You are safe here." Hassar hurried off and William took stock of his condition. His side was stiff from tightly wrapped bandages, but the pain was manageable. His weapons were at arms reach, with his clothes clean and stacked neatly beside them. He searched for his memories. They came in mixed pieces. The dream of his wife was near, but now faint. *She talked of a star, strange dream. Twenty years. It had been twenty years since she died. I miss her.*

He shook the dream from his mind and began to collect his thoughts of purpose. *Hassar said I have been asleep for a little more than a day. It is the third day, if all is well, Gaius should have Stephen, but does Stephen have the shroud? And, where is Ælfric?*

"I need to get to the Harbor of Eleutherion," he shouted to Hassar.

"I know, you have repeated that many times in your sleep, Templar."

"William, call me William."

"You cried out many times for the harbor and the name Stephen. Arabi is making preparations, he will return soon and he can take you to the harbor. There is still much madness about and it is safer to wait for his return. Anyway, I must redress your wounds before he arrives. Rest until then."

William sipped the hot tea and ate the dark bread with cheese. He could feel his strength returning. *Hassar was right; he should rest while he planned. He needed to know more. Perhaps Arabi would have some answers.* He finished the plate of food and dozed off again thinking of all the unfinished things he must do.

~

The Blood of the Shroud

Ibn al-Arabi surveyed the wreckage at the harbor. Many of the looters were busy loading the spoils of their depravity aboard the ships, while others continued to maim and rob the population foolish enough to venture out. Many of the crusaders lay crumpled in the streets too drunk to move. The pace of the attack had waned now that the city was firmly under the control of Boniface's men. It was no longer a siege, but a rape of a great city. Fighting seemed random and without purpose and often between men supposedly on the same side. The war was now for wealth, honor had long been forgotten. The Christians had laid waste to the center of Christendom. The judgment of their foul deeds would come to some in days and to others at the end of their days, in this he was certain. He wore the garb of a beggar and most had ignored him, intent on finding what treasures remained or simply to find more intoxicating drink. He made his way from the rooftop by a series of jumps and tumbles until he was once again upon the ground. He ran from the site and headed back to the Forum Bovis, an area largely untouched by the invaders who had confined themselves to the riches of the political center, near the Cathedral of St. Sophia. He avoided the central corridors in favor of the side streets. His pace was quick. Within a block of the forum one drunken invader foolishly attempted an attack. Arabi left him largely intact breaking only his nose and a wrist before he ran off. He arrived back to his quarters in time to find Hassar dressing William's wounds.

"It is good to see you well again, William."

"Your friend Hassar would make a fine physician."

"That would be because he is one," Arabi returned, "Hassar is my friend, editor, physician and can write and read in seven languages. His only failing is that he worries incessantly and nags me like an old woman."

Hassar looked squarely into the face of William, "Arabi mistakes the wisdom of an old man as nagging. As a scholar few can match Arabi, but his lust of travel and adventure often place him in jeopardy for reasons beyond my comprehension. Scholars study and write, they don't continually relive their days as a warrior. It is no doubt the failing of his father who felt the warrior-scholar would serve him better than one before the other." "Take no heed to his philosophical ramblings William. My father thought while spiritual knowledge without learning was possible, he had never met anyone who had achieved it. He believed men must experience the world beyond books and lectures. To do so meant I would need to travel this world and meet the great men of it. However, one often meets the lesser men in such travels, he simply prepared me for when I would." William gave up a laugh, "Yes, I have seen the results of his training. No doubt a great warrior your father." "Without peer some have claimed. Enough of the past we have much to accomplish this day. I trust you find your garments in fine condition. It seems you had stepped in something. I had them cleaned and mended for you. Do you feel well enough to dress?" said Arabi.

"Hassar your wrappings are excellent, I can move well enough to fight," William said, rising from the bed, while stretching his limbs.

"You are blessed, your burns are not much more than a bad day in the sun. Your shoulder wound required more attention, but I believe you will live. I would provide you with cautions, but no doubt they would fail to enter your ears with any greater influence than they have on Arabi. May Allah provide you protection for your travels."

"Thank you Hassar, I am in your debt."

"Repay me by returning my friend safe to me."

William stood and dressed in the morning light. The Templar was imposing at any time, but the majesty of his garb was pronounced in the golden hues of the morning. He stood a head above the two men. He was covered from shoulder to ankle in grey woolen cloth covered over by the finest metal mail. Over this was his white tunic bearing the Templar cross over his chest and the embroidered wolf on the rear. Tying the tunic to him was a grand leather belt with a silver buckle, half-a-hand's width, which wrapped him twice making a cross at his right hip and designed to hold his long sword and Gladius dagger. A smaller belt of matching brown leather ran from his left shoulder going under his right arm and held his axe to his back. From his sword belt hung a large silver cross on his right side, held firm by an iron chain looped through his sword belt. His look was finished with fine beige leather gloves and boots to match. He pulled his sword from its sheath and swung it slowly, side to side, to test his bandages.

"Excellent, I feel whole again. How far is the harbor?"

"Close, William. I have secured cloaks for us should we need to disguise ourselves. Here," he said, handing William a hooded cloak, matching the color of his mail, "I will be ready in a few moments. Hassar please bring me the chest." Hassar left and returned with a plain, ashen colored chest, four feet long with delicate and ornate iron handles on each end. He opened it to reveal two thin and curved Damascus swords, sheathed in black and silver, a white costume of fine silk, and a belt of black leather, black form fitting gloves and short boots with wide straps to secure them above the ankles. Arabi dressed in this manner resembled a lethal dancer. Arabi looked at William to see his expression of surprise and said, "I see you expected always the part of the beggar for me. I think perhaps the role of warrior will serve us both better today. Besides, I will need to be dangerous if we plan to visit the harbor."

"Dangerous," the incredulous William replied, "what were you before?"

"A mere annoyance."

The men said their goodbyes to Hassar in a manner that suggested the outcome of their journey was too uncertain to promise a safe return. Once the horses were made ready, the men mounted and headed to the harbor with William following Arabi. They made little effort to hide their presence, as the streets remained quiet for most of the journey. But, within a few blocks of the harbor gates, the sounds of active men could be heard. They slowed their horses to a walk and then found themselves a safe vantage to inspect the action. Men could be seen carrying and dragging goods through the harbor entrance to load onto the waiting boats. Crows and dogs feasted on the dead that dotted the streets like garbage. The scene played out like a macabre play from the underworld. The guards at the gate took little notice of the men flowing through, preferring to trade jokes and drink, leaning against the walls casually. Then William noticed him.

"That one I know," pulling his dagger to point at the Abbot Martin.

"The holy man?" Arabi asked.

"The Abbot dresses only to hide his sins, but lives to do Satan's work. He is one of the two that wanted the shroud. We will wait and see if his partner the assassin shows."

"Assassin?" questioned Arabi.

"Yes, Ælfric. I had hunted him for killing my brother, yet God has found him for me. I can end his useless life today."

The Abbot looked well worn and trudged along as if injured. He stopped at the gate and questioned the guards.

"Has Ælfric returned?"

"Once. But, he has left again with three men heading for the Golden Gate," one of the guards answered. The Abbot was about to ask more questions when the loud screams of a girl could be heard, "Stephen will kill you when he catches you!"

"The boy is already dead," Ælfric answered, "and I will have his head for you to admire soon."

The words stung at William, *Stephen dead?* Ælfric's arrival soon attracted many men from the docks. "Take this harlot and place her in the hold, but harm her not, she is for me alone." The men pulled at the screaming girl and moved her through the gate as she fought them, much to their delight. Ælfric then acknowledged the Abbot, "So you have survived Abbot, I shall have to reassess your abilities." The glow of his anger filled his face and the Abbot screamed at him, "You left me to die, you bastard." "Now, now, Abbot, in truth I had more pressing obligations at the time. Your fate couldn't concern me then." "I will tell the Pope…" "What will you tell him, of your failings, how you almost lost the shroud? If it were not for me we would not have the shroud now," Ælfric said, as he held the leather bag high. "You will say nothing more of the matter or face a future without your tongue," Ælfric threatened as he pulled his dagger to accentuate his point. The Abbot, red-faced, silenced himself. "See, isn't that better. Friends again. Board the ship and find something to push down your gullet. You will soon see that the past is just that." Ælfric turned his horse through the gate and moved out of the sight of William and Arabi.

"I need you to do something for me," William said.

"What is your request?"

"I must find Stephen. Do not lose Ælfric and don't let him escape with the shroud. Gaius may be here, find him if you can. The harbor master would know if he is here, as they are friends. Gaius is a Greek, old and leathered, like an old hide. He will help you. Here, show him this cross, he will know it is mine." William removed his cross and solemnly handed it to Arabi with both hands, "I will return here and seek you out. If I cannot find, you I will leave word with Hassar for where you may find me. God be with you."

"I will not fail you. Allah be with you my friend," Arabi said.

Arabi watched the gate as the Templar rode-off-hard to the west and contemplated his next move. Men of all types moved through the gate freely. The only unifying characteristic of the thieves were the bundles they carried through. He dismounted, stripped to his loincloth, and made a bundle of his clothes and armaments with his cloak. He freed his mount allowing him to run off without saddle and then staggered off to the gate with the bundle on his shoulder and the saddle slightly dragging the ground. The guards began to eye him suspiciously, but he did not avoid their look, meeting it and then moving towards them. He looked at them sleepily as he passed and stopped at the center of the gate dropping his saddle, staggering to the left and right as if drunk, as he manipulated the package on his shoulder. He then moved on leaving the saddle where he had dropped it. One guard started to warn him of his mistake, but the other pulled at him and said, "We will make a few deniers on that, let the drunkard pay for his passage." Once through the gate, no one took notice of him and he slowly changed his gait, leaving the role of drunkard slowly, as he walked towards the ships moored at the dock.

He could now take in the full scale of the thievery. Hundreds of men formed large lines to board three ships moored at the dock. He moved along the walls thinking someone would take note of him, but the attackers were too enthralled with their treasures or too drunk to notice him. So he moved freely along the dock unimpeded by the warriors. He saw Ælfric near the largest ship, giving instructions to a squire and then allowing the young man to take his horse. Ælfric then climbed the narrow wooden ramp and boarded the ship. At the top he glanced back and seemed to look into Arabi's eyes, before turning and moving from his vision. Arabi moved slowly past Ælfric's ship and took in her features. He estimated that it would hold a crew of forty or more. It was fitted to sail, but could be assisted by oar should the need arise. It was not meant for speed, but cargo, and from its height in the water it was fully laden. As he made his way to the final beach of the harbor, he reached a boat badly damaged by fire. An old fisherman tended to a net nearby and he approached him.

"I look for the harbor master, is he near?" Arabi asked.

"He live in wall, there," pointing to a weathered door in the western sea wall, "He no come out more now. Hide, wait for men to go, he fear death outside."

Arabi went to the door and pounded on it, but no one would answer. He pounded again. He inspected the door and noticed a weathered rip at its base large enough to fit his hand through. He took from his bundle William's cross and passed it beneath the door leaving the chain that held it on his side. He pounded again with greater intensity. He looked down just in time to see the chain pass through, as the door was quickly pulled open and the tip of a blade placed against his chest, "You are not William!" Arabi looked at the man unafraid, "William has described you well Gaius, I am Ibn al-Arabi. I have been sent to find you." Gaius looked over the thin man with disdain, ready to kill him, "You look like a Muslim, why would William send a Muslim?" "Perhaps inside it would be safer to explain," Arabi answered calmly. Gaius looked over Arabi's shoulder to see the great lines of men and allowed his dagger to drop and tersely said, "Perhaps, but watch your words carefully, I am in the mood to kill." Gaius turned aside to let Arabi in and quickly closed the door bolting it tight after him. With the door secure, he grabbed a torch from the wall, turned to his right, and followed a tight corridor until they came to a small room lit by a single candle. The room stank of sweat and stale air. The furnishings were meager, housing only a narrow bed, small side table and a three-legged stool.

"Sit," Gaius barked, "Tell me, where is William and Stephen?"

"William seeks Stephen now. A warrior named Ælfric may have killed him."

"Ælfric the assassin, is here in Constantinople?"

"Yes. Here on these docks right now. I have seen him only moments ago. He has the shroud as well."

This news confused Gaius.

"But, who are you and how do you know William? He has not mentioned you to me."

"We met here in battle against the invaders, allies by need, friends by choice. William has traveled west to seek Stephen and sent me to find you and delay Ælfric by any means."

Gaius rubbed his rough beard and thought for a moment before speaking.

"How did you find me?" said Gaius.

"Fate. William told me to seek out the harbor master," Arabi replied.

"I have failed them," Gaius uttered, moaning the words out.

"You cannot fail that which is not finished. This is far from complete. There is more to tell," Arabi replied.

"More?"

"William in his haste to find Stephen did not tell me who the girl is?"

"What girl?"

"The one who knows Stephen has been taken by Ælfric. She is his prisoner aboard his ship."

"I know nothing of this girl."

"She spoke of Stephen when she arrived. She is the prisoner of Ælfric and she is now in danger. We must save her; she is part of this somehow. If we do not act swiftly, I fear she will suffer greatly at the hands of Ælfric. I need your help."

Gaius looked up at Arabi and renewed his purpose before speaking.

"Of course, you are right, it is not finished. If she be friend of Stephen it is enough, do you have a plan?"

"Regrettably no. Are you armed?"

"I can fight," Gaius replied.

"Then all we need to do is gain control of a ship protected by thirty or forty men."

"There is always a way to take a ship," replied Gaius, "Follow me."

Gaius led Arabi through the narrow tunnels that comprised the quarters of the harbor master. "Where is the harbor master?" asked

Arabi. "He is safe now. My friend and his family have escaped. This place was built with many secrets. Follow me." Gaius moved quickly through the narrow maze of tunnels constructed into the sea walls of the harbor until they came to a flight of stairs. They were so constricted that it was difficult to keep their shoulders from touching the sides as they climbed. Short and steep, the steps made the trip to the top seem endless in the dark. As they rose the smell of the salt air filled the corridor and finally a small window appeared on the right. Gaius peered out and then said, "Which ship is she on?" "The one closest to west end of the harbor. It is the largest of the vessels and carries the banner of the Pope." Gaius grew silent remaining at the window with a fixed gaze and then said, "They are preparing to leave. We must hurry. Can you swim?"

~

Ælfric was pleased with the preparations aboard his vessel. *We will leave soon and I will be liberated from the stench of rotting flesh.* He turned and looked back one last time at the carcass of the metropolis. *I have done well, my ship is laden with gold and gems and the shroud is firmly in my hands. I will be the hero for saving the shroud. I must extort something grand from the Pope. Where should I settle? Rome is soiled. I will be king somewhere where the climate and women are warm.* His thoughts were interrupted by the navigator's words.

"When do you wish to leave?"

"Is everything at the ready?"

"The men still bring treasures aboard, but our hold is full and we are beginning to stow things on deck. The ship will not hold much more."

"Stow only the gold now. Leave as soon as you are ready. Have someone prepare me a bath in my quarters. I will take enjoyment soon and I wish to be clean of this damn city. Have the harlot sent to my room in an hour."

~

Christina was shackled to the side of the ship, too high to lie down and too low to stand, so she was forced to crouch to rest. The roughness of the rusted shackles cut into her skin, but her thoughts were all for Stephen and Appa. *Stephen would succeed. He will come for me.* But, doubts crept into her and she wept quietly. Time passed like a leaking jug—slowly with no good to come of it. When the men came for her she was too weak to fight and allowed herself to be dragged to Ælfric's quarters. Ælfric saw her bleeding wrist and barked, "I told you she was not to be harmed, who did this?" One of the men confused replied, "We did nothing, the shackles…" Ælfric moved towards him and threw him against the wall and proceeded to pummel him with a gold candlestick until he was a bleeding mass, to the horror of the other men. "Clean this mess quickly, I wish to be alone with her." The men hurriedly moved their companion from the room smearing his blood across the floor as they left. Ælfric turned and walked to her side, "Extend your arm, let me look at your wound." Christina hesitated and he gently reached for her arm and pulled it forward, "Please, I need to look, you will not be harmed." He carefully inspected the injury and declared, "It should not scar. I will send for the physician to tend to it. A bath has been drawn for you, it is just beyond the curtain." Christina was perplexed by his concern and a look of confusion hung to her face. Ælfric took in her state and said, "There is no need for us to fight. Certain exchanges are required to keep men such as these in order. There is fierceness even in a flock of sheep. Please have the bath. Are you hungry?" Christina muttered, "No." "I will have something brought anyway. Perhaps your hunger will return when you are clean and rested." Christina moved around the curtain to be free from him and found a brass tub from which rivulets of steam rose like wisps of smoke. Beside it, a small table was filled with rose soap. Moving slowly towards the tub to inspect it, she felt the warmth of the water with her forefinger. Lingering for a moment she danced her fingertips against the surface. Turning her palms to her she examined the filth and decided to quickly wash her hands and face in the tub. As the filth vanished she began wiping higher to include

The Blood of the Shroud

her arms and neck. Now the clean parts made the unwashed areas seem dirtier and she attempted to clean herself without removing her clothes. Ælfric began giving orders to someone outside the door and left the room. *Perhaps, if I just get in and out quickly it will be enough.* Removing her clothes she stepped into the hot bath. Like sun on a summer day she melted to the blissful feeling of the warmth. She began to quickly wash herself, taking care to be quiet. Only the distant sounds of men working could be heard and she began to relax and enjoy the bath. She finished washing, but lingered to enjoy the warmth for a few moments more. She gazed around the room. Everywhere she looked gold, silver and gems overflowed from every container. Looking up at the walls, a brightly polished shield projected the leering face of Ælfric back at her. Startled she reached for her clothes to find them gone. She sank into the water and covered her breasts with her arms.

"You are a fiend."

"Come now, you could not think I would leave you unwatched to cause me harm. Wash more or I will be forced to wash you," Ælfric replied with the grin of an executioner.

Faced with his threat she washed defiantly, agitating the water to prevent him from a clear view of her. His reflection turned from her and she contemplated her recourse, but none appeared. He came around the curtain with a cloth in hand for her to dry. Standing out of arms reach, he held the cloth, forcing her to rise, and expose her body to him to take it from him. "If you stay in any longer, I will have my men dump you from the tub and they can also take delight at your nudity." She rose and submitted to his stares, "Take your shame, you are nothing but the droppings of a pig." Ælfric struck her with the back of his hand. Christina fell backwards landing hard on the wooden floor and then felt the cloth drop on her. "Clean the blood from your face before you present yourself to me," Ælfric ordered as he left her. Christina was barely conscious from the blow. She pulled the cloth towards her. *I will kill myself before he touches me again.* She pushed herself up and wrapped the cloth around her. Grabbing her resolve like a weapon she walked around the curtain and spotted her destiny immediately. *The dagger in his belt!* She brightened her face with a smile and walked gently towards him. If he could see through her farce it did not show. But, before she could reach it he took it from his belt and tossed it on the floor, "Take it. It is what you want. There, pick it up," Ælfric said, motioning with his hands towards the dagger. She hesitated. "PICK IT UP," he screamed. Keeping his eyes in view, she bent and retrieved the dagger and timidly held it in front of her. Ælfric laughed, "Now what have you gained, do you intend to kill me princess?" Christina stared him down and then drew the dagger to her throat, "No, it is I who will die and by my hand." The grin left Ælfric for a moment as he gauged the truth of her intent, "Why do you wait?" Then, she saw it. In the cornucopia of objects in the room she had missed it when she had entered. She stared at it in disbelief. Then, she howled in laughter, "You are a fool. You will not have me or the shroud!" Ælfric turned to look at the shroud strewn across his chair and screamed for his guard to come, "Get me the Abbot, now! Drag him to me if necessary."

~

The Abbot was about to bite into the leg of a roasted duck when the guard interrupted him, "You must come quick, Ælfric demands to see you." "He can wait. I have just started to eat." The leg slipped from his grasp as the guard boxed him hard in the shoulder, "You fool, he is in no mood to wait for anything." Abbot Martin looked at the leg trapped in the dirt of the floor and cursed the birth of Ælfric silently and then said, "The lord has spoken, let us bask in his glory."

When the Abbot entered, Christina was pointing a dagger at Ælfric and taunting him.

"You have nothing and you are nothing, he has bested you…"

"What is the meaning of this," the Abbot demanded, interrupting Christina's rant.

"What is this?" Ælfric asked, holding the dirty cloth high.

The Abbot squinted and cocked his head to divine the meaning of this strange test.

"I said, what is this," Ælfric repeated.

The Abbot still not understanding the meaning to his question replied with one of his own.

"The rag?"

"This is not the shroud?"

"Why would you think that rag is the shroud?" the Abbot questioned.

Ælfric glared at him and then grabbed a plate, flinging it at him, striking his forehead, drawing blood that ran into his eyes. "Have you gone mad," the Abbot said, clutching his head. Ælfric called for the guard again, "Bring me the navigator and chain the harlot below. Christina held the dagger out from her and the guard hesitated. "Why do you delay?" Ælfric demanded. "She has a dagger." Ælfric marched towards her and Christina attempted to spear him. Ælfric turned quickly and grabbed her wrist with his right hand wrenching the blade from her with his left. "You do not have the taste or skill for death. I shall decide when and how you die. You will show me where the shroud is!" Christina spat in his face, "I would rather die." He returned her favor with a punch to her gut causing her to fall clutching her waist. "That will be true soon enough, but only when you beg for its relief from my punishment. Take her below now and hang her hands high." The guard grabbed her by the hair and dragged her from the room as she screamed in pain. The Abbot was still nursing his head wound when the navigator arrived. "We must leave immediately," Ælfric ordered, "tow the small boats, we will make a landing to the west beyond the city." "As you wish," the navigator said and then turned and left Ælfric and the Abbot alone. "This is your mess," Ælfric said. "Mine?" "Had you not lost the shroud, I would not be chasing it now. Get out of my sight and be ready for the landing. I will need you to identify this worthless rag for me. I will not be fooled twice."

~

"They are taking the landing boats," Gaius said, "that is our opportunity. Gather your things." The pair worked quickly and left the safety of the walls to venture out. The crew of Ælfric's ship ignored all, in preparation for their departure, giving Gaius and Arabi the opportunity to push Gaius' boat out into the water, unnoticed.

"She will no longer sail and hopefully she will not sink until they have passed."

"What do you intend?" Arabi asked.

"We must grapple the passing landing boats and pull ourselves aboard. Hopefully they will be too engaged to watch their trailing boats. The winds are not yet strong and they should not make more than two knots as they pass us. If they move much faster we may not be able to catch them."

Gaius and Arabi pushed the burnt wreck into the water and boarded as the shallow waves pushed against it. "Grab an oar and make for the sea, we will hide outside the harbor's west sea wall where the channel is narrow and make our attempt there. We will get one chance, if we fail we have no hope to catch them in this." The men made for the entrance far ahead of Ælfric's crew and turned into the open waters of the Marmara Sea. Here the water was rougher. No longer protected by the harbor's channel walls Gaius' boat bobbed excitedly. Gaius directed the boat around the sea wall and out of the sight of Ælfric's crew. Gaius dropped anchor and the men prepared their bundles for their backs and waited. Gaius sharpened the ends of the grappling hooks with a rough file, one final time, and coiled the ropes carefully on the deck. He noticed the bow hanging lower than normal and went to inspect. The boat was taking on water fast. *Should they have to wait much longer they would be swimming,* he thought. He returned to Arabi's side, "We are running out of time, load up and prepare yourself." With their gear stowed upon their backs the men waited holding the dangling grappling hooks by the rope. Once the ship passed, they would have only moments to swing their hooks to speed and toss them onto the passing boats. The men stood apart to prevent their lines from tangling and waited for the passing ship in a solemn silence, serenaded only by the cries of seagulls and lapping waves. Dark clouds anchored the sky and the day and the passing time began to weaken their spirits. Gaius had taken the spot closest to the bow to gain more time should Arabi's toss fail. Soon the deck was covered in water and the men stood calf-high in the brine. It was then the bow of Ælfric's ship appeared. Gaius quickly estimated the speed of the vessel and winced. *It is going three or four knots!* "Get ready," Gaius shouted. The ship moved past them at alarming speed and the lines of the landing boats in tow came into sight. The men began to swing their hooks in anticipation. The bow of one of the landing boats appeared and Arabi made his attempt. The hook made its target and Arabi leapt over the side clinging to the wet rope wrapped around his right arm. With no hope of catching the end of Arabi's fast moving rope, Gaius swung his own hook, but the wake of Ælfric's ship caused him to slip on the wet deck and he lost his aim. The hook sailed through the air and caught Arabi in his left shoulder, digging deep into his flesh. Arabi released his left hand and grabbed the rope of the offending hook to ease his pain. On the deck of Gaius' boat, the line entangled Gaius' leg causing him to fall to the deck. He slid upon its wet surface frantically grasping for the rope, but was taken over the side of the sinking boat, striking his head as he went over. Arabi in severe pain looked back and could see Gaius bob in the water behind him, feet first. Arabi pulled at the line hauling Gaius, in an attempt to bring him forward, but the drag caused by him, in tow, was too great and he could only manage to hold on, as he was whipped by the waves. He attempted to free his right arm, but the wet rope was wrapped too tight and he could not find release.

So the men, like hooked fish, were dragged through the rough waters, behind Ælfric's ship.

The Blood of the Shroud

Constantinople – 1204

Fourteen – Those standing that shall not touch death.

The hooves carrying his impending doom softened and sounded like raindrops to him. He could no longer hear the laughter of the drunken men cheering his demise. The blades of grass moved in cadence to the voice of the wind above his crossbow. His face drew a relaxed smile. Calmness settled in him and he calculated the arrival of his deathblow, with attentive detachment. "If you have only ten breaths before your end, waste none in the worry of death," his father had once preached to him. Stephen drew in a slow deep breath and waited—carefully watching the warrior ride down on him. If he moved too soon his assailant could correct and slice his back. A delay too long would cost him an arm or worse his head. His attacker needed to be fully convinced of his victory over him before Stephen could take his action. One stride would be all that he would be allowed. He let out his breath and sat into his legs. *One, two, three, four*—soon it would be his time. His attacker let out a sound of agony, wrapped in hate, and raised his sword higher. Then his sword started its downward move and Stephen sprang to his right, diving down towards the ground. He hit the ground and folded himself, rolling over his right shoulder, carrying his legs above him. Tucking in his knees, he finished his roll with his feet below him, and pushed himself off the ground with his legs and left hand, while his right pulled the crossbow from its resting place. He stood quickly, turned and took aim at the astonished warrior being carried fast past him. The quarrel left the slide piercing his attacker through the back of his helmet. As he crashed forward, Stephen ran after him. The dead warrior fell off to his right, pulling the reins with him, forcing the horse to a stop. Stephen reached them and leapt to the saddle pulling the reins from the dead man's hands. The disbelief of Stephen's victory delayed the drunken warriors advance and Stephen charged off and away from Appa, as they confusedly gave chase. He took the reins into his mouth and clamped down hard as his horse galloped away from his pursuers. With his hands free, Stephen twisted the handle of the crossbow to reveal the last of his quarrels and mounted it into the slide. The two warriors having regained their reason were now in mean pursuit with swords at ready. The cover of the forest provided too much risk for error and Stephen knew he would need to be out of the forest to use his crossbow effectively. He headed straight for the edge of the forest in the direction of the village, hoping to reach it and lose them there, amongst the buildings. He made it to the meadow, but the men had gained on him, and he found himself with only the option to shoot. The men pursued in a side-by-side formation. Their intent was clear to him. When they reached him they would split to attack equally from both sides. He cranked back the quarrel and readied it to fire. He released the lock and pulled the crossbow to his chest. Taking the reins from his mouth with his left hand, he prepared his mind for the impossible shot. He listened until he could clearly hear the breathing of his attacker's horses. They were close and would soon split around him. He leaned back and rested on the horse's back extending his right arm with the crossbow and took aim. The warrior in the lead seeing the danger attempted to pull off to his left, but was too late, Stephen had him in his sights and released the quarrel. Striking him in his side, he fell quickly from his horse. The last warrior energized by the attack kicked into his horse for greater speed. Stephen pulled himself forward, looked at his crossbow one last time, thought of his father and then tossed it to the side, to free his right hand. He could afford no delays. It would take everything to reach the village ahead of his attacker. Stephen could begin to see the edge of the village and pleaded with the horse to move faster. As he crossed the meadow, his pursuer taunted him, "Not long now— little one." He looked back over his right shoulder and saw the savage grin on the face of the warrior a horse length away. He turned forward and could only watch the distance to the village shrink, unable to modify his circumstances any further. The hoof beats of his horse syncopated with those of his heart and he became one with the beast, gaining a little on the warrior behind him. As the village came into clear view he contemplated his passage through the maze of buildings and decided on his path. Twenty breaths and he would be there. He reached the trampled dirt of the village's main street and headed for the first building, rounding the corner to his right and then making a quick left through the crops that grew behind the home. He remembered the ironsmith had an axe and tried to force the memory of the path back. But, the warrior dogged his every movement, staying only seconds behind, and the path to it could not be brought to his mind. He continued rounding corners searching for anything suitable for a weapon but none appeared. *He would need to outdistance his pursuer,* he thought and decided the central path through the village would be faster. He recognized a building near that path and coaxed his steed towards it. Rounding the corner he made his first mistake and headed into a cart. His horse balked and threw him from the saddle. He flew through the air and struck the cart's wheel with his left shoulder. A loud crack erupted inside him, and his arm suddenly felt loose. He attempted to push himself up to run, but the pain was too great, and he fell back. Turning towards the warrior he waited stoically for his end. The warrior warned of the obstacle by Stephen's rider-less-horse had slowed in time to save himself the same fate. He looked down upon Stephen from his steed and spoke, "Your games are done boy. I will cut you slowly and make you beg for your end." The warrior dismounted and moved towards him, confident in his malice. When he reached Stephen's feet he stood over him and contemplated where to plunge his blade for maximum discomfort.

Stephen knew the sound well. The wisp it made as it turned, end on end, seeking its target. It gave little warning to the uninitiated, rendering them dead long before they could even ascertain its might. It struck hard and the warrior was moved two feet forward, pushing him against the cart, before he dropped at Stephen's feet with William's axe embedded in his back. The dying warrior looked him in the eyes confusedly before closing them for the last time. Stephen looked at the horizon to see William in saddle twenty feet away smiling back at him. "Are you hurt?" William asked. "My shoulder, I cannot move my left arm." William dismounted and came to him, "Can you stand?" Stephen considered his condition and answered, "With help." William assisted him to his feet and helped him into the nearest home. Like the rest of the village, this too was ransacked, but afforded a bench for Stephen to rest. William removed Stephen's clothes to look at his shoulder and from the bruising and swelling, realized the signs, "Your arm has moved from its path, I can mend it, but it will hurt greatly. Rest now, I need to find some things."

"Hurry uncle, Gaius is gone and we must get back to the forest quickly."

"If Gaius is gone, why should our journey return us there?"

"For Appa and the shroud," said Stephen.

"What is an Appa?"

"The girl from the village, she has the shroud."

William had many more questions, but Stephen's shoulder needed his care, so he held them, and left the building in search of supplies. He returned sometime later with a cut branch and cloth in hand and set to work. He cut the cloth to length and then came to Stephen, "I need to

The Blood of the Shroud

pull your arm into place, and it will hurt much. Bite on this," William directed as he handed Stephen the small stout branch. Stephen did as told and William gently raised his arm and placed his left foot into his armpit, as he pulled firmly outward on the arm. Stephen winced hard, as his arm popped into place, and then spit out the branch when it was done. William placed his arm into a sling and asked, "Now tell me of this Appa and the shroud."

"It will need to wait. We have no time uncle, Ælfric has Christina and she is in danger."

"The auburn headed girl, what has she to do with this?" William said, realizing immediately whom Stephen spoke of.

"You know of Christina?" Stephen shot back.

"I saw Ælfric with a girl, screaming your name. By now she is aboard his ship."

"We must go now," Stephen demanded, as he rose in obvious pain. The determination of his look stalled William from asking more questions and allowed him to go. Stephen led them riding the horse left by his now dead pursuer. He traced his path backwards in order to retrieve his quarrels and crossbow. But, was disappointed to find the bow bent from his toss and no longer usable, in its present condition. The same was true for the quarrels, and so he took one of the fallen knights swords for his own. He inspected the fitness of the sword and found it wanting. Poorly balanced and without the grace of his father's design. Still the need to be armed outweighed any misgivings he had about the weapon, so he stowed it and moved on. When they arrived back at the hollow Stephen was surprised to find Appa outside it, gathering wild flowers and humming an unknown but happy tune.

"Appa, are you well?" Stephen asked from his horse. Appa looked up and held her flowers towards him, "I wait good. Flowers get for you when come back. Happy see you." Stephen dismounted and went to inspect her. He held her head feeling for fever, as she smiled back at him.

"He say back you come, worry no."

"Who said Appa, who said I would come back?"

Appa turned from him to seek out more flowers and sang out sweetly, "Shepherd come, tell Appa soon you back, tell no worry." Stephen shot William a perplexed look. William shrugged and asked, "Where is the shroud?" Stephen crawled to the center of the hollow to find his tools and the shroud rolled in the leather bag carefully. This too confused him, for he had left the shroud over Appa to cover her and now it was wrapped carefully and ready for travel. *Who was this Shepherd?* He gathered the bags and left the hollow to question Appa more, but felt time pressing against him and decided the occasion for his answers would need to come later. William placed Appa before him and the three rode back towards the Golden Gate, at the western wall of the city. William noticed the gathering clouds and said to Stephen, "A storm comes can you ride faster?" Not answering, Stephen kicked into his steed and pushed beyond his pain, to gain on time. His thoughts filled with dread at the thought of Christina held captive by Ælfric. He cursed himself for not killing him in the church and vowed given a second chance he would not delay in sending him back to hell. The sting of his thoughts dominated his pain and he moved towards Constantinople in a desperate rage. William mirrored Stephen's worries with his own for his friend Gaius. *What has become of him? Has he died? I should have insisted he stay in Athens. What will I say to his wife Basina?* He stopped his mind's chatter to pray to Christ. He reached to touch his cross and remembered that he had given it to Arabi. This refreshed his hope and he thanked Christ for sending Arabi to his aid.

The time to the gate passed quickly and soon it was in view. William slowed his steed to a walk and Stephen mimicked his efforts asking, "Why do we slow?" "There have been changes, the walls are manned again and the gate is guarded now. It was empty when I passed it before," William said, as he motioned towards the walls with his finger. The pair stopped their horses to inspect the scene further. "There is danger here, hide your dagger in your boot Stephen. If there is trouble, leave me and find the Forum Bovis. Look for a man there named Muhammad al-Hassar. Tell him I need his help. He will aid you." "A Muslim?" "It is too much to explain now, just trust me, we must find Gaius I fear he is in trouble. Take Appa from me." Appa was happy to be at the side of Stephen again and hugged him in appreciation.

They made the balance of their journey to the gate slowly. William took note of the number of men and the armament each bore. *Too many to kill*, he thought, *and too well armed*. Men either feared or hated Templars but dared not kill one openly, apprehensive that the brotherhood would hear of it and send severe retribution. William led his procession to the gate slowly and the main guard eyed the Templar suspiciously but waved him through without speaking. But, as Stephen made his way past the guard, he was ordered to stop, "Halt, where did you get that horse?" The guard's alarm aroused the men around the gate and all drew-to-attention with their weapons drawn. "I said, where did you get that horse, boy?" William turned and spoke, "It wandered in the village beyond, and we were returning it." "Surround them!" the guard ordered and soon twenty men surrounded the trio with pole axes. "You lie Templar, that is my brother's horse. He would not leave it. Where is he?" the guard growled. William stared him down and calmly said, "We know not of your brother." "Dismount and we will seek for the truth in your words," the guard angrily ordered. Appa clung to Stephen and whispered to him, "Bad man hurt." "Worry not, I will protect you." But she remained unconvinced and gripped him tighter. With no place to run Stephen and William dismounted and then helped Appa to the ground. They were pushed through the gate and into the city, forced to follow the wall to the right, prodded by the pole axes. Leading them was the guard whose brother William had killed. Soon they were directed to a small open cell built into the walls. The guards stripped them of their weapons and belongings and pushed them into the dirt floor enclosure locking the iron gate behind them. The guard looked in and said, "I will seek the truth in this, you should pray now. If you have lied to me it will not end well for you." The guards ignored their belongings dumping them into the cell next to theirs. In sight but well out of reach. Appa looked at Stephen and whispered, "No good here." "It is alright Appa. We will be well, worry not," but Stephen was unconvinced by his own words as the clouds above him darkened both his mood and the day.

A young guard was stationed with them to prevent their escape, but seemed indifferent to their actions. Stephen took in their surroundings seeking weaknesses. Moving towards the back of their small cell he inspected the bars that separated him from his tools and the shroud. He tugged at the bars with his one good arm, inspecting for flaws, but could find none. Appa followed closely, too scared to leave his side for even a moment and in an effort to help him tugged at the bars with her skinny arms, pulling a faint smile from Stephen. William was also bent on finding means of escape and turned all his attention to the young guard. The keys to their cage hung out of view. He determined even with the guard gone, it would prove most difficult to gain access to them, unsure where they hung on the wall. But, any attempt to escape required solitude from the guard's prying eyes and he would need to be eliminated for them to have any chance at escape. The cell also remained in clear view of the other men guarding the Golden Gate and the chances of removing the guard in daylight would not go undetected for long and he determined that an attack by him at night would be his only option. William joined Stephen at the back of the cell and whispered, "Have you found any weakness?" Stephen turned to him speaking in hushed tones, "Our enclosure was built well, but if I can get my bag I believe I can unlock our cell. The lock is old and poor in design. Its large size

The Blood of the Shroud

was made to intimidate fools. It should be simple to manipulate it but I need my bag to do so." "We can do little till dark. Make your plans for the retrieval of your bag and I will set my mind to the elimination of our company so that we may work in peace," William said. As they spoke the guard overheard their mumblings and said, "Silence! Your plotting will do no good here. Keep still or I will add chains to your waiting." William glared back at him, but held his tongue.

The day, although late, seemed to drag itself slowly towards the night and they could do nothing but think of possibilities, as storm clouds gathered above them.

Constantinople – 1204

Fifteen – The eyes of the wicked shall fail.

It felt like acid and he began to choke. His brain alarmed came forward violently. *Where am I,* Gaius thought, struggling to make sense of his position as he bobbed violently in the open sea. His nostrils burned as the brine forced its way into him. He flailed out with his arms in panic. He felt a rope touch his right hand and grabbed at it from instinct alone. He pulled the rope across his chest and grabbed it with his left hand, pulling at it like a madman. The force of his tugging twisted his body and he freed his head from the punishment of the moving sea long enough to take a clear breath. Gaius still coughing and choking regained some composure and looked forward to see Arabi looking back at him in great pain. Pulling more upon the rope, he inched forward towards him. The sea seemed to blaze past him as he struggled to move forward, bleeding from his head. His arms burned from the effort and every muscle turned against him. But, he did not stop. He reached a point where the force upon his legs lessened and he kicked to free himself from his entanglements. This eased the pressure against him some and his forward progress improved. He stopped long enough to see Arabi release the grappling hook from his shoulder and toss it off. The realization of what had transpired took hold and he renewed his efforts to reach him. Hand over hand the journey-of-inches through the open sea seemed endless. When all his energy had left him he felt a hand upon his wrist and looked up to see Arabi on the landing boat. Once aboard, the men fell back and rested, unable to move their battered bodies any further.

The rain was gentle upon him and Arabi opened his mouth to catch it. *Life from a drop,* he thought. It was dark now. He raised himself and touched his shoulder. *It's not too deep, I will live,* he thought to himself. His eyes adjusted and he reached over to his companion to wake him. Gaius was slow to stir and it required some effort for him to right himself.

"Are you hurt?" Arabi asked, quietly.

"My head aches, but the worst is gone, and you?" he replied.

"I have no time for my pain, what is your plan now?"

Gaius thought and said, "Plan?" He stared at him for a moment and then looked towards the ship. "We climb that rope that holds our boat, save the girl, return and escape in this vessel." "I was concerned that you had planned something more intensive," Arabi said, with a narrow grin. Gaius started to mumble something angrily back, but stopped himself with a tired grin and replied, "No, that will be enough." Arabi unpacked his wet bundle, dressed and stowed his weapons upon his back. Gaius had carried an old Greek war tunic, a belt, woolen leggings, and a short sword and when dressed, resembled an ancient Spartan. Gaius tossed the grappling hook at one of the landing boats and drew it near. With it within reach, he untied the rope holding it to the ship and allowed it to drift off unnoticed by the crew of Ælfric's ship. He tied the loose line to their boat and then repeated the action with a second and final landing boat, leaving their boat as the only transport to the shore. "Sit," Gaius commanded as he handed him the freed line. He then took a seat beside him with the second untied line in his hand and instructed, "Pull in unison we must draw our boat closer so that we may climb. Follow me." Gaius hooked his legs under the short bench to anchor his body to the vessel and pulled on the rope, gathering it in. Arabi followed his action and slowly their vessel crept forward. A boat's length from the side of the larger vessel, Gaius called out, "Stop." Handing his line to Arabi, he tied off the end to the bench with a slipknot and then did the same for Arabi's line. "We will climb from here, I will go first, follow when I reach the middle. When I tell you, release my line by pulling it here. Allow it out some, but keep the end," Gaius instructed, pointing to the handle of the slipknot. Gaius grabbed the rope hoisting himself up and away from the landing boat, drawing their small craft closer to the larger vessel from his weight on the line, "Release it now!" Arabi did as commanded and Gaius was propelled towards the hull of Ælfric's ship. Landing with his feet against the side he began his climb. A distance of four large men standing foot to shoulder stood between Gaius and the deck. *What waited for him at the top could only be a murderous encounter should he be detected,* he thought. Arabi watched as the older man climbed slowly to the deck and prepared himself for his turn. Gaius reached the middle of the ship and motioned for him to follow. Arabi grimaced as he pulled himself up. He stopped for a moment, focused on the center of his pain and then removed it from his mind. Midway, Arabi looked up to see Gaius slip over the edge. He heard a muffled groan and then silence. As his head came over the deck he saw Gaius lifting a dead man over the railing, allowing him to fall into the water. The deck was littered with sleeping men. One crewman reacted in his sleep to the sound of the lifeless body hitting the sea, but did not wake fully, instead drawing an old canvas tighter to him.

"There are too many to kill and it will be dangerous to walk among them," Gaius whispered.

"Together yes. But, alone I can do this. Stay with the tiller. I may need a diversion should I have difficulty returning. If I am not back before dawn, leave."

"I will leave when you return, go now." Gaius said.

With Gaius at the tiller, Arabi crept forward stepping carefully between the net of bodies. A large pot over a fire, set on short stilts, burned mid-ship giving him pause. *A fire would be tended to,* he thought. But, he saw no one tasked with the job. The drizzle stopped for a moment and the waves could be heard lapping against the anchored ship. Then he heard steps coming from below, so he crouched down between the sleeping men to hide from view. The eyes of one of the crew resting against the railing opened. He stared at Arabi for a second and then attempted to give warning, but was silenced by Arabi's knuckles thrust quickly into his larynx and then killed by a rapid twist of his neck before he could move. The sound of the steps stopped and a bundle of firewood could be heard being placed carefully on the deck. Arabi raised himself slowly to spy on the crewman feeding the fire, mindful of his noise. Pulling one sword carefully from his back he moved half-crouched towards him. He was within swords reach when the man turned and Arabi was forced to slice his neck. Before he could fall upon the deck Arabi leapt forward to catch him and place him on the deck softly. He propped him up near the fire as if asleep and moved on. With the advantage of the fire at his back he could now see the steps leading below and made his way towards them.

Ælfric could not sleep and spent the night ruminating about the events that had led him to this moment, drinking his mood into a fierce rage. Full of anger and wine he decided that now was the time to extract what he needed from the auburn-headed-wench. *Once her flesh had been salted a few times by his whip, she would relent and give him the information he needed.* Grabbing his favorite flogging whip and a cask of wine he made his way to her chamber, staggering against the narrow walls as he went. The guard was asleep against her door, angering him enough to apply a swift kick to his temple, killing him. Grabbing the keys from his lifeless body Ælfric opened the door and staggered through to see Christina chained, standing naked, forced to face the hull—lit by a single dim lantern. The weariness of her position had caused her to slump and hang herself by her wrists in an unintentional effort to rest. The locks around her wrists had torn into her flesh, causing blood to drip down her arms. Upon hearing him, she forced herself upright. He lurched towards her and spoke softly into her ear, "Perhaps now you are ready to please me with what I want to know." "I don't speak to swine," she replied. "Where is the shroud?" he screamed into her ear. Christina turned her head quickly and bit his nose, clamping down hard. Ælfric screamed out in pain and punched her in the kidneys, causing her to release him. He staggered back holding his bleeding nose, screaming, "You witch, I shall beat you till no man will ever want to look upon you again." Christina screamed back, "Then you will rid me of the curse of my life." Christina's retort held him back for a moment and then he replied, "We shall see after the sting of my private humor has robbed you of your flesh." He removed his whip from his belt and proceeded to beat her methodically, pausing only to enjoy her cries and drink more.

Arabi moved quickly towards the screams of the young woman, maneuvering the narrow hallway quickly, unperturbed by the darkness. The dim light of her cell stood out in the darkness and he soon found the open doorway to her room-of-torment. Ælfric was about to lash her again when he arrived. Grabbing the ends of his whip he spun the larger man around, knocking him out with a punch to his face using the heavy guard of his sword's hilt. The sound of Ælfric crashing to the ground alerted Christina to his presence and she uttered, "Who is there," before falling unconscious from her pain. Looking around the room in search of something to release her he spotted the key ring on the floor next to Ælfric. Unlocked and in his arms, he laid her gently down and then set upon finding something to cover her. *She would swim in Ælfric's clothes,* he thought and remembered the guard outside the door. Stripping the smaller man of his tunic and leggings he quickly returned to Christina and gently dressed her. He then placed her over his shoulder and began the dangerous trip back. When he had reached the stairs leading to the

The Blood of the Shroud

deck, he could feel her stir and set her down. Feeling poorly equipped to defend and carry her; he hoped she had sufficient strength to move on her own. She opened her eyes and began to scream, forcing him to cover her mouth firmly with his hand and say, "I have come to save you, be still." Christina wide eyed inspected his face and judged him truthful with her calmness and he released her. "Did Stephen send you?" Christina asked. "There is no time to explain, can you walk?" Arabi said, pointing up the stairs. Christina lifted herself with his help and grimaced out a small, "Yes." The pair moved at a pace Christina could manage and found the deck still peaceful when they arrived topside. They had reached the fire, when the alarm to stop was shouted by Ælfric from the top of the stairway passage. The men still fused to their slumber, awoke confused and stood at attention, not knowing where to look or what to do. Arabi kicked the pot hard, scattering the fire, putting one man in flames immediately. The lit-man panicked and ran towards Ælfric. Turning and pushing the flame-with-legs from him, Ælfric unintentionally steered him to the stairway where he crashed down loudly. The man now in severe agony, screamed as the flames grew upon his body. At the end of the stairs he met the stout wall that made one side of the stair's landing. His neck broke killing him immediately. The force of his crash brought down the small-unlit oil lamp that hung on the wall dousing the wall with oil. Mixed with his flames, the wall began to burn. Here, where the wood was drier, the flames took on new life and filled the lower deck with smoke and flames rapidly.

Arabi slashed the nearest man and grabbed Christina by the hand pulling her towards him and into his arms. Another crewman attempted to stop him, but only succeeded in having Arabi drive his sword through him. Leaving his sword in place, Arabi lifted and cradled Christina and then leapt over the railing, holding her tight. They met the water with their legs—plunging deep into the darkness of it. When the brine met Christina's freshly torn flesh, she screamed in pain expelling what little air was inside her and started to panic. Arabi sensing her distress kicked swiftly and returned them to the surface. Choking and coughing, Christina clung to Arabi only half-aware of what had happened. Seeking cover from the arrows Arabi was sure would arrive at any moment he moved them near the hull taking refuge in the darkness. The men above moved loudly in confusion and above it all he could hear the voice of Ælfric screaming, reminiscent of a mad-dog.

Before their arrival on deck Gaius had been busy cutting the ropes to the rigging leaving only threads holding them in place. One pull on any of the lines and the rigging would be rendered useless, giving Ælfric's men little opportunity to give chase easily. But, the alarm and fire inspired him to do more damage immediately and he released the sail and cut the boom line. The rapid release of the sail forced the boom around knocking four men hard to the deck. With one passage towards him cut off he hurried over the side, making his way down the rope hastily to the landing boat. He untied the boat quickly and made his way towards Arabi and Christina. Hugging the hull to avoid detection, he moved slowly towards them. In the shadow of the ship, the night appeared black, and he could not see them. As he reached mid-ship the pandemonium of the crew had reached a pinnacle and the din of it made him fearful that his companions had drowned. It was then the hand of Arabi grasped the edge of the boat. Hurrying to his side, he first hoisted Christina up and then assisted the weary Arabi. He rowed slowly to the aft of the ship and then calmly away from it. As they looked back the fire had turned into a conflagration, consuming half the deck, and had started up one sail. At a distance the fire wrapped them in an amber glow of triumph and the men relaxed, as Christina slumped into exhaustion at the front of the small boat.

~

She heard the noise of thunder and grew fearful of what was to come.

"Do not be afraid, the thunder is not for you Christina," Arabella said, in soft tones.

"Who are you," Christina asked, recognizing something familiar in her face,

"I am your past that you no longer remember."

"Am I dead?" Christina asked.

"No, you dream the dream-of-souls."

"I don't understand," Christina replied.

"You have grown so beautiful," Arabella said, stroking her face gently.

"Where am I?"

"Think not of that now, our time is short. I was sent to tell you something. You must listen carefully. You will survive all. What suffering you have here will matter little later. Your faith will be challenged again, be strong and you will survive."

Fog rose around Arabella and obscured her from Christina's view.

"Where have you gone? Come back!" she pleaded. But, Arabella did not answer.

Christina then heard the voices of men talking far in the distance.

"...It will be dangerous to return to the harbor in this boat," Arabi cautioned.

"We will not have to directly. There is a beach before it. We will land there. The harbor master told me of a secret passage that leads to his quarters from that beach. Once we are back, we can find aid for our passenger."

Arabi looked down upon Christina to see that she was back among them, "She is awake," he said to Gaius and then turned to her, "Remain still, we still have time to our travel. Rest." Christina looked at him, but was too weak to speak and remained still, lacking any will to do more.

With the darkness as their cover the trio traveled undetected quietly past the first sea walls of the city and then Gaius turned them towards the shore. A small beach with an outcrop of large rocks appeared to them under the dim light of the moon and Gaius rowed to it, landing the bow against the rocky sand. Arabi jumped out and dragged the line to the rocks, using them to anchor the boat to the shore. He returned and both men carried Christina to the wall. When they reached the wall Gaius returned to the boat and set it free to drift off. He returned and said to them, "We wait now. I will need the light of dawn to find the hidden door."

The night had passed quickly into morning and soon the yellow light of dawn etched the edge of the indigo night. Gaius stood and spoke, "Stay here, I must inspect the wall for secret markings." Arabi nodded and then looked at Christina and found her eyes meeting his. She righted herself with much distress and then asked, "Tell me who has saved me." "There is more than can be shared now. Know this, I am Ibn al-Arabi and I have come as your friend and protector and know of your Stephen from his uncle William, whom I call friend. We will leave soon and I will find you aid for your wounds." "Then Stephen is alive?" "Rest now, we will talk more when you have been tended to." Lying on her side once more, she sobbed, not for herself or from her pain, but for Stephen, whom she was sure was gone by the absence of Arabi's answer.

Gaius returned with news of his success and the three returned to the secret passage he had found. Christina resisted the urge to walk on her own and allowed the men to carry her. The door to the passage was guarded by an over growth of high bushes. While Christina rested, the men set to work pulling the growth away from the door. With the wooden door free of its entanglements, the men discovered it barred with stout iron bars. The bars appeared fixed in the wall requiring the work of several men working with hammers to detach it. Perplexed, Arabi looked at Gaius half-squinting to convey his puzzlement. Gaius laughed.

"Beautiful is it not? Look carefully my friend."

Arabi it inspected closely, but could see no simple method to free it.

"I cannot find your amusement."

"It must be lifted and moved a hands width to the left and then we can pull the right side forward. The bars are locked neither top nor bottom. It is set in a channel at the right, we need only clear it."

"Ingenious," replied Arabi.

"It is clever, but still heavy, it will require both of us to manage it. It is the weight of two stout men, I was told. Will your shoulder allow it?"

"It will require the attempt to know," Arabi replied.

The men stood side-by-side and spent some time finding suitable hand holds. They dug into the sharp walnut sized rocks at their feet, in hopes of finding more forgiving footing, but discovered only sharper rocks. When the best-of-the-worst conditions prevailed Gaius gave the command to lift. When they had freed the bottom edge from the rubble, the men slowly moved the gate to the left. Arabi's shoulder screamed at him to stop, forcing blood from his wound to accentuate the need. Gaius' head began to throb and his arms to quiver. Under the weight of the iron, the required hands-width-distance grew in length in the men's minds, but they did not falter and finally freed the right edge dropping the gate roughly in unison. Now with the bars resting on the ground again the effort to pull the gate forward seemed effortless in comparison. With the gate open the men rested for a moment and Arabi mused aloud,

"Two giants."

"What giants?"

"The two they compared this gate to."

Too tired to laugh, Gaius could only nod in agreement. The wooden door required no effort to open, as it was fitted with a secret push lock near the base. With it open, Gaius inspected the passage. It was narrow and without light. He traveled twenty feet in and returned slowly to report. "We will spend some time in the dark. We cannot carry her, she will need to walk." Arabi turned to help Christina, but she was already up and said, "Let us begin then."

～

Boredom. Imprisonment weakens even the toughest of men—crumbling their will with time. Even the contemplation of escape dims the mind in the repetitiveness of a seemingly impossible activity. Stephen could not sleep staring at the bars that separated him from his tools. His ideas grew tired of racing through his mind. If the answer to their freedom was there, Stephen could not see it.

William stood guard at the front gate, familiar with long waits that end in death. He watched the guards, looking for their patterns and their weaknesses. He turned to Stephen.

"If we cannot open the gate, we must have the guard open it for us."

"How?"

"Annoyance. Retrieve your dagger."

Stephen puzzled, moved forward with it in hand.

"They are about to change shifts. The weakest of them will be set to guard us."

"How do you know?" asked Stephen.

"It is the last shift till dawn. It will be given to the lowest man. I have watched him. He is sloppy in dress and manner, suited only to guard. His brains rest in the mud. When the others depart to retire, I will provoke him over."

Stephen peered through the bars to see his uncle proved correct. The final two guards departed, leaving only the sloth to watch over them. William waited until the guard had settled in to sleep his duty away and then shook the gate loudly causing the iron to roar against the silence. The guard infuriated by the interruption called out and ordered William to stop. Ignoring him, William intensified his actions, moving the guard to action. The guard rose and pulled a pole-axe from the wall and came over to their cell and thrust it through to push William back. The mistake of his action grew apparent as William leapt to his right, twisted, turning

The Blood of the Shroud

back to grab the wooden shaft, pulling it tight against the bars. The pull unseated the guard's stability and William then pushed forward hard, knocking the man to the ground, simplifying the matter of taking the pole-axe from his hands. William swung the pole-axe above his head and returned it swiftly through the bars stopping short of piercing the man's neck, allowing the point to rest uncomfortably through his skin. "Shout and you are done," said William. The guard stunned, looked back at him not daring to move. "Drag yourself towards me," William ordered. The guard fearful of his end complied in silence. "Put your hands through the bars." The guard did as told trembling. "Stephen tie his hands with his belt." Stephen rushed to the guard's side and did as instructed, as William pushed the pole-axe deeper into the guard to guarantee his cooperation. The guard now bound, William drew the pole-axe back and said to Stephen, while staring into the guard's eyes, "Kill him with your dagger if he utters a sound." William turned and then used the pole-axe to drag Stephen's bag towards him from the other cell. Pulling it through the bars, he returned and handed it to Stephen. "Free us." The guard looked on in wonderment as Stephen worked the lock, opening it quickly with his tools. Now free, they tied and gagged the guard with his own clothes, retrieved their belongings and headed quickly away from the Golden Gate. William reasoned that they needed to regroup. He needed time to think and plan. There was too much he did not know. *Where was Gaius and the boat; had Arabi found him; and had Ælfric escaped his grasp again?* He decided they would head north, away from the congestion of the city and into the farmlands, travel around to the east and head back in when they were close to the Forum Bovis again. As the buildings thinned and it became apparent that they were not heading to the harbor, Stephen protested, "We need to find Christina, she is in danger." "Stephen our circumstances lead us elsewhere. We need help, your shoulder, this child, we have friends here and we need them now if you wish to save this girl. We are not even sure where she is. We came for the shroud and we knew it would not be without cost. She may be part of the price. But, I promise you, if she lives, we will find her, but for now it cannot be." Stephen knew his reasoning was right, but he wanted none of it. Trapped by the futility of any other action, he followed William with a sadness he could only describe as grief. They passed into the farms of the city as the dawn arrived. Empty and peaceful, the war seemed far removed and William tried to plan on how they would escape from Constantinople without Gaius and a boat. Stephen had become nearly lifeless, burdened by thoughts of what Christina was enduring at the hands of Ælfric. Appa followed both peacefully, no longer burdened by anything, remembering the Shepherd's words. "Be like the flowers," he said. She liked flowers.

The Blood of the Shroud

Constantinople – 1204

Sixteen – Exiles from the lion's den.

The weight of time hung upon Hassar like a prisoner's yoke. He prepared for the wounds he knew would show, in a false hope that the spirit of his actions would prevent the future. Ibn al-Arabi was the warrior who became a scholar and his only friend. But, Arabi could never quite leave the role of the warrior, not while injustice reigned upon this world. Hassar had died when his wife and child were lost to him. It was the scholar, who saved Hassar's life, not the warrior. He had wandered aimless and soulless before he met Arabi in Fez. Arabi's teachings had given him his faith back and in return he pledged himself to Arabi forever. Arabi was his master, not that he would tolerate such a title. They wandered the world as friends and learned together at the feet of the greatest minds the world had brought forth. If Hassar shined now, it was only because he was lit by Arabi's light. And now he was worried that his lantern through this world would not return.

The attackers ignored the true things of value in Constantinople and so Hassar had no difficulty in securing the medicinal supplies he wanted. *What good was gold, if a fever could rob you of life?* After a day of trading his knowledge and money freely, he had gathered all that could be found. Hassar planned for now and the future. They would leave soon, he was certain. Now that Constantinople had fallen completely, it would never again rise to the heights it had once known. The center of the world was gone and reason was made weaker because of it. What would take its place frightened him.

The Forum Bovis was eerily quiet when he returned. The innkeeper met him, beseeching him to come to his quarters quickly. When he entered, he saw a young girl badly wounded, lying upon the only bed, with her mother crying next to her.

"What has happened?" asked the horrified Hassar.

"She escaped her mother's care to play outside and was found by the invaders who did this to her. Can you save her," he pleaded.

Hassar went to her side, dropping his bundles by her bed and inspected the young girl no older than seven years.

"I will need clean water, wine, straight branches and honey. Bring them quickly." Hassar ordered.

The girl looked torn apart, an arm broken, cuts riddling her body and she had been ravaged. Hassar thought of his own dead child and went to work to save this one. For six hours he tended each wound carefully, until he could do no more that would be of use.

"She is in the hands of Allah," he said, to the innkeeper and his wife.

"I will return in the morning. Pray."

The mother returned to her child's side and sobbed in a way that put cuts on the souls of those who could hear it.

"Your time here will be forever free, thank you," said the innkeeper.

Hassar returned wearily to his quarters and sat to rest and reflect on the day when Arabi and Gaius burst through the door, carting the half-alive Christina.

"Hassar she has a bad fever and cannot be revived. She needs your help," said Arabi.

Hassar arose and spent the balance of the night tending to them all— his strength renewed by the return of his friend.

~

Hassar was awakened by the pounding on the door, piercing the dream he was having of his family. He heard Arabi say, "They have returned."

The Blood of the Shroud

Hassar arose to greet William and meet Stephen and Appa for the first time. He began to speak when he was stunned into silence by the half-hidden face of the young girl in bandages. *Appa was the embodiment of his dead daughter,* he thought. "Have you nothing to say Hassar?" Arabi asked. *It is an illusion.* Regaining his composure he replied, "The child's bandages are filthy, I will tend to them now." He drew off to the corner and began to remove her bandage tenderly, inspecting her face for differences that would expose the falseness of his hopes. But, the more he unveiled, the more she held the face of his lost daughter. This of course was a falsehood of want. The reality was that time had robbed him of his daughter's face. But, the substitution from need crafted a space for Appa in his heart. When he discovered no reason for her bandages, he grew confused. She bore no mark or wounds of any kind, yet the bandages were caked with dried blood. He called out for the men to come and asked, "Why has this girl been bandaged?" Stephen held Appa's smiling face, twisting it gently from left to right and said, "She was cut across her face. I saw it. She could not have healed in this time. It is not possible." Hassar looked back upon her, "She shows no sign of a cut, perhaps it was just blood splattered across her face that confused you." Stephen had no firm answer and replied with a tentative, "Perhaps." Appa looked at the men and spoke, "Food?" Hassar said, with a smile, "Yes, I will get some food for you, my little miracle. Arabi, I have gathered provisions in the chest there. I must check on Christina." The men separated and began to set the table to dine. Stephen followed Hassar to Christina to check her progress. Christina was face down, unconscious, her torso covered by bandages. Hassar said, "Her wounds were bad and infection has set in. I can do no more for her, but keep her clean and comfortable. I fear she will not make another day." Hassar saw tears well up in Stephen's eyes and added, "But, I cannot read the future, certainty is never wise in these matters, she has shown much strength to get here, perhaps things will change." Stephen looked down upon Christina and Hassar left him alone to sit with his friend, in what he believed to be her final hours. Stephen left her to return shortly with his bag. Pulling the shroud from it, he whispered to her, "We have saved it. You saved it Christina!" He placed the shroud beside her, tucking it carefully under her arm, "As soon as you are better we will take it to a safe place together," and then he cried quietly beside her.

The men gathered at the table and began to eat and talk.

"Arabi, I owe you much. We are done in Constantinople. As soon as we can, we will take our leave," William said, turning to Gaius, "Where is our boat now?"

Gaius looked at William with some concern.

"At the bottom of the Marmara."

"What?" said William.

"There was some trouble in taking Christina from Ælfric," Arabi added.

"Where is that demon now?"

"We left him with his burning ship," Gaius replied, "Perhaps he too lies at the bottom of the sea."

William bit off some bread on this news and chewed it slowly saying nothing. Unnoticed by the men, Hassar had taken charge of the young ward, Appa, cutting her food into pieces and watching her carefully as she ate. He spoke, "You all need rest and to wash. No one is tending the baths in the forum, but the water is clean. It will help your wounds and allow me to redress them for your future travel." Cleanliness appealed to the men and all except Stephen agreed to the action, refusing to leave Christina's side even for a moment.

~

The baths of the forum were dark, lit by seven small skylights, creating undulating spotlights on the water's surface. The torches along the wall had not felt fire for many days. The black and silver marbled floors fed the echoes from the men's movements. The ceiling hung four men high, with high arches, and was supported by fluted columns. And, in the dark expanse that made the bath's chamber, the men felt uneasy, the room defined purgatory in their minds. The large cool pool fed by the river still remained, but the fires that fed the hot baths were no longer lit—the attendants scared off long ago. William built a fire under one of the cauldrons and the men waited on a nearby bench for the water to warm.

"Gaius can we secure new transport?" William asked.

"I will need to scout the harbors. But, in this climate the costs will be severe."

"Your costs will be covered," Arabi interrupted.

"I promise you will be repaid in Templar gold for anything you risk," said William.

"We will worry about repayment when we have freed ourselves from here," replied Arabi, "I should go with Gaius and secure a boat with him."

"I will go alone. I will travel faster without anyone. If a boat remains that can be bought, I will find it and return it to the Eleutherion Harbor," Gaius said.

William was about to object, but Gaius' look suggested better uses for his words and he consented to the plan reluctantly.

"Besides, I will need you all to scour the city for supplies for our journey home. Tend to your wounds, and gather what we will need. If I have not found anything in two days time, there is nothing that can be had and we will need to make new plans to escape this crucible," said Gaius.

The men relaxed in silence and washed themselves in the warm water, bracing for the uncertain future that they would soon meet.

⁓

Hassar left with Appa to check again on the innkeeper's daughter leaving Stephen alone to watch over Christina. Stephen had exhausted his tears and was left only with a heavy sense of dread. His shoulder ached and he pulled a bench next to Christina so that he could rest at her side. Exhaustion and pain overcame his will and he drifted into a deep slumber. When he awoke his eyes met the gaze of Christina.

"You live," she whispered.

Stephen groaned as he lifted himself upright.

"How do you feel," he asked.

"Much like I had been married to death."

"I will find Hassar."

"Hassar?" Christina said.

"I will explain later, rest."

Stephen found Hassar in the courtyard giving Appa a language lesson.

"Come quick, Christina is awake."

When they returned, Christina was upright sitting on the edge of the bed. Hassar felt her face.

"No fever. I need to check your wounds."

"May I have something to drink first?"

"Of course," he said, leaving to prepare her tea.

Stephen looked upon her with guarded optimism.

"Stop staring at me like a sad dog. Where am I?" she asked.

"We are in Constantinople. We have saved the shroud and plan to leave soon."

"Where is the shroud?"

"Next to you," Stephen said, pointing to it on her bed.

Christina turned her head and reached for the bundle. She picked it up and examined it closely for the first time.

"It does not look as I imagined. It is so plain."

Stephen for all his efforts had also failed to study the shroud before now. Christina offered it to him saying, "It should be protected now. Place it somewhere safe." Stephen took the shroud from her and suddenly the weight of it seemed greater than before and with it in his hands, the magnitude of his responsibility grew. Hassar returned and ordered Stephen away.

"I must undress her. Allow her some privacy, while I tend to her wounds. It was then that Christina noticed Appa.

"What is cannot be. She bears no mark, what miracles do you offer physician?" she said, staring at Hassar in disbelief.

"I have done nothing. She came to me bearing no mark, no wound, unharmed and beautiful as you see her."

"It is true Christina. I witnessed it all. She bore nothing," said Stephen.

Christina looked at the men confused and then towards the cheerful Appa who hugged her legs.

"Enough of this talk. I must see to your wounds," ordered Hassar.

Stephen moved from the room, shroud and Appa in hand, and waited outside. Hassar carefully unwrapped Christina. Washing the blood from her back, he discovered most of her wounds had knitted themselves together.

"Is it terrible?" Christina asked.

"I thought you dead a day ago. Now you have nearly healed. This is not my doing. I cannot explain it."

"Then I should be thankful that your hands are blessed Hassar," Christina replied.

~

The men returned from the bath and a table was set for one final meal before the group would begin the work necessary for an escape from Constantinople. As the men sat, Christina rose to thank them for her life.

"I now know the meaning of this life is not measured by our triumphs, for each achievement falls through our fingers like sand. Should we fail or succeed in this task will matter little, should we forget that we are all part of whom God has given us to be with. Thank you all for saving me."

D.B. Sanders   183

William turned to Stephen and said, "I see now why you have been taken by this enchantress. She sparkles like the stars of heaven." Stephen turned red, but was saved from reply by Gaius, "What man among us seeing a fine jewel, does not admire it? And, perhaps even dream of possessing it."

The meal turned to party and as the group dined they began to share agreeable stories of past times.

"Christina, has Stephen shown you his fire, the one that hangs from his neck?" Gaius asked.

"Fire?"

"When I first met him, he signaled me with a medallion he made, that was bright like a fire. Show her Stephen."

Stephen withdrew the mirror that hung from his neck and handed it to Christina.

"It is beautiful, but I do not see the fire," she said.

Stephen rose and stood by a candle, directing the light back at her.

"More star, than fire," said Christina.

William stopped mid-drink and turned to his nephew, staring at the mirror.

"May I see it, Stephen?" he asked.

"Take it uncle, if it please you," Stephen offered, noting his interest in it.

"I will hold it for a time and return it to you later," William replied, hanging it around his neck.

The party dwindled as the food was finished and Hassar, Christina and Appa cleaned the dishes away.

"I will leave tonight," Gaius said.

"How will we know you have secured passage," asked Arabi.

"Someone will need to return to the harbor master's quarters and wait," said Gaius.

"I will take that duty," said Arabi.

"Then it is left to you William, to secure our supplies," said Gaius.

"He will not be alone, we will prepare with him," Christina said.

"She will rest. Stephen and I will help William," Hassar corrected her.

With the assignments divided the group broke as Arabi handed Gaius his cloak.

"It will be cold tonight. Take care my friend."

"I will see you no later than two days," Gaius said and then left.

William prepared to leave after him, while Arabi watched.

"What are your plans?" said Arabi.

"Gaius is a stubborn old goat. I must watch over him, this is too much for one man. I trust Hassar can manage the supplies," William asked.

"Yes, with Stephen it will be enough. Go with Allah. I will see you at the harbor," Arabi replied.

Arabi secured the door and the group prepared for the evening rest. Hassar finished cleaning and the lights were put out. Christina and Stephen with Appa between them took the one bed and Hassar and Arabi took to mats on the floor.

"Milan," whispered Christina.

"What?" said Stephen.

"I want to see your home."

"I will take you wherever you wish."

"Milan."

"It will be done," Stephen promised.

New Harbor lay south and close and Gaius reached it unnoticed. It had been designed for the city's fishing fleet and Gaius knew it would have a vessel suitable for the journey home. Largely undamaged by the invaders, the fishermen continued their trade, finding the invaders excellent customers for their catches. When Gaius arrived the docks were empty, save a few fishermen tending to their nets and lines. He approached the pair nearest him.

"I look for a boat to purchase," Gaius said to them.

"You will find none here," one said, but the other corrected, "Zoilus' wreck can be had."

The fishermen laughed.

"At the end," one said, pointing to the south, "see Zoilus aboard the Sappho."

The harbor made a tight semi-circle around a small bay and was dimly lit by torches that hung from the walls. As he made his way around looking for the Sappho, he felt unseen eyes watching his movements, putting him on alert. He finally spied the Sappho and could see the humor behind the fishermen's laughter. The Sappho's prime was gone years before and all that remained was a floating carcass in need of much work. Gaius tapped his dagger against her stern. A giant with a flowing beard made his way into the light.

"Away from here before I crush you, little man."

"I wish to buy your boat."

This brought a smile to Zoilus.

"Ahh, the Sappho is a fine vessel."

"I wish to come aboard to inspect it."

"You may inspect it when you have paid me for it," Zoilus said, his grin turning menacing.

"Keep your boat, I will look for another."

"Then payment for my time," Zoilus demanded.

Gaius ignored him, turning to find two men behind him with knives in their hands.

"Now you'll pay with your life," said Zoilus.

Zoilus leapt from the boat, with a club in his hand.

"My money now," he demanded.

Gaius attempted to stab him, but Zoilus was faster and struck him on the head dropping him to the dock. "Search him." The villains swept over him, pulling Gaius' heavy pouch from his belt. Zoilus pulled the bag from their grasp and stood to count it as the men grunted at him in anger. "Silence you curs, you will have your share," Zoilus said, pouring the contents into his hand, as William's sword pierced his abdomen. The clatter of coins sprinkled around them as the fishermen moved back, knives at ready. "Leave now," William ordered as he moved further into the light. The larger of the two ignored him and moved to his side to give advantage to the pair's attack. But, in William's eyes he was a clumsy fool and attacked him before his partner could thrust at him. Cutting off his jaw from its mooring the man stared at him with a garish grin before William took off his head. In a continuous motion he turned and sliced the neck of the other man, frozen in fear, who dropped clutching his neck in a futile attempt to stop the spurting blood. The attackers now dead, William rushed to Gaius' side to see if his friend remained alive. He found him breathing, but bleeding badly from his head—his scalp torn from the clubbing. He moved him onto the boat and looked for bandages to hold his blood in. The Sappho was a wreck, like the man who owned it and all that William could find were dirty rags that he hastily washed in seawater. As he wrapped his head, Gaius regained his mind.

"Stay still, your scalp is torn," William ordered.

"I should have stayed in Athens. I am too old to be of use now."

"I still have much need for you my friend. Rest and I will see if I can move this vessel from the dock," William said.

Gaius touched his head and groaned more from his stupidity, than from his pain. He moved himself to the railing and watched the ineptitude of William struggle with the rigging. Gaius pulled himself up and said, "Untie the dock line, you cannot manage this." As soon as they were away from the harbor Gaius surrendered the tiller to William.

Pointing to the north he said, "Keep her bow there. Let her drift until morning. We will not go far. I just need a little rest." And then, Gaius lowered himself to the deck and fell into the slumber-of-the-injured.

Arabi spent most of the day peering from the harbor master's window seeking William and Gaius. The balance of Ælfric's warriors had abandoned the harbor to rejoin the fleet, their coffers now overflowing with stolen relics and treasures. Some of the city's defenders had returned to repair the damage that remained in their wake. But, in the city's center Boniface's men ruled supreme and travel through the city remained treacherous. Hassar with Arabi's help had moved most of the supplies to the harbor master's quarters in preparation for William and Gaius' return, but Stephen and the women remained in the relative comfort of the forum. *It was time for Hassar and him to return home,* Arabi thought. He had much to think and write about. They would go as far as Athens with his new friends and then find passage back to Egypt from there. *Perhaps, Hassar was right and it was time to put his sword down, could not the injustices he saw be removed as easily with his words?* Arabi took notice of a small vessel that stood out alone in the distance and wondered if it could be Gaius and William. Two men moved on the deck, but they were still too far away for him to recognize. Whoever they were, they were heading towards him and would be here before sunset. Taking the chance that they had returned, he left to retrieve the balance of the supplies and return with Stephen and the women, before the boat arrived.

The cramped quarters of the harbor master overflowed with bodies and supplies as the group waited for Gaius and William. Their wait was short and soon the men began loading the Sappho and making it ready for sea. They were not quite done when the noise from the gate at the far end of the harbor started.

"Everyone load something, we must leave now," William ordered.

The invaders had returned in force, swords drawn, screaming in anger and moving towards them quickly.

"Everyone aboard now," said William.

"We don't have everything loaded," Gaius said.

"Leave it, we must push off now."

William and Stephen were charged with the deck lines and once boarded, they remained aft, looking back at the Harbor of Eleutherion. They were a mere thirty feet from the dock, when the soot covered and wounded Ælfric appeared, pushing his way through his men, brandishing his sword high and screaming derogatory epithets at them. Stephen became enraged at the sight of him and screamed at Gaius to turn back to the dock, but William held him by his arm and said, "Later we will deal with him, we cannot take them all now. We must leave this place." Stephen huffed, pulling himself from William's grasp to turn and glare at Ælfric, but said nothing. They could still hear the faint cries from Ælfric and his men as they moved from view and out into the Marmara Sea. Only the soft touch of Christina could bring his mood back to the present, "It is alright Stephen, you have saved the shroud." Stephen turned to her and said, "But he must be made to pay for what he has done." "He will, just not now and perhaps not by you, but he will pay. Come away now, rejoice in what we have," she said. The words stuck to him and he relented to her wishes, moving away from the stern with her.

Gaius who tended the tiller, called for William and Arabi to join him.

"I have little faith in this vessel. She is scrap at best. For our safety I will need to hug the coast until we cross for Athens. I think she would sink in the open sea. Once home I will fit you with one of my best boats for the balance of your journey."

"We can take our time, no one knows where we head. Do as you see fit," William said.

"I agree," said Arabi, "my time is my own. I have no hurry and can use the rest to good advantage."

When sunset arrived they had reached the final resting place of Ælfric's vessel. But, they could not tell, for it lay far beneath the water's surface, removed from their sight. Fire, mistakes-of-judgment and the weight of its stolen treasure had conspired to pull her down.

Taking with her those who would not abandon her gold, even for life. As the darkness became the blanket for their thoughts, the crew of the Sappho relaxed and found their amusement in the bright stars above. Christina watched in amazement as Stephen constructed a cot from nothing for her to lie upon.

"You are most clever Stephen, thank you," she said.

"I see what is not hidden and yet others find this some greatness. Mine is a commonplace talent. But, you see the nature of our souls—that is true greatness. Rest now," Stephen replied.

Christina planted a gentle kiss on his cheek and then sat in comfort upon her bed of nothing. With the fears of the past behind them the group rested easily as Gaius guided them along the coast—sleeping lightly with one hand resting on the tiller. Stephen moved slowly among his friends checking for their comfort before returning to rest alongside Christina for the night. The great city vanished from view and with it the challenges of the past were lifted from their minds. The sea air was cool, but not cold. The air wet, but fresh to their noses. No longer did the soot of the burning city linger, hugging them with her arms of danger. Time moved slowly past them and they marveled at the wonders of the heavens that now twinkled brighter above them. When their eyes finally closed to slumber, no one aboard the Sappho could sense the danger that moved rapidly towards them.

The Blood of the Shroud

Marmara Sea – 1204

SEVENTEEN – THE SHADOW OF DEATH.

Cardinal Ugolino vomited again. *Damn this sea,* he thought. His eruption into the brass pot filled the room with the aroma-of-the-damned. "Take this away and bring me another," he ordered his servant. He hated traveling. *When I become Pope, the world shall be brought to me,* he thought. His only enjoyment on this journey would be watching the smug Byzantines on their knees before him. But he was unsure what could be accomplished beyond that, after all the sack of the city would be complete by now. The Venetians would be in control and there would be little influence he could bear on the city's future. But, if his uncle the Pope demanded it, what could he do? He at least came with the strength of force. The new Sicilian war galley that bore him would be the embodiment of his influence. If they would not bow to papacy right, they would at minimum respect its power: one hundred and fifty knights, fifty archers, forty oarsmen and a three-mast vessel that rivaled the best of the Venetian fleet. *Here, he was the Pope!* The arrival of Abbot Bryce interrupted his thoughts.

"Cardinal we have passed the gate to the Marmara. We will arrive in Constantinople before noon tomorrow."

"Have we any news from there?"

"The landscape is bare. Even Gallipoli shows no signs of activity. But, one small boat has been seen in the distance, coming from the direction of the city."

"Have the pilot stop them. I want to know something of the city before I arrive," ordered Ugolino.

"What if they will not stop?"

"Not stop? Have the pilot order them stopped. Fifty archers should influence their minds. Leave me! Your imbecilic prattle disturbs my prayers. Not stop? This is the Pope's galley..." Cardinal Ugolino carried on loudly, acting as his own audience, as the frightened Abbot scurried off to deliver his order. Then he felt the turbulent rumble inside him and reached for the non-existent brass pot, cursing his servant before expelling the last of his breakfast onto the floor.

~

"She has turned twice towards us," said Gaius to William, "I have tried to avoid them but it is clear they wish to meet."

"Then let them. They are not part of the invader's fleet. A ship that size would be leading them, not following. Whoever commands her will not take kindly to us forcing them to chase much longer. Head towards them and look friendly," said William.

Gaius guided the Sappho to intersect the ship and the distance between the vessels quickly shortened. William recognized the colors first, "It is from the Pope's fleet. Stephen, my weapons." Arabi came to him, "You will need this again, I think," handing him his silver cross. William kissed it and then installed it on his belt. Stephen returned with his weapons and a stiff brush and proceeded to clean his boots. Then William placed himself at the bow so all aboard the ship would see the emblazoned cross of red upon his chest. They moved alongside the ship and soon a rope with saddle board was lowered. But, William refused to sit, preferring that he reach the vessel's deck standing upright on the board. As the boom raised him, he twisted in the breeze exposing the wolf crest on his back. Some among the crew knew the mark and a flurry

The Blood of the Shroud

of chatter spread from man to man. But, Abbot Bryce knew nothing of it and motioned for one of the men to come to him.

"What are the men saying?"

"It is the Wolf of Acre!"

"What do you mean the wolf?"

"William Arc, Commander of the Templar forces at Acre. It is said, he once killed a thousand men in a day of battle."

"Preposterous, no one man could kill a thousand men in a day," said the Abbot. But, he knew well that such rumors held the seed of truth and that the Templar should be treated gingerly. As William was raised high above the men to clear the deck railing, he appeared as a giant. *What is he doing here,* the Abbot thought to himself? Firmly on deck, William looked detachedly down on the Abbot, who tried not to cower from him.

"Cardinal Ugolino commands an audience with you."

"Then have him come to me."

"Have him come to you, are you mad?" the Abbot exclaimed.

"Most find it unwise to call me mad."

"I meant no disrespect. It is just that, the Cardinal has been ill. It would be a kindness for you to visit him in his chambers. There will be more privacy," the Abbot said.

"Have we something private to discuss?" William said.

The Abbot ignoring his question motioned for William to follow him, with a slight bow. William drew a thin smile and followed the little slinking man to the Cardinal's quarters.

~

"William Arc, Master and Commander of the forces at Acre," Abbot Bryce announced.

"Leave us," ordered Cardinal Ugolino and then turned to William, "They told me your vessel was a wreck, better fitted for firewood than travel. Why would a Templar of your standing travel such?"

"I travel in secrecy to meet my ships in Gallipoli."

"I was told that Gallipoli had been abandoned."

"Your information is incorrect. Two thousand of the finest Templars are waiting for my return," said William.

"I was unaware that the Templars had joined the crusade."

"We have not. We are merely protecting our interests."

"What interests are those?"

"Templar interests," William returned quickly.

"Why does your tongue wear a veil? Are not Templar interests the same as the papacy?" said the Cardinal.

"Why have you summoned me?" William demanded.

Cardinal Ugolino's forehead grew lines from folded flesh.

"I need information before I arrive. What are the facts on the ground? What has happened to Constantinople?"

"So now the Pope wishes knowledge of the mad dogs that he has unleashed on Christians. The town is in ruins. Much has been burnt. Nuns have been raped in the streets. The churches have been desecrated. The innocents defiled and killed. Those are the facts on the ground!"

Cardinal Ugolino grew silent for a moment then replied, "That was not the papacy's doing. We did not sanction such acts."

"If the master is not responsible for his dogs, who is?" William asked.

"You dare lecture me?"

"You dare hide your culpability, while innocents die?"

The Cardinal's ruddy face turned a darker shade of crimson.

"You may leave me now, I have no further use for you."

"Nor I, you," said William.

~

"The Abbot was right, you are mad," said Gaius, "You challenged the nephew of the Pope, who has control of a Sicilian war galley, larger than any I have seen."

"My prudence on the battlefield often fails me in the company of pompous fools. One of many reasons I will never be Grand Master."

"Well you have achieved something, we are free to go," said Gaius.

William nodded, feeling an ugly tightness in his belly, as his eyes followed the Pope's galley moving towards Constantinople. The Sappho traveled lightly upon the Marmara and the group cheered as they passed Gallipoli and into the Aegean Sea. Gaius decided to hug the eastern edges of the Christian empire to find a shorter crossing to Athens. It was a gamble that midway along the coast the Aegean would be calm enough to allow them safe passage. But, to travel directly across from the gate would place them on the open sea, far away from the safety of the coast, for too long a time. *No, the pinch of the continents would be their best option to cross safely,* Gaius thought.

Pus mixed with blood as it dripped over his lips. The skin under his eyes took on the hues of indigo and reddish purple, making the swelling appear larger. He coughed frequently to clear his throat from the blood that trickled down it. His once perfect nose was bent halfway down and proudly displayed Christina's teeth marks in the torn flesh. Ælfric was not happy. The physician readied himself to straighten his nose, to improve his breathing and stop the bleeding. He tried to steady his sweaty, shaking hands; half-afraid that Ælfric would impale him, should the pain prove unjustifiable. "Must I drown in my own blood before you heal me physician?" Ælfric growled. The physician answered by pressing his palms against Ælfric's nose and twisting the protrusion sharply to the left, with a quick snap. If it pained Ælfric, he did not show it. He did not flinch or twinge even as the flax twine was led through his nose by the coarse iron needle. Ælfric's mind was elsewhere, plotting the long painful demise of the Templar and his conspirators. The beauty of his torturous plans for them overshadowed any discomfort he felt from his treatment. *They would pay most beautifully,* he thought.

"It is done," the physician said.

"A mirror!" commanded Ælfric.

"Perhaps later, when the swelling has settled."

Ælfric pushed the physician from him and grabbed the mirror from the table and stared at what remained of his once handsome face. The coarse stitching crisscrossed his nose making a grotesque quilt from the flesh of his nose. The color under his eyes gave him a grim appearance. He laughed loudly, frightening the men nearby, by the unreasonableness of his humor. His face now beamed the diabolical horrors of his mind. His thoughts turned to Christina and he delighted at the notion of her forced to view this monster, as he mounted her. "A ship comes," said a warrior motioning to the harbor entrance. Ælfric turned and tried to settle his double vision into one coherent view. A garish blood covered grin formed on him, as the beauty of the Pope's vessel took shape in his eyes. The instrument of his revenge had arrived unexpectedly. *Perhaps there is a devil*, he thought. "Meet the landing boat and secure it. I must have audience with its master immediately," ordered Ælfric.

Cardinal Ugolino tried to avoid his stare.

"I need your ship," said Ælfric.

Even when Ælfric was well, the Cardinal was apprehensive around him. He had never understood the influence he carried with the Pope. But now that he had become a gargoyle his presence unleashed a firm sense of dread around his heart.

"Impossible, I am here under the Pope's direction."

"As am I," replied Ælfric, "A Templar has taken Christ's shroud from here. The Pope has ordered it returned to him."

"A Templar? I have just seen a Templar."

"Where?" demanded Ælfric.

"He was carried on a wreck towards Gallipoli. He intends to meet his forces there."

"He lies. There are no forces at Gallipoli. We have time to capture this thief now. In this vessel we will overtake them in a day and can return as quick. You are not safe here even with your men. There is no

The Blood of the Shroud

love for the Pope here and without me you may find yourself hung as an effigy for him," said Ælfric.

"Impossible, they would not dare," replied the Cardinal.

"A whore reigns over Santa Sophia and you think the papacy's will can stretch to protect you here? Only I can protect you in the midst of these wolves. If you think me a liar, please yourself, and walk through the city of the damned. I will happily watch as your limbs are crushed under wagon wheels and your eyes are fed to the crows."

The Cardinal shivered under his robe.

"Perhaps this delay was ordained. A day you say?"

"Yes, no more than a day and then we will return and complete your duties under my protection."

"Very well then, we shall take a day to retrieve the shroud," said the Cardinal.

The sun fed the air. Clouds drifted westerly, painting pictures of snow-covered mountains across the sky. It filled all, but Gaius with peace. *A storm was coming!* He would hug the coast tight and pray that it would form far from them. It was a naïve wish, but he did not want to hold to thoughts of danger right then. He was happy that he would meet his family again. No more adventures for him. He would spend the rest of his days filling his nets with fish and leave the journeys of blood to others. He allowed the feelings of peace to fill his mind, while ignoring the muffled shouts of danger from his belly. Stephen and Christina took to spending their time watching the skies from the bow. Hassar had taken the role of teacher in an effort to strengthen Appa's vocabulary, much to her delight. The resemblance of father and daughter could not be avoided and soon they became inseparable. Arabi and William tended to their weapons and shared stories of victory and defeat enforcing the bonds between them. The world aboard the Sappho was perfect for those few hours.

Appa saw it first, "Boat, there," pointing aft with her thin arm and finger. Hassar squinted but could not see it, calling for Arabi to come look. He was answered with the footsteps of the group.

"She is right, it is a ship. It is large. It looks like the Pope's war galley, but I cannot be sure yet," Stephen said.

"It is coming fast towards us, a few hours away at most," said Gaius.

"Can we hide?" asked William.

"Give me Gregory's mirror." William looked confused, but complied without question.

"Stephen is this map accurate?" asked Gaius.

"My father was meticulous in all things."

"Then this mark would be Smyrna?" asked Gaius.

Stephen studied the design and answered.

"Yes, that is the port of Smyrna. But, if we go there we will be trapped. The bay before it is long and the exit is the same as the entrance."

"Perhaps, but that port is a busy one and we can hide ourselves in the open, amongst the many ships and boats. The war galley will need to anchor and send men in to search for us, if they believe us there. If they do, they will not easily be able to set sail again until their search is done. All we will need to do is wait until the first night and then pass them as they sleep," said Gaius.

~

Founded by the Greeks, the city of Smyrna was located at a central and strategic point on the Aegean coast, in what was Roman Asia. It was a venerated ancient city. Six centuries old when Christ was born. It was so old that no one aboard the Sappho knew its true origins or of the many battles that had been fought on its shores. Now it was a Christian and Jewish settlement and busy trade town. Here far from the thoughts of war, the busy port of Smyrna flourished and Gaius' gamble proved correct. The Sappho found a home among a small fleet of equally worked fishing boats and hid without effort in plain view of any who should look. If the war galley came, it would be most difficult to see them. Close to the docks the air was filled with the sweet smell of fresh bread and pots of seasoned fish stew prepared for the fishermen by their wives. The catch of the day was piled high and sold to merchants who haggled loudly, infusing the docks with excitement. Other merchants pushed carts of assorted wares and shouted for customers to come, adding to the chaos. And the attentive eye of Christina captured it all. She jiggled against the railing and craned her neck for a better view. She had started to stand on the railing, when Gaius stopped her, "It would not do to have you drown after we have just saved you." Christina looked back at him dejected and asked, "Can we go into the town?" The idea of going ashore had an appealing ring to everyone, but William and Arabi. Stephen wanted to find a blacksmith's shop to repair his crossbow, Hassar wanted to feel the earth beneath his feet, Appa would not leave his side, Gaius wanted more supplies, Christina just wanted to see the world, and under their combined pressure William and Arabi relented reluctantly.

The entrance was guarded lightly and no one stopped them for tribute or inspection. The ancient and modern stood together. Buildings built before Christ served as the material for new foundations and the remaining rubble served as informal forums, dining areas, and merchant quarters. The city was active with tradesmen of every race. Men preached in many languages, while wagons and camels were loaded for journeys to distant lands. The smell of spices and incense filled some areas with the aura of mysticism. Children laughed and played, running through the crowds undisturbed. Groups formed to hear the news of other lands while drinking tea or wine. Laughter and arguing could be heard in equal parts. Smyrna had the feel of peace and the group relaxed. They drew apart to their separate pursuits under the watchful eyes of William and Arabi. Christina followed Stephen while Hassar relaxed with Appa by a vendor serving tea.

"It is good to be here," said Arabi.

"I will not feel well until the shroud is under the protection of the Templar brotherhood," said William.

"You have not far to go. Your journey is almost done. Have you made plans for after?"

"My plans are the dictates of the Templar Master. I may be returned to Acre, but I do not know. So much has changed. And, you, what are your plans Arabi?"

"I will follow you to Athens and then depart for home. I think it is time to rest my—" As Arabi was about to continue Hassar broke into their conversation excitedly.

"Arabi, I have found us passage home. A caravan leaves tonight for Jerusalem and from there they will head to Mecca," said Hassar.

Arabi looked towards William.

"I am in your debt Arabi, feel no hesitation to leave us, perhaps it is time," William said.

"Arabi you can continue and I will follow as you wish," Hassar said, seeing Arabi's thoughts upon his face.

"No my friend, take the caravan, I will meet you in Mecca. I must finish this to have peace."

"William, I wish to take Appa with me," said Hassar.

"She is not mine to give or keep. It is her choice and based on how she clings to you I believe she has made it. She is in good hands with you my friend."

"It is settled then," said Arabi.

"We should return now to help Hassar with his things."

William looked up and could see Stephen busy with the blacksmith, but could not see Christina.

"Arabi take them back, I will see to the others," said William.

Stephen had returned to his old world and was lost in the work of craftsmen. He had just finished straightening his crossbow when William arrived.

"Where is Christina?" William asked.

Stephen looked up from his work and scanned the horizon.

"She was with me only moments ago; she cannot be far."

Stephen cried out her name, but no answer returned. Then the murmur of the crowds swelled causing them to look towards the docks. People began to run towards the gates excitedly. William and Stephen took a position away from the blacksmith's shop, allowing them a view through the gates. On the horizon the Pope's war galley came steadily towards them.

"The galley will be here soon, return to our boat now; I will find her," said William.

Stephen hesitated.

"Worry not, I will find her, but if we are delayed, leave without us." William ordered.

"No, I can not," said Stephen.

"You must, the shroud must be protected. I will find safe passage to Naples, if the need comes. Do your duty! Delay no more, go!"

Stephen turned from his uncle and began to run back to the boat, but stopped halfway, turning to take a final look at him, suddenly fearful that it would be his last. His gaze could find no view of him and so worry began to fill his mind.

～

She had not planned to run off. It was the church that had beaconed her. The church of Smyrna, one of the seven churches of John's revelation was here before her. She needed to touch it. Polycarp, John's own apprentice had been martyred in Smyrna. The spirit welled inside her and she desired to pray to Christ in this sacred spot. This was no accident that they were driven to Smyrna; she could feel the hand of God in this. She saw nothing, heard nothing as she walked towards it. She knew why she was here, the lesson of Polycarp. The lesson of the faithful was here. Even when the sword of evil pierced his chest, Polycarp would not save his life by cursing Christ. She would not fail Christ either. The doors were open and many stood and prayed in silence. She moved past them, seeking a better view of the altar and the wood carving of Christ. Hung high above he faced them, head turned and eyes closed. His suffering displayed clearly, looking thin and worn. She bowed her head and prayed for strength and forgiveness, completely lost in her veneration of Christ.

William became agitated, *where is she?* The marketplace was abandoned for the docks as the crowds awaited the arrival of the war galley. In the absence of crowds, it became apparent that Christina no longer occupied the area. He cursed his luck and stopped to think. He knew nothing of this girl and her habits. *She could be anywhere.* He needed to find her fast, before the Cardinal's men arrived. It was no mystery to him that they were here; he was sure that Ælfric was behind this. *Why else would they be chased,* he thought. He cursed himself for challenging the Cardinal. He saw a small hill and headed for it to gain a better view of his surroundings. From this vantage he could see above the walls. The galley would anchor soon. He turned his head back and saw the church beyond. *She had prayed often aboard the Sappho, she would no doubt wish to do the same at the church,* he thought. The congregation had not yet heard of the arrival of the war galley and still filled the church, blocking his view of the altar. William moved slowly among them searching for a view of her. But, Christina had taken to her knees to pray and could not be seen through the haze of people filling the atrium. A rumble of whispers began to fill the church as they noticed his tunic. He had not expected to go unnoticed, but he certainly did not want to become part of the daily gossip. Some closed in on him to touch him as he passed. Templars were revered by the faithful. But this admiration would only serve to cause him trouble when Ælfric's men arrived. He could wait no longer for Christina to appear to him and decided to shout her name, even though it would destroy the aura of sacredness and possibly provoke some of those around him to protest his presence. His shout was loud and echoed and as expected the congregation turned in unison to look upon him. The city's elders hurriedly moved towards him with scolding looks married to their faces. But, he was saved from their trouble when Christina appeared, parting the sea of troubled souls with the beauty of her face.

"Your actions have placed us in grave danger we must leave now," said William.

"I meant no harm."

"You are naïve to think your intentions matter in this. It is your actions that endanger us. You must cease your recklessness if we are to survive. Ælfric will arrive soon."

"Ælfric is here?" Christina said.

"I suspect it greatly, for there is no other reason for the Cardinal to give chase. He is no doubt under the influence of that demon."

William held her back at the church doors and ordered her to wait while he surveyed the landscape for Ælfric's men. None were seen and he motioned for Christina to come. "Can you run?" William asked Christina. She no longer ached and nodded, yes. With the gate no longer in view William could only guess at the whereabouts of Ælfric. He mentally traded places with his nemesis and calculated that Ælfric would first check the docks for their boat. Failure there would send his troops forward into the city with guards left at the gates to block their escape. Being such, their only chance was to make it to the boat before the landing boats arrived. But William's calculations mattered little, for as they reached the grassy edge of the merchant's area he could see Ælfric's men pushing their way past the crowds, intent on finding them. He pulled Christina down and they hid in the grass watching as the warriors piled into the city. As the count reached twenty, William decided they would need to act now or be confronted with their end.

"We must go back, deeper into the countryside, we can not make it back to the boat now," said William.

"How will we get back to the others?"

"We cannot. We must leave here now if we are to escape. Hurry!"

Christina held a look at the harbor gates and the setting sun cast a sharp golden beam through the dust of the milling men, pointing, she thought, to a direction they should take. She grabbed William by the arm and pointed to the light.

"We should go there."

"Why?" asked William.

"I know not, but I sense it is right for us."

William lacking a better plan thought, *at least that direction offers some cover,* so he ceased his questioning and followed Christina blindly.

～

Stephen arrived at the boat winded, but well ahead of Ælfric's men, who were still on the water in the landing boats. Gaius had covered much of the deck with old sails and was ready for his arrival.

"Where are William and Christina?" Gaius asked.

"She is lost. William searches for her."

Gaius felt his frustration move to the back of his neck and he cursed something in Greek that Stephen did not understand.

"Where is Arabi?" asked Stephen.

"I sent him for fish guts."

"Fish guts, what for?"

"You will see soon enough. I need you under the sail. And, lay low! You must be well hidden before they arrive."

Stephen was in no mood for hiding, but the sense of Gaius' plan began to unfold in his mind much to his chagrin. *Fish guts,* he thought. He could hear Arabi arrive and soon they sat side by side, near the bow, under a sail, listening for the tenor of danger. Ælfric's men scurried along the deck looking for them. As they neared, Gaius grabbed one of the pots of fish guts and turned in on end. Plop-thwast-thasss. The fish guts hit the deck covering it in a smelly slime. Gulls swept down immediately and covered the deck pecking at each other and the bounty, while Gaius turned over the second pot. He then leaned on the railing's edge and pretended to mend the outstretched sail. When the warriors arrived the squawking of the skirmishing birds made hearing an impossible task. "We need to search your boat," the warrior ordered. Gaius pretended not to understand, forcing the warrior to repeatedly scream his request, until Gaius could no longer feign the malady of deafness. "Search as you will but watch your step, you will find it slippery." The warrior stepped onto the boat as the birds loudly protested his arrival. Some of the birds not satisfied to just vocalize their discontent took to diving at his head causing him to lose his balance and slip, forcing him to crack his head and helmet loudly against the railing. His companions laughed raucously at his misfortune and he righted himself in anger. Once back upon his feet he gave a cursory look around without moving and then climbed back to the safety of the docks, moving swiftly away from the Sappho.

"You may come out, they have gone," said Gaius.

Stephen and Arabi crept carefully from under the sail attempting to avoid the treachery of the slimy deck. Stephen realized that Hassar and Appa were no longer aboard.

"Where is Hassar?"

"Appa and Hassar have joined a pilgrimage to Jerusalem."

"Perhaps that is best given our circumstances. I only wish that Christina and I could have wished them well," said Stephen.

"Appa told me to give you this," said Arabi handing him the small carved knight, "she told me to tell you to bring it to her."

Stephen gripped the toy tight and then placed it with the treasures of his bag, while tears welled in his eyes.

"What was William's plan?" asked Gaius.

"There was no time for plans. He instructed that we are to leave if he is delayed. The protection of the shroud was foremost in his mind," replied Stephen.

"We will not leave for many hours, I will look for him," said Arabi.

"You will not. We can lose no others and leave here safely. He is in the hands of God. We will prepare to leave and do his will. Besides, we must rid ourselves of these stowaways if we are not to be heard leaving," Gaius said, pointing to the gulls.

~

"There is no sign of them," the warrior said. Ælfric said nothing, contemplating this news. *It is not possible; they must be in Smyrna,* Ælfric thought.

"It will be dark soon, should we call the men back?"

"Yes, call them back but leave guards at the gate," said Ælfric.

The exiting warrior bounced Abbot Bryce harshly into the wall as he attempted to enter with instructions for Ælfric from the Cardinal.

"There is no respect left for the clergy in these modern times," Abbot Bryce said, as he rubbed his shoulder.

"What do you wish to burden me with?" snarled Ælfric.

"The Cardinal wishes to know when we will return to Constantinople. He says you have had your day."

Ælfric rose quickly and shoved the small man aside, slamming him into the wall again, as he left the room.

"No respect at all!" the Abbot screamed.

~

"I did not call for you. Why are you here?" questioned Cardinal Ugolino.

"I came to give you your answer. We will leave when I say."

"This is impossible. I must finish my mission. I was not sent for this. You must find transport here for your private crusade and I will take my chances in Constantinople with my men. I can spend no more time on this."

Ælfric drew his dagger and sliced the back of the Cardinal's hand. The Cardinal drew his hand rapidly back.

"What demon has possessed you? You have cut me!"

"I have had enough of your prattling tongue. It is you that shall find transport for your journey. I am taking control of your ship now."

"My men will not stand for it."

"They will once you have given the order."

"I will do no such thing."

Ælfric thrust the dagger at him and held it tightly against his throat.

"Then you will not see tomorrow."

"Wait, hold your blade. I will do as you wish," begged the Cardinal.

Ælfric turned from him and before he left the room, turned back.

"You think now that my blade no longer touches your neck, you will be able to renege on your promise, so I shall make one to you. Should you send me trouble, I will make sure my men avenge me a hundredfold."

The Cardinal trembled under the fierceness of Ælfric's glare, swallowing his plans of treachery.

Eighteen – The fishes are chased into an evil net.

All was quiet on the hill. The will to succeed outweighed William's desire to rest, but Christina could go no further. Her spirit was as strong as his, only her legs refused to comply with her wishes. As she lay upon the grasses to rest, William looked for signs of life on the horizon. Only bitter blackness greeted his gaze. The sky was clear, but his thoughts were dark. He knew his arrogance had sharpened his tongue against the Cardinal rashly and brought this plague against his companions. He pulled his sword from its sheath; kneeling before it, head bowed and began to pray, not for himself, but for the protection of his friends. *Punish me for my sins lord, but spare them from the debt of my transgressions.* He remained silent hoping for a sign that he had been heard. None came. As William sheathed his sword his fingers slid across the inscription placed by his brother's hand. Although, he could not see them, he remembered the Latin words of Disticha Moralia by heart, "In adversity do not lose heart; hold on to hope: hope alone does not desert a man even at death." Here on this desolate hill came his brother's counsel. He looked up and saw a star fall from the heavens. He followed its path to the ground and saw a fire. "Christina wake, we must go now."

They reached the small fire ring and were met by an old monk, cooking a rabbit over it. He looked up and motioned for them to sit without word. "This is Christina and I am William." The old man returned no answer, but offered the roasted meat by means of gesture. They sat upon the ground staring into his weathered, but peaceful face. "He has taken the vow of silence," announced William. The stranger offered no guidance on this and instead took to cutting slivers of the meat and handing it first to Christina and then to William. They ate in silence, grateful for the meal. Something moved in the darkness and the snorting of a horse could be heard. William stood and moved towards the sound and discovered a large farm horse. He returned quickly to the fire ring and removed his dagger. He sat and began to cut at the seams of his tunic near its base. Working quickly he succeeded in exposing a small pocket, which held a small Templar gold piece. "I wish to purchase your horse. This coin is worth several horses," William said, while thrusting the coin forward towards the old man. But, the man pushed his hand away gently and rose walking away from them, only to return leading the horse back to William. He offered the reins to him.

"I don't understand, this gold will buy three fine horses for you," William said.

Then the monk stretched out his finger and touched the cross upon William's chest.

"He wants nothing from us," said Christina, "you are a Templar, that is enough."

"We must go my friend, but may we have your name before we do?" said William.

The monk knelt and drew into the dirt with his finger a name in Hebrew. But, William could not read it.

"His name is Isaiah," said Christina.

"Thank you Isaiah, you will be forever in our prayers," said William.

The pair mounted the workhorse and rode off slowly into the darkness and as they rounded the hilltop Christina looked back, to see only darkness where fire once burned. She started to tell William, but suddenly felt the hand of Christ upon her and fell silent.

~

"Trust me it will work," said Gaius.

"You will pull us from shore?" asked Stephen.

"Me and the donkey. But, you and Arabi must keep us away from the shore with the poles. If we run aground we may not be able to pull ourselves free."

"Is there no other way?"

"We can not row ourselves from here. The guards on the war galley will hear us. And, there will be no wind till dawn. I must pull the boat past them from the shore. It will work, have faith."

But, Stephen had little faith in anything now. Already their plans were turning to ashes in his eyes. William had not returned and now this. He wanted to wait. He was sure the war galley would move on once their search was complete. They had already searched the dock and found nothing. But, Gaius was convinced that there was greater safety by distance between them. He was also sure that they would search the docks again, giving the Sappho time to reach the Aegean, before the galley would move on. As Stephen thought it over, it became apparent that both positions were a gamble and gave into Gaius' idea uneasily. They pushed the Sappho from the docks, allowing it to float freely, and then pushed it past the other boats into position near the south shore, where Gaius waited with the donkey. Arabi tossed the rope to him and Gaius tied it to the animal and then they began their slow journey past the war galley. Fires beamed from the galley's deck giving the vessel an undeserved glow of beauty. The Sappho stood in strong contrast to it— encrusted in darkness. Every item that shined was hidden. Things that could rattle were tied tight. The Sappho was a ghost upon the water. Even their breath was muted while the difficult work of keeping them apart from the shore was undertaken. Slowly the inches turned to feet and the Sappho found itself past the war galley and around a corner, safely from the sight of the guards. But, what was gained in distance was lost in time. While they were safely from sight, they were not safe by distance.

The Blood of the Shroud

Should the war galley leave now they would be caught easily by benefit of forty oarsmen. The time to dawn drew near and the horizon began to glow. Gaius began to take shape upon the shore and Stephen could see him signal for them to hold the Sappho steady. Untying the donkey Gaius entered the bay and Stephen and Arabi pulled him towards them with the rope. Once on deck Gaius pulled the sail taut, but the wind was lacking and the Sappho remained still in the water. "If the dawn does not bring the wind, we may need to abandon the Sappho here," said Gaius. "It is too early for such plans. Allah will bring us what we need. You will see," said Arabi. Stephen looked back and prayed that the Pope's men would remain occupied with the search for them, for another day.

Ælfric could not sleep and ordered a landing boat readied at dawn. He would go ashore and inspect the docks himself. He was sure they had not gotten past him. They were close. Smyrna would have been their only choice. *They hide so plainly my men have ignored them.* Ælfric ordered the landing boat to make a sweep of the docks. The dawn pulled at the blackness gently and the unseen shapes began to take form. Fishermen were preparing their boats for the day's journey and the smell of hot tea began to fill the air. The boats were crammed in tight everywhere except where the Sappho had been. Ælfric ordered the oarsmen to the spot and they pulled into the dock. He could hear the fishermen on both sides speak Greek as he moved in and asked them in their native tongue who had been there. But, the men pretended that his tongue was foreign, giving up the location of the Sappho with their unspoken lies. He smiled and ordered one man to shore to gather the men and he returned to the war galley. Soon the galley was a hive of activity as the warriors prepared to depart. The Cardinal had taken most of the knights leaving him only the pilot, his thirty warriors and fifteen archers. But, all the oarsmen who were slaves and useless to the Cardinal on land, their backs now bent permanently to their task, were left to him. It would be enough. The Templar's end was near. His revenge, if not sweet, would surely be filling.

~

Her head bumped his axe handle repeatedly as they rode. She tried leaning to the left and then to the right to avoid it. But, the strain of holding those positions proved too hard and she finally resigned herself to the bruising she would receive.

"You squirm, do you need rest?" asked William.

"Your axe handle," she said, hesitantly.

"Ahh, forgive me, you should have spoken sooner. Lets us rest some and I will arrange it better."

They dismounted and William used his cloak to bundle the axe and then tied it to the horse. Christina watched his careful manipulations. He moved with an assurance crafted from years of training.

"Are all Templars like you William?" asked Christina.

"Templars are just men. Some are good and some pretend to be good. We allow God to separate the chaff from the wheat. It was not always so. In our beginnings only the purest of hearts stood together. The road of the Templar Knight has always been hard and marked us for a painful death. Those who join for the glory of our name, meet their end badly."

"Do you fear your end?"

"I fear only that I will not have served my lord well before I am taken. My failings are as great as my virtues. I can only pray that I am forgiven when I stand before him."

Christina started to ask another question, but William stopped her.

"We are almost there, we must continue. The Sappho should pass soon, we may still have a chance to join them."

From the crest William could see the small peninsula that guarded the inlet to Smyrna. The dawn of new beginnings was forming on the horizon. They mounted again. "Hold my arms tight," William ordered and then he kicked into the horse to force more speed from her. Christina could feel his massive muscles flex under his covered arms and felt safe in his care. Brightness fell upon her cheek and she looked to her right to see the shimmer of the inlet. She began to feel the wind at her back turning her long locks into a maelstrom of hair. The moment seemed perfect. She was happy. William moved sharply off the crest and for a moment she lost her grip and nearly fell, but William caught her without effort and shouted, "Hold tighter," continuing downward unabated at a speed that both thrilled and frightened her, causing her to scream aloud in the pleasure of the moment. She felt alive and connected to everything around her. The blur of the landscape settled finally and she found herself at the shore with her heartbeats thumping loudly in her ears. She laughed and felt free of her past.

"Now we will wait until nightfall. If they have passed we will continue on to Acre," said William.

Christina's stomach loudly uttered its desire for food and William took from a small pouch a crust of bread.

"It is not much, I will hunt for us later. Rest and pray that our friends are near."

That crust represented their provisions and their horse needed water and rest as much as them. William was worried if the Sappho had already passed, the road to Acre would be hard and dangerous. They would need to return to Smyrna for supplies before they could make that journey. It would be unlikely that Ælfric would not leave men behind to watch for them. The dawn was replaced by morning and the sunlight danced off the ripples of the Aegean, unfazed by the plight of their struggle. Sea birds dived at the surface returning to the air with their morning meal. Christina lay back on the grass and rested while William stood watch over the inlet. He could see the shore across the inlet and was confident that the Sappho would not escape his attentive eye should they pass. But, he felt it was late. Past the time for their arrival, he turned to inspect the landscape around them in hopes of a more rewarding view. He saw Christina had risen and was intently staring past him, "They are here," she said. The Sappho came slowly into view, pushed by light winds. William withdrew his sword and waved it high. Stephen responded in kind motioning towards the Aegean. It became apparent to William that Gaius would not stop and wished them to follow. "Gaius seeks a better shore to join us—we must follow," said William. They could not follow along the shore, as it ended into a shear cliff surrounded by harsh high rocks. "We must go over the hill, Gaius will know to follow. We will meet him on the south side of the peninsula."

~

Gaius hugged his friend.

"I thought you had passed us," said William.

"Our delay is the plan of the almighty. If we had passed sooner we would not have been rejoined now."

"Has the galley moved?" asked William.

"She lay still when we left," said Gaius.

"Then let us make our escape."

"This cove will provide us cover from their eyes. I think we should wait until the galley has passed, so we may see their direction. We cannot outrun them, but knowing where they head will allow us to take passage away from them," said Gaius.

"Your idea has merit. We will wait then for the serpent to chase the empty wind."

As the sun hung low in the sky, the war galley passed them heading straight across the Aegean, while the crew of the Sappho watched anxiously for signs of detection. But, Ælfric's galley made consistent progress away from them, until it fell over the horizon and out of their view.

"They head west, we will head south for a time and cross the Aegean when at least a day has passed," said Gaius.

"Take us how you see fit Gaius. But, we should remain vigilant and take watch at all hours," said William.

"I agree the galley is not our only threat here. We shall stay near shore and wait for our time."

It was not the threat of the galley that worried Gaius now. Signs known only to him were present. A storm was near. He hoped to travel south away from it and then cross the Aegean below it. He tried to relax. He had made this crossing many times. But, worry gnawed at his gut, like dry rot. He took in the Sappho. Deck planks were loose, sections of railing moved under weight, she leaked and the mast bore a crack at its base—she would not survive a storm. *She needed steady winds, on a calm ocean, if she was to deliver them to Athens unharmed,* he thought. He would guide them south and wait for the weather to favor them.

"Gaius seems worried," said Christina.

"There are many concerns at sea," said Stephen.

"What concerns?"

Stephen's thoughts turned to the pirates, but held his worries from her.

"Uhh, the wind, our direction, the conditions of the sea and other things known only to him."

"Oh. Yes, those would be worrisome," said Christina.

"Fear not, there is no better man at sea. He will guide us safely," Stephen said, to bolster his will. *Pirates. This time if they come, he could not save them with Greek fire,* he thought.

"I need to stand watch," Stephen said, as he turned and moved towards the bow with intensified purpose.

~

Two uneventful days passed. The Sappho moved lazily south along the eastern edge of the Aegean Sea, near the shore of the Byzantine territory, under light winds and the firm hand of Gaius. The storm remained safely northwest of them and Gaius decided that the long journey to Athens could begin. He would keep them safe by skirting the calm waters near Crete. And only begin the northern leg of their voyage when he was at its western tip. From there, the trip to Greece could be accomplished in two days. The winds of the Aegean turned against them and punished them for three days with Gaius fighting to maintain their course, through the liberal use of profanity and willpower. He acted, as a man possessed, giving up the tiller only when forced to eat. At night he would sleep sparingly, checking their position endlessly, as if the stars might deceive him this time. As dawn was created for the seventh day all the land vanished from view. The wind withdrew and they held still in the water. To the north the storm abated and refreshed itself continuously. Gaius walked the length of the boat repeatedly and prayed for good wind. The others hid themselves under makeshift tents to escape the punishing flames of the sun. On the ninth day the wind returned, but pushed them north. The storm had ceased and Gaius allowed the Sappho to move gracefully with the wind. As the day turned to dusk, Stephen sighted a disturbing mark on the horizon from the east. "Gaius can you see that?" Gaius squinted and said, "No." But, before Stephen's image could be identified, day became night. That night Stephen planted himself at the stern with Gaius and peered out at the dark ocean guardedly.

The morning rose to brisk winds and dark skies. The swells grew and the crew began to lose sight of the horizon as the Sappho intermittently fell into the valleys of blue and green. Christina's stomach turned and she spent her time with her head over the side with Arabi watching over her. Stephen secured the shroud near him. William secured his weapons. Gaius cursed the sea and tried to find a path away from the swells. But, it was too late, the storm was building around them and he could see no course to calm. It was then that Stephen saw it. As they crested a swell the war galley took shape in his eyes. She lay close, but Stephen could not be certain that they had been spotted. Stephen clawed his way to Gaius' side to shout.

"The galley is near," Stephen said.

"What direction does she lay?"

"She comes from our stern."

Gaius' arms rippled under the strain of the tiller, as he forced the Sappho to his will.

"Tell everyone to lash themselves to the boat. This will not pass easily," Gaius ordered.

Soft rain began to fall. But, as the winds increased, the drops turned to blades and their faces were stung by its briskness. Gaius tied the tiller and moved forward to drop the sail. The wet rope was cold against his calloused hands. The sail dropped roughly around his feet and whipped at him as he gathered it in. He was king here and he was determined to lose no one in his kingdom. With the sail tied, Gaius fought his way to the stern and positioned himself for a rough day. The swells began to tower over the boat and he could no longer determine the Sappho's direction. Now it was a matter of navigating the swells so the boat would not capsize. He would worry about their course when they had survived the storm. Worse storms had challenged him and failed to stop him. For a moment it seemed as if his arms would cramp, but the feeling left quickly and he ignored the warnings they gave. The swells grew, turning into mountains. The day appeared as night and the sense of time vanished to all aboard the Sappho. Water hit the deck with such force that some deck planks vanished before their eyes. The roar of the storm masked the loud groans of the Sappho's distress. They were blinded and deaf. It was as if the known world had vanished and they were now held in the monstrous hand of a sodden ogre. However, Gaius was affected by none of it. His will overshadowed the elements and he kept the Sappho in the slender zone of safety. He had no time for fear, guiding the boat over the crests by will alone. As he crested another watery mountain the Sappho took to the air, only to land harshly against the surface moments later, taking them into another valley. They slid quickly across the surface and faced another mountain growing, as they fearfully watched. When they had reached its base the crest of the mountain began to split and suddenly the bow of the war galley appeared; like a dagger through a cloth the galley pushed through twenty feet above them. The moment froze in the eyes of Gaius and he calculated where the galley would land. He pushed hard against the tiller and succeeded in turning the Sappho parallel to the galley's hull. The galley fell solidly against them and the Sappho began to capsize. Gaius looked forward to see his companions contorted by their bonds as the boat turned on its side. Losing his grip he began to fall into the sea. He grabbed his dagger from his belt and turned his fall into a dive. The water was black and Gaius fought his way to the surface. He reached it in time to see the mast heading towards him. He bent to dive, but was caught by it, ripping a wide tear down the length of his leg. He kicked in excruciating pain back to the surface and found the hull. He swam to its edge and then dived in an attempt to save his friends. William was struggling to free himself when Gaius found him. He cut the ropes that held him and then pulled him to the surface. They reached the edge of the Sappho's hull and clung in desperate act to find safety. William looked into the face of his friend to see the color drain from it. Gaius said something that he could not hear and then loosened his grip to fall under the sea. William shouted and reached for him as he sank, but could not find him.

William looked around and found Arabi and Christina clutching the edge near the bow, but Stephen remained from view. William hoped that his nephew clung to the opposite side. Rudderless, the Sappho bore them harshly through the seas. Arabi shouted something to Christina that William could not hear and then sank below the surface. William fearing that Arabi was lost attempted to reach her, but the water proved too forceful and he made no progress. They watched each other helplessly, as they clung for life. Arabi struggled beneath the surface searching the inverted deck for the bowline. The Sappho twisted violently in the water and the bowline caught him at his middle, forcing most of the air from his lungs. Seconds remained to his life as he withdrew his sword and cut the line near his feet. As the tension released he dropped his sword and wrapped his arm around the line. He sank further in the water as the Sappho moved over him to his left. Clear of the boat he kicked to the surface to gasp for air. The line on his arm grew tight and the stern of the boat began to twist towards him. Helpless to move, he watched it move rapidly at him. He judged the distance and braced for impact with the inverted rudder. It met his side hard and he felt his ribs crack. In anguish he reached up to meet the ledge that supported the rudder and pulled himself out of the water. Now perched on the ledge he tied the bowline around his waist as the water crashed down hard on him. Arabi looked up and spied the small keel affixed at the center of the hull. He prayed to Allah and then pounced upward on to the hull running past the keel on the left and then jumped towards the right side where William and Christina clung in desperation. Her strength was failing and she began to lose her grip as he reached her. He grabbed her from behind and pulled her towards him. They dropped beneath the surface and then returned above it with Christina coughing and choking on the brine. This succeeded in awakening her will to survive and she regained some strength. Arabi twisted her to his back and then climbed back to the keel. With Christina clinging to the keel Arabi jumped in again to retrieve William. He hit the water and submerged, but found he had no more strength and lost consciousness—unable to feel the large hand of William on him.

The squawk of gulls intruded on their dreams. Clouds loomed large in the cerulean blue sky and moved gracefully over them to the north. Arabi awoke to find himself tied with Christina and William to the keel. William shook his head slowly as he woke and then looked his way. Arabi's once beautiful white suit looked gray and fresh blood covered his left shoulder. William untied the knot that held them and stood to inspect their surroundings.

"Look there, the war galley," William said, pointing to the south, "that is Crete they head to."

"Is that all you can think of, the war galley? Gaius and Stephen are gone," said Christina.

"What would you have me think of right now? We have no food, nor water. Our boat is useless and if another storm appears we will most likely not survive. Think not that I have forgotten them, for I have not. But, my grief must wait. I believe Ælfric is in control of that war galley and he for certain, means us harm," replied William.

"Do you think they see us?" asked Christina.

"It matters not, they head away from us. They may be damaged and need repair. For now they have no want of us," replied William.

"They may change their minds once they see us," said Arabi, "for we are drifting towards them."

"Without supplies it is for the best. Crete is our only chance to survive," said William.

William began to remove his clothes.

"What are you doing?" Arabi asked.

"I will fetch Stephen from below, no doubt he is still lashed to the railing. I will not have him the bait of fish."

"I will go with you," said Arabi.

The men lowered themselves into the water slowly for the grim task of retrieving Stephen's body. William's eyes focused slowly in the dim water beneath the boat. Arabi motioned to him and the pair inspected the cut ropes where the boy and the shroud should have been. Returning to the surface, Arabi said, "He freed himself, but where is he?" William did not answer, but instead turned his head to Crete to ponder the question for a moment before saying, "Let's retrieve my weapons."

The Blood of the Shroud

Nineteen – Death swallowed up in victory.

The water rushed forward and then swiftly pulled away from the shore. His right hand was half buried in the sand. A gull thinking him dead approached cautiously, wishing to peck at his eyes. Others of his kind began to join him, singing a nasty chorus of delight. The pain in his head finally awakened him and he looked up to exchange stares with the gull. Stephen pushed himself off the wooden chest and attempted to stand and fell back onto the sand. Looking around dazed he hoped to see something familiar. Pushing himself up slowly again he found he could stand this time. Grabbing the chest by its end he dragged it protectively from the lapping water. Stephen made it to the dry sand when his strength retreated, forcing him to rest again. His bag was still around him and he pulled it off to inspect its contents. Only the carved knight remained, but its walnut shell helmet was missing. Stephen gave out a hollow laugh and then looked out at the sea to see the demon coming towards him. Considering his options, he found them all wanting. Standing again, he looked inland to see the shore surrounded by large rocks and high hills. He unlocked the chest to find the shroud intact. Removing it from the chest, he rolled it carefully, tossed it over his shoulder and then dragged himself towards the hills. A small animal trail led upward and he followed it with his legs screaming for rest. He turned to look once more at the war galley and attempted an estimate on when they would arrive. *No time for pain,* he thought, ignoring the demanding objections of his legs. His thoughts turned briefly to Christ's last hours. He summoned his will, but could only trudge slowly upward. He prayed for help and then wondered if his companions were dead. *This is my duty now.* The hills provided no cover. The grey and yellow grasses were too sparse and thin to hide him. Here he was naked to the world. He turned to his right and saw the galley preparing to drop its anchor. He tried to run, but failed before he started. Praying for a miracle he looked up the path. A snake slithered across the trail, stopped halfway, looked at him dismissively and then scurried through the grasses. Moving forward he stumbled on nothing and nearly crashed down the hill. Step by painful step, the crest came towards him. His tongue was dry and he licked his parched lips. The taste of salt reminded him of the storm and what he had lost. The landing boats were coming and Stephen made more effort, but little progress. *Is this my final hour?* Stopping for a moment he looked out at the sea and marveled at the grace of God. Thirty men were coming for him. They looked small from where he stood. *I will be safe at the crest. The shroud will be saved and I can rest.* Gripping the shroud tightly he prayed out loud as he walked. The gulls squawked loudly and he knew the men had arrived at the beach without looking. Dragging each foot forward he dug small trenches with his toes, before he lifted his feet. Men were shouting below him. He looked down and saw two groups moving at him from two sides. The crest was not far. The clatter of their weapons grew louder. He wanted a drink so very badly. *Perhaps, there will be a cool creek on the other side.* The men moved in unison and their feet pounded out a fierce percussion against the ground. He could hear Ælfric's voice. It grated against his pounding head, making him wince. The crest was close. *I will be safe there—thirty-feet at the most.* Stephen reached behind for his crossbow and then remembered it was still attached to the Sappho. His foot touched the crest and he smiled victoriously. He moved forward six feet and could see that the other side

222   The Blood of the Shroud

was sheer rock and fell to his knees. He could hear the men running towards him and he looked up to see Ælfric leading them. He pushed himself up, to meet him standing. Ælfric slowed his approach and glared at Stephen.

"You have made much trouble for me boy."

"Of that I am glad," replied Stephen.

"Keep your spirit, you have much use for it soon. Your prison waits. Bind the boy," Ælfric ordered.

The men tied him at his center with thick ropes and when they were done jeered at him. He was pushed roughly and forced back down the trail.

"I almost forgot, I have something of yours," Ælfric said.

Stephen began to turn towards Ælfric as his quarrel was plunged into his thigh. Stephen staggered, almost falling, but Ælfric caught him.

"Did I place it too high. No, that is the spot, I am sure of it. If I remember correctly it burns when you move."

Ælfric then pushed Stephen forward and he began a painful staggering march down the hill.

"Where are your friends?" Ælfric demanded.

"They are dead."

"Then how did you get here?"

"By miracle."

"You will tell me the truth of it, soon enough."

~

At the beach, Ælfric ordered the men to set up camp and for a large post to be erected in the center of it. The shroud was stripped from Stephen and he was left under guard while the preparations were made. Soon tents surrounded him and he watched the men work on the post. Absent stout trees the men erected a ramming post upright in the ground and Stephen soon found himself tied to it. Ælfric returned to inspect the work and then entered a nearby tent, returning with drink in hand. Ælfric looked out at the sea and said, "It is a fine day. I will sleep well tonight." Stephen made no reply and Ælfric approached and twisted the quarrel in his leg, causing him to scream out.

"Ahh, you have found your tongue again. Where are your friends?" Ælfric asked.

"They are dead!"

Ælfric twisted the quarrel again and enjoyed more of his screams.

"I assure you this is the most kindness I will show you today. Now, where are your friends?" Ælfric demanded.

"I assume them dead. The storm took them from me," said Stephen.

Ælfric glared at him for a moment and then said, "You look parched, perhaps a drink," and then offered Stephen the cup. Stephen took a sip, spitting the vinegar out instinctively.

"It seems the wine has turned like your fate. We will talk again when you have rested. Should you need something ask my men; you will find them most accommodating," Ælfric said, with a laugh, turning to vanish into his tent, leaving Stephen to ponder his future.

Fires were made and the men made a show of the food and drink, taunting Stephen as they laughed and ate. The long day turned to night and the cold wind began to blow against him. He shivered and wondered how long it took to die. A large fat warrior came to him, drinking from a wooden cup, while staring at him. When his cup was dry he tossed it aside and drew close, then lifted his tunic and began to urinate on him. He finished and retrieved his cup, returning to the fire to drink more. Stephen looked up and out at the ocean. He thought he saw a glint, but it vanished too quickly to be sure. He slept at times, but was awakened frequently by his guards. The moon hid itself behind the clouds and blackness became his only blanket. He dozed off again, but was awakened by something near him. He lifted his head slowly and noticed his guards slumped together at the fire. William whispered from behind.

"Do you have the strength to walk?"

"I do not know. Where are the others?"

"Close, we must go now." William said, as he cut his bonds.

Stephen moved forward to find his legs collapse under him. William lifted him, tossing him over his shoulder and carried him from the camp. They reached the far end of the bay, hidden by darkness and a few large rocks to join Arabi and Christina.

"He is badly hurt, he needs this water. There is some food as well," William said, tossing the items to them.

"We all are in need of it, thank you William," said Christina.

"Most of all we need to leave this beach. Dawn will be here soon and they will discover the wreck and us soon after," said Arabi.

"I will return to the camp and steal a landing boat," said William.

"I will go with you," Arabi replied.

"No, you must stay here and protect these two. If I fail, find a way to escape."

"Ælfric has the shroud," whispered Stephen.

"Worry not of that right now," said William, "I will return soon."

Only the lapping waves could be heard as William crept back to the camp.

"All will be made right Stephen," said Christina.

"How can you be sure of this?" Stephen replied.

"It was promised to me. We must keep our faith."

She stroked his face gently and he fell asleep under her touch.

"I must remove the quarrel from his leg," Christina said, "I need you to hold him. Make sure he cannot be heard."

The pain of the extraction woke Stephen, but Arabi held Stephen's mouth tight and only muffled cries could be heard, as Christina cut her dirty dress away and bandaged him.

"That will need to be cleaned or he will die from that wound," she said. And then, she held Stephen in her arms until he slipped into unconsciousness again.

~

"He should have returned by now. Something is wrong," Arabi said, as the dawn approached.

The shuffle of many men could be heard in the distance.

"They are coming this way," said Arabi.

"We must run," urged Christina.

Arabi looked around and said, "To where?" motioning to the high hills surrounding them. Stephen awakened by their rustling said, "What has happened, where is William?"

"Ælfric must have him. They are coming for us," said Arabi.

"How many?" Stephen asked.

"Too many to fight," replied Arabi.

Stephen looked around and saw his crossbow near him.

"You found it!"

He reached for it and twisted the handle, placing the bloody quarrel inside its hidden compartment. Then they came out from their hiding place, amongst the rocks, and met Ælfric.

"I have the Templar and now I have you. Take them," Ælfric ordered.

They were pushed back to the camp and saw William sitting and tied to the post. The sun had passed over the horizon and the beach was now bright. Ælfric looked his captives over and recognized Arabi.

"You. The fire killed my horse."

He struck him hard, dropping Arabi to his knees and then withdrew his sword to plunge it into him when one of Ælfric's men shouted, "Look," stopping Ælfric. He turned and focused on what the man pointed to. Three ships were heading their way. Ælfric studied them carefully for a moment and then turned to his men.

"We must leave now," Ælfric said and then turned his gaze back to Arabi, "Perhaps it is for the best. I think a slower death for you, will be more enjoyable for me."

When they reached the galley Ælfric's bound captives were hoisted to the deck and pushed along to the bow of the ship. The crew taunted them as they were pushed along. Arabi noticed a break in their line. He feigned a movement towards his right, causing the guards to follow him and then ran to the break and leapt over the railing.

"Archers kill him," ordered Ælfric.

The archers moved hurriedly to the railing and waited. Stephen took the opportunity to inspect the approaching vessels. He nudged William and nodded in the direction of the ships uttering softly, "Pirates."

When Arabi did not return to the surface, Ælfric announced, "He has drowned. Let the fish have him. Take them below." They were placed into a small hold below deck, under the bow of the ship, to be left in the damp darkness.

"A few weeks here and you will find your will gone," said Ælfric.

"Fire tempers metal, misfortune God's warriors," William replied.

Ælfric slammed the door and screamed at the guard.

"Let them eat their misfortune, give them nothing."

William could hear his companions struggle with their bonds and said, "Do not struggle. Rest. You will need your strength soon enough."

"Strength for death?" asked Stephen.

"No, strength to fight," replied William.

"How can we fight, we are captives? Ælfric will kill us," said Christina.

"Do you think this is some accident? That chance has placed us here? We have been guided here. Draw from your faith again and you will see through the darkness that surrounds us. The shroud is here and now so are we," replied William.

Loud noises from the deck could be clearly heard by them. Muffled orders were shouted and it was evident that the galley was preparing to leave.

"They think they can outrun the pirates," said William, "we will need to escape when they are engaged. Stephen is there anything we can use in here?"

By now their eyes had adjusted to the dim light coming through the door's edge. Stephen felt the floor and walls for anything of use, as William did the same, only to fail. William tried slamming against the door to test it. It failed to give, but did elicit an angry response from the guard. They sat back in failure and listened to the oarsmen's pace.

"They will not hold that for long. They will need good wind and luck to escape the Bedouins."

"Can we do nothing?" asked Christina.

"Yes, we can wait and pray," said William.

~

Arabi pulled himself tight together and entered the water as a ball. Straightening quickly he allowed himself to drop and looked upward to see the shape of the hull. Arabi centered his focus and kicked to return to the bow of the ship. Breaking the surface he took in a large breath and then sank beneath the surface again to work out of his restraints. The wet fibers swelled, as he contorted his body to free himself. Working feverishly he succeeded in freeing one loop over his shoulder, loosening the entirety of the mass holding him. He returned to the surface again and finished the work of freeing himself. With the rope free, he wound it around his body making a sash of it. Above, the sounds of men preparing the vessel to leave, was evident. Now freed of the rope, he inspected the vessel. He saw his chance to return to the deck: the anchor. He dove under the vessel to remain hidden from the crew while his eyes searched for the chain that held the anchor to the vessel. Finding it, he returned to the surface and waited until the chain began to move. It began its ascent and he dove under the water, following the chain to the bottom. Free of its sandy mooring the chain drew tight and the anchor nearly caught him in the chest. He twisted around it and kicked furiously to get above it, in order to grab the chain that held it. As his head exited the water, he quickly looked for a spot on the hull that he could cling to. The anchor entered a hole through the ramming post, fitted at the bow. Two iron rings straddled the opening that he could cling to, if he leapt

The Blood of the Shroud

from the anchor at the correct time. Missing meant having a limb cut off by the anchor's blades or falling back into the sea. He quickly slid down the chain and found his footing on the anchor and waited for his rapidly approaching moment.

~

Ælfric studied the approaching vessels, while the men took to their stations.

"We cannot outrun them without creating an opening. We will have to go through them. I suggest we head for the smallest ship and ram it," said the pilot.

"No, head for the largest, it is closer and with it gone the others will move off in fear," ordered Ælfric.

"Her deck line is as high as ours, she will be able to board us quickly if we miss," replied the pilot.

"My men will hold them off. Just make sure you place her hull wound properly to sink her quickly."

Ælfric returned to the Cardinal's quarters and ordered his Marshall with him.

"How are the men?" Ælfric asked.

"They are fed and ready for battle. The Cardinal's men less so; I do not trust them."

"They will fight to live, worry not of them. Besides, this battle will be over before it has begun. Of more importance is how we ransom the Templar."

"Ransom?" asked the Marshall.

"Yes, that fool and his companions cost me my ship and bounty. I expect to be repaid. The Templars have gold and it will be mine."

"They may pay, but they will also seek revenge against us. It will be better to toss him and his friends overboard."

"And return home empty handed, the men unpaid? No, I will have my due. Have the Templar brought to me."

~

William gave out a sarcastic laugh and said, "The Grand Master will pay nothing for me. I provoke him far too much. He will find his life easier with me gone."

"I did not ask your opinion of your worth, only his location," replied Ælfric.

"He is easily found."

"Perhaps if I remove the ears of the boy you will be more forthright in your speech."

"You touch the boy and I will feed your entrails to you before I kill you."

"I tire of your empty threats. Trust me, I make none of my own. Give me his location."

"He is in Naples. But, realize the boy is under the protection of the Templars and is considered one of us. Harm to him guarantees your end. Your ransom will be nothing but pain."

"And the girl, is she also a Templar?"

"She enjoys my personal protection. Harm her or the boy and you will be hunted the rest of your days. You will know no peace, until my sword plunges through your heart."

"You Templars are all arrogance. Your glory days are far behind you. The world is changing and you will soon find the Templars are no longer needed in the new empire."

"That day is not here. I will live long enough to see you dead before me."

Ælfric grabbed him by his ropes and tossed him hard against the table. He crumpled over it, scattering objects to the floor with him following. Then Ælfric kicked him in the head until he seemed unconscious.

"Guards take this cur back to his cell," Ælfric screamed to his men outside the door.

Dragging him roughly below and through the oarsmen's deck, William noted the guards and their position, through half-closed eyes, before he reached the cell. They tossed him roughly in with the others, slamming the door behind him.

"You are hurt!" said Stephen.

"All is well. I took some pain to secure us a blade," William said weakly, as the blade dropped from his clasped hands. He then let out a deep sigh and grew silent.

"William speak to me!" said Stephen.

The darkness answered him, with the stone silence of dread.

~

Leaping from the blades, Arabi stretched out his arms and grabbed at the iron ring with one hand—his body swung forward and then backwards violently. The blades of the anchor dug into his back, to punctuate the success of his grasp. Writhing in pain, he looked down at the sea, regained his composure and reached up to secure himself with both hands. He dangled for a moment and then twisted himself around to face the anchor. Placing a foot on the blades for support he began to loosen his rope sash, releasing a few feet of line. He then thrust the line through the iron ring and began the slow process of creating a rope sling. He could feel the galley turn swiftly, as he worked, but ignored its new direction, concentrating on his task. When he was seated in his creation he rested and looked out at the water to see the pirate vessel on a collision course with the galley. His seat would provide an excellent vantage for the destruction that would soon come, and guarantee his death if he remained. He looked back at the galley and saw the edges of the deckhouse above him. He swung his remaining rope and attempted to throw it above and over the ramming post. It required several tries before success was his. With its end secured and the loop firmly around the post he began his climb up the side. His shoulder disagreed with his course and he slid back twice to his starting position, nearly falling into the sea. His third and final attempt seemed destined to fail as he reached the top, feeling his grip unintentionally fail again. But then it seemed as if the hand of God had reached below him and hoisted him up and over. Prostrated on top of the ramming post he stopped for a moment and looked forward to see the pirate vessel near the moment of impact. The pirates were turning away hastily as the war galley followed. Impact was imminent. He crouched and turned to face the war galley and then moved swiftly towards the deck. Fixated on the pirate ship, the crew of the galley was unaware of his approach and he reached the hull undetected. He looked over his shoulder and prepared to climb the railing, as the ramming post neared its target. He found a foothold and gauged the distance to the first handhold. Mere feet remained between the vessels as he climbed quickly upwards. He grasped the top of the railing as the ramming horn entered the pirate's vessel and the force of the impact threw him backwards. He fell onto the ramming post and barely held on. Regaining his balance he climbed again, reaching the deck of the war galley this time. His entrance startled a nearby warrior who mistook him for a pirate and moved forward to slice him with his sword. Training overtook thought and Arabi moved sideways avoiding the attacker's blade as he struck the man in the neck with his forearm sharply—grabbing the man's sword with his free hand. Now armed, Arabi sliced the man's exposed leg causing him to drop. He had no time to enjoy his victory, as another two warriors set upon him. He killed them quickly and gained another sword. The ramming post had entered the bow of the pirate's vessel too high to sink her and only succeeded in creating a bridge between the two vessels. Wasting no time, the pirates cast their lines across to tie the vessels together, as the opposing archers began to take each other's crew down. The pirates followed the volley of arrows, with some warriors charging along the ramming post joining Arabi in his fight against Ælfric's men. The ramming post tore away from the pirate's vessel exposing a gaping hole in its side. The vessels now tied by rope and grappling hooks could no longer drift apart and the pirates worked to draw them tight together. As his unintentional allies joined the fray, Arabi worked his way around the deckhouse seeking the entrance

The Blood of the Shroud

to the lower deck. He succeeded in making it to the aft of the deckhouse when a giant warrior guarding the entrance confronted him. Armed with mace and sword, the beast of a man attacked. Unable to dodge the mace heading for his chest Arabi raised his swords as a shield. The contact lifted him and threw him backwards onto the deck. The giant charged forward with murderous intent. Arabi threw his feet backwards over his head and rolled over himself until he was standing again. The giant swung his sword wide with a sweeping motion. The sword swept across his chest cutting through his clothes, barely missing his flesh. The motion exposed the giant's left side and Arabi thrust one of his swords into the man. If the giant felt the wound, he gave no indication of it, twisting again with the mace in his right hand, heading for Arabi's head. Arabi's sword tore itself from his hand, as the giant twisted, leaving the blade firmly in his side. Arabi raised the sword in his left hand to deflect the blow. The mace slid along the blade, avoiding his head, but the force was so great that he was thrown into the deckhouse and he crumpled to the deck. As the giant reset his weapons to finish him, an arrow entered his right eye, throwing him back temporarily. He staggered for a moment and then stared at Arabi once more with his remaining eye and moved back towards him with his sword held high above him. The break in the giant's attack allowed Arabi to find an opening in the giant's movements and he thrust his sword into the man's groin. This blow was sufficient to cause Arabi's attacker to howl in pain, but not to eliminate his threat. The giant stopped, dropped his sword and then pulled Arabi's weapon from his groin, as Arabi watched in astonishment. Weaponless, Arabi moved back, as the giant moved forward with the arrow in his eye and the sword still firmly in his side. Seemingly unstoppable, Arabi looked for a place to escape his wrath, but the deck was now a maelstrom of fighting, leaving no space for movement or escape. The giant's remaining steps towards him were lumbering as he raised his weapons. With his death imminent Arabi's vision held the clarity of his end and he waited in peace for the final blow that would mark his end. The mace began its descent first, but Arabi noticed it was uncontrolled and merely falling from the giant's hand. As it descended, Arabi twisted into the giant, securing the weapon in his hand finishing his turn by delivering a blow to the giant's head. The blow from Arabi would have been a killing strike, had not the giant already succumbed to death.

With his path clear Arabi moved quickly to the passage that led below, with mace in hand. The shaft of steep stairs led directly past hollows of weapon caches. When he reached the bottom he could see the narrow hallway leading to the oarsmen behind him. Before him a short hallway led below the deckhouse and a dim light could be seen. He moved forward and shouted William's name. Muffled cries were returned to him in reply and he moved towards them, unaware that a guard stood in the shadows ready to impale him with his sword. The noise from the battle on deck cloaked the sounds of the guard's thrust and Arabi was ignorant of the attack being made upon him. The mace in Arabi's hand deflected the thrust away from his torso unintentionally. Still the blade succeeded in slicing lightly across the top of his hand as it moved away from him, causing Arabi to drop the mace. The guard drew back the sword again. But now with the advantage of surprise removed, Arabi was on him before he could thrust again. Arabi pushed forward with his left hand moving the guard's right arm towards his chest and his own sword against his throat and then Arabi kneed him in the groin rapidly. Arabi's right hand moved above the guard's head forcing it down, while his left hand pulled back on the guards arm, drawing the sword against his throat, cutting deep into it. The guard slumped forward, as his blood erupted onto Arabi. With no impediment barring him, Arabi found his friend's prison, removed the wooden bar crossing the door's face and opened it. William looked up, cradled by his friends and said, "Impossible."

"No, merely difficult. We must leave now," replied Arabi.

"We need weapons," said William.

"You will have your choice, follow," said Arabi.

Finding his crossbow with William's axe and sword stored in the weapons cache at the base of the stairs, Stephen said, "William they are here."

"The shroud is held, at the aft of the ship, in Ælfric's quarters. The passage past the oarsmen leads there. Two warriors guard the passage and the oarsmen, one aft and one at the entrance to the chamber. I will meet you in Ælfric's quarters," William said.

"What do you mean—meet us?" asked Stephen.

"I must find Ælfric and end this."

"Hundreds of men are fighting above. This risk is unnecessary," said Arabi, "come with us."

"No, it is time. He will pay for my brother's death now," said William.

"I will come with you," said Stephen.

William looked down at his nephew, "The shroud may now be the last proof of our savior's sacrifice—it cannot be lost to this world. We are his warriors. You must do this. It is our duty. Go now."

William turned and headed up the stairs, while Arabi led the group down the hallway to the oarsmen's chambers. When William reached the deck the fighting was now a conflagration of swords. Bodies were strewn across the deck contorted in a grim contempt of life. Ælfric's men had succeeded in cutting loose some of the lines binding the ships together and the pirate's vessel had drifted askew. Now the vessels no longer stood side-by-side making it difficult for the pirates to send reinforcements. However, the remaining two vessels in their fleet-of-treachery had nearly arrived. Through the maze of flying arrows and clashing swords, William met Ælfric's eyes as he shouted orders to his men. Ælfric stood in front of the aft mast protecting his backside, while he dispatched scores of attackers with a deftness born from his experience. His movements showed no defect and now with his audience of one, he became flamboyant to show his strength, while William struggled his way towards him. All before him were enemies and William fought with a single-minded purpose, giving no quarter, leaving a trail of blood so thick the deck behind him became slippery. The bodies opened up before him exposing Ælfric and William sent his axe after him. Ælfric moved quickly to his left and the axe imbedded itself deep into the mast. Ælfric smiled at him, beckoning him forward, while making a show of impaling a pirate. William felled three more men, while Ælfric did the same, clearing the space between them. Ælfric thrust forward first, nearly slicing through William's right side. William parried his thrust and twisted into him, slicing Ælfric's leg. Ælfric returned the favor by nicking William's ear, as he pushed him away. A pirate stumbled between them and both men relieved him of his life and then returned to their private battle. William stumbled and Ælfric shouted at him.

"Your end is near, Templar."

William answered with a thrust, catching Ælfric in the left shoulder, pushing him back, and then followed with a slash meant to remove Ælfric's hand. But Ælfric was undeterred, twisting his sword quickly, nearly freeing William's sword from his hand and then followed with a thrust of his own that caught William in his left side, causing him to double over from the pain. Ælfric now at advantage, pummeled his head, felling William to the deck. Finishing with a quick slap, with the side of his blade, at William's sword hand, relieving him of his sword. Ælfric guaranteed of his victory, paused to savor its moment. He moved forward and said loudly, while holding his sword high for the killing blow.

"Where is your savior now, Templar?"

Ælfric unaware of his blunder-of-hesitation, in his effort to gloat, allowed William to push himself up and forward, grabbing Ælfric's sword hand, moving him backwards to the mast. The spike of William's axe imbedded itself deep into Ælfric, pushing through his ribs and into his right lung. Ælfric's stared into William eyes, gurgling words of blood. William pulled Gregory's sword from his hand and said, "You are not worthy of living," thrusting the blade through Ælfric's heart to finish him. Ælfric reached out frantically and then dropped his arms to his side, as William moved away to retrieve his other sword.

The pirate's reinforcements had arrived and their lines soon found the war galley, causing Ælfric's men to abandon his cabin, in defense of their sides, giving William clear access to Ælfric's quarters. When he entered he saw the Cardinal's royal chest, but no sign of his companions. He exited and found the aft passage to the oarsmen's chamber. Oarsmen and smoke left the chamber and William fought his way past the fleeing men to discover Arabi and Christina fighting flames caused by broken lanterns and Stephen working passionately to free the slaves. William fought his way to Stephen.

"We must go now."

"We cannot leave them chained, they will die."

"Hurry then."

William rushed to Arabi's side handing him a sword, "You cannot succeed here. Guard the girl to Ælfric's quarters. We will follow when the men are freed." Arabi looked back at the swiftly advancing flames and then tugged at Christina to follow him and the pair moved with the freed oarsmen to the deck. Stephen unlocked the last of the chains as the flames and smoke licked his boots and the oarsmen scrambled away.

"We must go now," screamed William.

When they reached the deck, oarsmen littered it, killed both by pirates and the crew in their attempt to escape. Fighting remained fiercest at the rails, as the crew fought back the attempts of the pirates to board the galley, leaving Ælfric's chambers unguarded. William and Stephen entered and found Arabi in battle with two pirates, as Christina was attempting to assist with a club. William gently swept her aside and plunged his sword into one of the pirates, allowing Arabi to finish the other.

"Stephen block the door," ordered William.

Stephen closed the door quickly, securing it with a wooden bar. An ornate stained glass window graced the rear of the quarters. William pummeled it with a golden candlestick smashing it outward, until the opening was clear. They looked out and saw the blue of the Mediterranean complemented by the golden shores of Crete. Two landing boats remained in tow, while three cut free by the pirates, drifted slowly off to the west. To the side of the quarters lay the Cardinal's gilded ornate wood chest on top of a table. William motioned to it and said, "The shroud must be in there. Stephen can you open it?" Affixed to the chest was a large lock. Stephen looked around for anything that could be used to pry it apart, when the pounding of a ram against the door began.

"You need to get to the landing boats. Take the chest with you. Hurry," William ordered. Arabi looked out the opening and said, "We will have to dive to the water, it is too far to climb."

"I cannot swim," said Christina.

"You will dive first, hold your breath and I will find you and take you to the boat," said Arabi.

"I don't think this chest will float, it is too heavy," Stephen said.

The door began to flex under the pounding.

"There is no time to wonder, throw it over, you must leave," William ordered.

"What of you?" asked Stephen.

"I will stay until you are safe. Now go, there is no more time."

Arabi helped Christina out the window to a small ledge below the opening and followed her. Then they were gone. William and Stephen watched as the two returned to the surface and waited until they were safe, before dropping the chest to the water. The bar across the door crackled, as it began to break.

The Blood of the Shroud

"Leave now. Go!" William screamed.

Stephen hesitated on the ledge for a moment and asked, "What of Ælfric?" William said, "His time is gone," as he pushed Stephen from the ledge. Stephen could hear the door fail as he dropped and the screams of warriors descend on William. When Stephen burst through the surface Arabi had already secured the chest to the landing boat's side and was hurrying towards him. Aboard the boat, the three looked back at the smoldering war galley and waited for William to leap. The smallest vessel in the pirate's fleet unable to moor itself to the side of the galley began to move to the aft of the ship and the pirate's archers spotted them and began to send volleys of arrows in their direction.

"We must move off before they find our range," said Arabi.

"No, William has not left," screamed Stephen.

But, Arabi ignored him, rowing the boat away from the arrows as the pirates moved in to finish the battle. Stephen was sullen as they landed on the shores of Crete again.

"Stephen we could not wait and save the shroud and ourselves," said Christina.

Stephen did not answer her, his tears thick in his eyes, as he pulled the chest from the boat. They could see the galley become engulfed in flames and the pirates move off, allowing it to drift off west. Stephen spotted a large rock nearby, lifted it, and then smashed the lock of the chest repeatedly in anger, until it was free of the chest.

"No!" he screamed in anguish as he lifted the lid of the chest.

Arabi and Christina looked into the empty chest and then looked back at the galley as the sun moved below the horizon. They watched in silent despair, as the burning ship carrying the shroud drifted from their view, now firmly in the hands of God and William to carry it to safety.

❖

Milan – 1242

Epilogue

Patrick entered the room carefully, uncertain if his father was awake. He found him slumped over in his work chair, resting his head on the worktable and decided to place the letter beside him and leave him to rest. He placed it on the table and turned to leave when his father spoke.

"What is it?" asked Stephen.

"A letter has just arrived by rider, a Muslim I believe," said Patrick.

Stephen stretched his arms above his head to wake himself and looked down at the paper. He recognized the script; it was from Appa. He began to tear the paper open, but stopped and looked up at his son.

"Have the rider stay and offer him lodging and food. I may have a reply for him to take."

"It is already done father, I know your ways," replied Patrick.

"Yes, of course you would. Stay for a time. This may be news of interest to you," said Stephen.

Patrick sat at the worktable beside his father and began to look over his father's drawings as Stephen read the letter silently.

S tephen, I send this to you with many prayers that my letter will find you with good health and cheer. The years that have separated us have grown longer than my wishes and with them more tales than I can recount in this missive to you now. Your letter of Christina's fate saddened me greatly, as I have held her as mother in my mind all these years. I hold a letter from her, sent long ago, but she included no mention of her motives or actions that would take place in her future, perhaps, to spare her protestation from me.

I would wish that my news would bring you relief from the sorrow you feel over her loss, but I can only add to it with sad news of my own. My father wished to write you of the matter, but I asked that he trust me with the task, so that in my words I could be drawn closer to you, if only in my thoughts. Arabi has died. As Hassar was father to me, Arabi was surely my uncle. I know this news will place much weight over your heart, for I know you held him as a close friend. The world demands much from us to live in it. Our struggles have defined us, but it is our friends and family who have given meaning to those trials. Arabi gave much meaning to all that knew him.

Write, when the seasons bring forth happier news for you to share with me and I will collect the sun from here to shine across my words in return to you.

With love and prayers, Appa

Stephen placed the letter on the table gently and said, "He is dead."
"Who is dead, father?"
"Ibn al-Arabi."
"The friend of your uncle William?"
"He was the friend of the righteous. He saved my life at Crete."
"I remember now, your tale of the shroud."
"It is no tale!"

"Of course not father, I meant no disrespect. I just remember when you told me of it as a boy, thinking it all so extraordinary—William surviving the battle with the pirates by clinging to a barrel, with the shroud of Christ inside. Being found by the Templars because of a mirror around his neck."

"Found by his friend, Gerald of Wales," corrected Stephen, "It is all true."

"I do not think otherwise. It is just—hard to imagine it all now. I seem to remember a girl in your story as well."

"Christina."

"Yes, a Christina. What became of her?"

"I am tired now, let us talk later of this," said Stephen.

"Yes father, rest now. It is best as I must attend to the afternoon deliveries now," Patrick said and then left his father to his thoughts.

Stephen felt old. *Soon they will all be gone and me with them.* He had not spoken to his family about Christina when the news of her death had arrived. It was private, feelings held secret for too long. Besides, he wished to spare his wife of all such talk. Christina. *Two years ago now. Fighting to save the souls of the Cathars at Montsègur.* He had not seen her in over thirty years, just before she became a nun. *She should not have died like that.* He had warned her against her foolishness. In reply, she wrote back only a single line of scripture to him, "For even the son of man came not to be ministered unto, but to minister, and to give his life a ransom for many."

Stephen pulled from his neck his father's mirror, now green with age, the sparkle long gone and reminisced.

FINIS

About the Author

D.B. Sanders has lived three lives. The one still held faintly by his mind's eye, the one he has embellished to share with his friends and the life that really materialized when few were looking—the life that crafted the writer in him. Graduating Summa Cum Laude, D.B. holds a BFA in drawing and painting. Soon after college he traded his paints for words, finding in them a divergent palette for his ideas. Sharing a fondness of antiquities and history, D.B. and his wife Kaye can often be found in musty places, seeking treasures to bring home and share with their three cats, Namaru, Hitchcock, and Earthquake (a thirty-pound domestic Bengal who stays by D.B.'s side when he writes.). The Blood of the Shroud is his first novel.

d.b.sanders.author@gmail.com

www.ingramcontent.com/pod-product-compliance
Lightning Source LLC
Chambersburg PA
CBHW031944240626
47153CB00003B/852